IRRESISTIBLE

"Why do you insist that you erred?" Lucy asked.

"For a dozen reasons. I am your guardian, for one. You are residing beneath my roof, for another. I have no serious intentions toward you. I am not courting you with the intention of marriage." He turned back. "Kissing you last night was wholly improper and imprudent."

Lucy had not slept well. She had rolled about on her bed, turning this way and that nearly the entire night, trying to determine just what had happened last night. She could make no sense of it. "You and I quarrel nearly every time we are together. So how did you come to kiss me?"

He stared at her. "In one sense, that is the most ridiculous question you could ask. You might rather ask how I keep from kissing you one minute out of two, or do you not know how beautiful you are or how desirable?"

BOOK YOUR PLACE ON OUR WEBSITE AND MAKE THE READING CONNECTION!

We've created a customized website just for our very special readers, where you can get the inside scoop on everything that's going on with Zebra, Pinnacle and Kensington books.

When you come online, you'll have the exciting opportunity to:

- View covers of upcoming books

- Read sample chapters

- Learn about our future publishing schedule (listed by publication month *and author*)

- Find out when your favorite authors will be visiting a city near you

- Search for and order backlist books from our online catalog

- Check out author bios and background information

- Send e-mail to your favorite authors

- Meet the Kensington staff online

- Join us in weekly chats with authors, readers and other guests

- Get writing guidelines

- AND MUCH MORE!

Visit our website at
http://www.kensingtonbooks.com

GARDEN OF DREAMS

VALERIE KING

ZEBRA BOOKS
KENSINGTON PUBLISHING CORP.
www.kensingtonbooks.com

ZEBRA BOOKS are published by

Kensington Publishing Corp.
850 Third Avenue
New York, NY 10022

Copyright © 2005 by Valerie Bosna

All rights reserved. No part of this book may be reproduced in any form or by any means without the prior written consent of the Publisher, excepting brief quotes used in reviews.

If you purchased this book without a cover you should be aware that this book is stolen property. It was reported as "unsold and destroyed" to the Publisher and neither the Author nor the Publisher has received any payment for this "stripped book."

All Kensington titles, imprints and distributed lines are available at special quantity discounts for bulk purchases for sales promotion, premiums, fund-raising, educational or institutional use.

Special book excerpts or customized printings can also be created to fit specific needs. For details, write or phone the office of the Kensington Special Sales Manager: Kensington Publishing Corp., 850 Third Avenue, New York, NY 10022. Attn. Special Sales Department. Phone: 1-800-221-2647.

Zebra and the Z logo Reg. U.S. Pat. & TM Off.

First Printing: May 2005
10 9 8 7 6 5 4 3 2 1

Printed in the United States of America

CHAPTER ONE

Hampshire, England, 1817

Lucy Stiles made her way through mounds of overgrown shrubbery, returning to Aldershaw's maze by her original path. If there was a more direct route to the house, she could not find it. So once again she passed by the shaggy home orchard before plowing through dense undergrowth to finally reach what was now an unrecognizable maze in the form of a tangle of yew shrubs.

She had just stepped into a clearing, which used to be the edge of a vast lawn, when she collided with the master of Aldershaw himself. "Robert!" she cried. How quickly her cheeks grew warm.

"Lucy?" He stepped back. "I do beg your pardon."

Did she see a look of welcome relief in his eyes?

"Hallo, Robert." Had it really been three years? How different he seemed, yet wholly the same. How different she felt. "How do you go on?"

"Tolerably well, thank you."

A sudden silence rose up between them. She wanted to

speak but all she could think of at the moment was that he was as handsome as ever, more so if that were even possible. He doffed his hat and in doing so a strand of wavy black hair touched his forehead. She knew the most ridiculous impulse to lift it gently back in place. Instead, she clasped her hands in front of her. Unsettled by the familiar if ridiculous *tendre* she had always felt for him, and afraid the gap would become uncomfortable, she spoke hurriedly, "I know that I should have sought you out at once upon my arrival but no one was about and I chanced upon your head gardener, Mr. Quarley. He insisted upon giving me a tour of the succession houses, which I must say were the only part of the grounds, save for the front drive, I found in tolerable order. I have been with him just now for this past half hour and more. Robert, the tales he told me of Aldershaw. I am still in a state of shock."

He smiled faintly, settling his hat back on his head. "Quarley always did favor you, but do you mean to tell me he took you through this terrible tangle of vines and shrubs?"

She smiled and nodded. "I was not in the least afraid. Besides, he wished to show me some improvements he hopes to make in your gardens, once he is given permission, of course." What would Robert say to that, she wondered.

He sighed. "I see he has been attempting to garner your support. I am well aware that he is grown frustrated that the acreage closest to the manor remains in this wretched state. However, I fear I cannot concern myself with his wishes at this point." His gaze drifted over her gown. "I trust in all this rambling about you have not snagged or torn your skirts?"

"I do not think so," she said, glancing down at the hem of her gown. Lifting her gaze to his face, she looked into his brown eyes and felt several butterflies flit suddenly about her stomach. How unfortunate that he was so very handsome and that, except for the anxious lines at the corner of his eyes, she thought he had never looked better. He was taller than most men and in her opinion had the perfect blend of lean athleticism and strength in his figure. His shoulders were broad, tapering to a narrow waist, and his legs were quite well turned. Whether in riding gear or formal black attire, he struck a commanding presence when he crossed any threshold, or appeared suddenly as he had just now, in a garden.

His face was bronzed, undoubtedly from riding about the estate, as Mr. Quarley had already told her he was wont to do for the majority of each day, but somehow his features seemed enhanced rather than diminished by the effect. His brows were nicely arched, his cheekbones high and strong, his nose straight, his jaw line a trifle mulish as it had always been, and his expression firm and confident. "You seem to be in excellent health," she stated, a new blush rising on her cheeks. Could she not think of something more interesting to say?

"I am well," he returned in an oddly quiet voice. He was staring at her but she was unable to determine in the least what his thoughts might be.

Robert Sandifort could not escape the quite poignant sensation he was presently experiencing at seeing Lucy Stiles again. He had been expecting her all morning, hoping to speak with her before the others in order to give some manner of explanation for what was going forward at Aldershaw. Now words escaped him, for all he could think was that he had forgotten how utterly beautiful she was, even wearing a frivolous bonnet with an enormous white ostrich feather curling over the front of the brim. Her features were far too delicate to bear the enormity of ostrich feathers and this one seemed inordinately grand.

Regardless of her hat, however, she seemed to have undergone some inexplicable change in the past three years. She had an air about her, which bespoke "the woman" rather than "the young miss." Of course she was four and twenty now, no longer a chit just out of the schoolroom, but had her eyes always been so blue and her complexion nearly the color of cream and sublimely ripe peaches? Her features were as they had always been, utter perfection. Her brows were light and beautifully arched, her lashes thick and full, her lips sweetly curved and the most beautiful shade of pink, ripe for kissing, surely.

She pushed a blond curl away from her cheek and smiled, if faintly. "I confess I am happy to see you again, though I hope we may not brangle as we were used to do in the past."

"I am certain we shall not," he responded. The strangest urge, full of affection and perhaps something stronger still, came over him. He wanted to embrace her, even to kiss her. Good God, where had such a reckless thought come from? Not that he would in any manner act upon his thoughts or urges, however strong. Lucy Stiles was, after all, his ward. His guardianship of her, as ridiculous as that happened to be, was a relic from the bond between their military fathers, something that should have been altered in his father's will when he became so ill. As it was, he was responsible for her until the end of the summer when she would turn five and twenty and come into her inheritance. After that she would be free to live however she desired.

"Robert, I must know," she said, interrupting his reverie. "What has happened at Aldershaw these past three years? I was never more shocked by the sight which met my eyes when the carriage turned up the long avenue."

He frowned. The question, as innocent and properly formed as it was, served to overset him. He desired nothing more of the moment than to strike something very hard with his fist. Dictates of his father's will prevented him from acting as he desired, as he believed was right and proper. Worse still, the cause of all the trouble lay at the door of his stepmother, Lady Sandifort, who still resided beneath his roof. To Lucy, however, he could not say these things. Instead, he expressed but part of the complexity of the problem. "My father was ill for a very long time, longer I believe than any of us knew.

During that time, he allowed a great deal of his fortune to be drained away in rather useless pastimes—"

"You must be referring to the very tedious task of keeping Lady Sandifort content."

"Did Hetty tell you as much in her letters?"

Lucy nodded. "But Mr. Quarley also explained some things to me about your stepmother, that she 'rules the roost,' as he put it."

"My stepmother," he cried bitterly. "She is but a year older than myself!" Lucy grew very quiet, perhaps in the face of his obvious frustration. "Well, I see that you are as perceptive as ever. As for Aldershaw, the staff is reduced to scarcely a tenth."

"A tenth," she cried, obviously shocked. "Well, that certainly explains much of the condition of the estate. I could not help but notice that all the furniture in at least two of the larger receiving rooms are covered in cloths."

"Aye," he returned, releasing a sigh. "I had hoped to make more changes once, well, once my father passed away, but the inheritance he left me had been depleted sorely."

There was a great deal more to the situation than he felt he ought at present to say to Lucy. Lady Sandifort ruled the roost, as his head gardener had so aptly put it, not just because she had used up most of the resources of the estate, but because his father had imprudently given Lady Sandifort power over his younger twin sisters, Anne and Alice, even to the arranging of their marriages, if she so desired. How often had he heard her threaten to do so when she did not get her way? At least she was forbidden any such course of action until they reached their eighteenth birthdays, but there was nothing to stop her from having betrothal papers drawn beforetimes. There was only one circumstance by which her power could come to an end: she would have to voluntarily quit Aldershaw, something she absolutely refused to do. At least she had agreed to refrain from making known the exact nature of his father's will, although he knew quite well she was simply waiting for the exact moment to reveal the truth to the twins. She was, if nothing else, calculating in every way.

Hetty and Henry both knew of the conditions of the will, so they understood quite to perfection how frequently he was prevented from giving his stepmother the dressing down she so greatly deserved. At the same time, he could not bear to have this information known generally. He did not want either Anne or Alice learning the truth about their father's truly hateful decision. It was hard enough that he was gone from their lives forever, but even worse that he had left each of their fates in the hands of a punitive, irrational stepmother.

There was only one ray of light through this dark expanse of clouds. For whatever his father's reasons for having jeopardized the future happiness of his twin daughters, Sir Henry had assigned to Robert the legal guardianship of his three youngest children, the offspring of Lady Sandifort: Hyacinth, William, and Violet. Lady Sandifort had no hold on them whatsoever. She could make no decisions for them concerning their education, nor could they be removed from Aldershaw unless Robert gave his permission, something he would never do, not so long as he drew breath.

Robert sighed heavily and continued, "I have every confidence that in time . . . Oh, the devil take it, you cannot know how frustrated I am."

"Since your complexion has changed more than once upon the introduction of this subject, I believe I have a glimmering of understanding."

Yes, Lucy was as perceptive as ever. "Beyond this," he continued, "the house is quite overrun at present and what servants have remained are sorely overworked." Instantly he regretted saying as much, since a new blush rose on her cheeks and a concerned light entered her eye.

"It was not by my choice that I am here," she stated quickly.

"And if I could change this ridiculous arrangement of our fathers, I most certainly would. But my solicitor said the will was quite explicit, that I must be under your roof until my birthday for a period of no less than three months if I am to receive my inheritance."

"Yes, yes, I know. My words were thoughtless. When I said the house was overrun I was not in the smallest way referring to your arrival, but to others. My brother George, his wife Rosamunde and daughter Eugenia have been living here for the past two years, and without end I am begun to fear, but of course Hetty would have told you as much in her letters to you. Lady Sandifort remains ostensibly because of her children, but I vow I have never seen a lady with less affection for or interest in her offspring." He regarded her for a moment, thinking that he was very happy she had come and that he could not recall why it was they used to brangle. He could not remember.

Lucy frowned slightly. "I must know, Robert. Is Lady Sandifort as cruel to your sister, to Hetty, as she was used to be?"

"Abominably so, made worse because they are of an age. It is a daily trial for Hetty, who is, by the way, quite looking forward to your stay at Aldershaw, but Lady Sandifort is never content unless she has said or done something to cause my sister to fly into the boughs at least once during the course of a day. Yet, I must confess to a degree of frustration with Hetty. She still shows no interest in matrimony even though, despite being four and thirty, she is still the prettiest lady in four counties and commands all degree of notice and attention. Of course, it is quite helpful that she is well dowered. At least my father was unable to touch the girls' dowries. Hetty, Anne, Alice, Hyacinth, and Violet, all are provided for." He was aware he was speaking to her as though they had last met but yesterday and that they were the greatest of friends. He wondered how it was he had fallen so easily into conversation with her.

"I am glad to hear it. You have not spoken of Henry, though. Hetty wrote to me in the spring saying he was going to take holy orders."

Robert felt nothing but disgust. "In May," he cried angrily. "He said he would do so in May, but nothing ever came of it and now it is June! He is one and thirty, he has lived in the same house all his life, he has refused the army, the navy, the law, and now it appears he is vacillating on the priesthood. I am out of all patience with him."

Lucy shook her head, her concern obvious. "Does Henry not wish to be a priest?" she asked.

"I have not the faintest notion. I have never understood him. I never shall. He rides like the devil but has refused a hundred times my offer to purchase a pair of colors for him. But come let me escort you back to the house. I know Hetty and the twins are longing to see you."

He offered his arm and she took it.

"So, Hetty is still steadfast in her refusal to take a husband?"

"Quite so," he said, wondering again why it was Henrietta, so pretty and lively, would have become a spinster. "She has a large enough dowry to tempt at least two hopeful suitors every year but she never allows any to approach her heart. I cannot for the life of me comprehend why she has not by now given up . . . that is . . . even if she had reasons earlier in her life for not marrying, I do not understand why she does not desire more than anything to have a home of her own, a family. Is that not what every woman desires?"

"I suppose to some degree, yes," Lucy responded. "And I believe you are perfectly justified in your bewilderment. Hetty is a delightful creature. She would have made any man an excellent wife these many years and more, for she is not only good-natured but knows how to speak her mind when necessary, which I believe a lady ought to do."

He glanced at her, at the openness of her countenance, and felt suddenly that he might be erring in encouraging so strong an intimacy between them. He thought it would be wise to shift the course of their conversation, so he teased her with, "This from an ape-leader of four and twenty?" He wondered if she would respond with her usual flash of eyes. He was not disappointed.

"An ape-leader, you say!" she exclaimed. "How very provoking!"

He chuckled. "Nearly as provoking as that absurd bonnet you are wearing. Your features are far too delicate to bear the burden of one ostrich feather, nonetheless two."

"How kind of you to express your opinion when I have not asked for it." She lifted her chin.

"You demand an opinion merely by wearing that horrid bonnet."

"And now my bonnet is horrid!" She withdrew her arm from his with a jerk. "That, Robert, is quite the outside of enough. I have not criticized your appearance, have I?"

"How could you when there is no need for criticism?" He stopped and threw his hands wide.

Lucy stopped as well, her eyes flashing dangerously. "I shall not lower myself to address the finer points of your toilette. However, if we are to discuss matrimony in its various forms I shall not hesitate to remind you that you have not married either, so how do you find the courage to recommend it to others or to judge them for refraining from it, as you clearly have done? Why have *you* never married?"

"Because I have no interest in taking a wife at present, though I suppose I must do so and that fairly soon, since it is certainly my duty to Aldershaw. Presently, however, I am far too busy to make a good husband."

She snickered her disbelief. "These are paltry excuses. I shall tell you why you are not wed, Robert, and 'tis not because you are so occupied. The reason you have never married is because you are cross as crabs nearly all the time. No lady would have you."

He narrowed his eyes in a manner he intended to be quite stern. "I see your tongue has not improved, Miss Stiles," he stated.

"Nor has yours, since you have already begun to find fault with me."

"Some things have need of correction." He was not certain why the tone of their exchange had altered so completely. He remembered now that this was how they were used to speak with one another.

"Indeed!" she cried. She did not flinch, not one whit, but remained standing before him as she always did when she came to Aldershaw, as though she owned every square inch of the property and all the inhabitants within. He never understood where her supreme confidence came from, save that he believed Lucy's sire had been of a similar temper.

The deuced fellow could command a room merely by raising an eyebrow, his father had once said.

Well, if Lucy Stiles thought to pass off such tricks today or any other day during her present sojourn beneath his roof, she was greatly mistaken. "I suppose you mean now to stare me down," he said, folding his arms over his chest.

"And now you are on your high horse because I told you why it is you are not married? I daresay you never even kiss one of your flirts except by permission."

This was going beyond the pale, but to his credit Robert held his temper strongly in check. "If you think to get a rise out of me this morning, *Cousin*—"

"We are *not* cousins," she cried, interrupting him. "I would never, not even if sorely pressed, claim the smallest relationship with you."

"As I was saying, *Cousin*, you shan't get a rise out of me today."

"I did not wish for any such thing. I was hoping for a kiss."

He was dumbstruck and saw the provoking, challenging light in her sparkling blue eyes. "You were hoping for a kiss?" he queried, stupefied. Some part of him knew she was playing at her games again, but the mere mention of a kiss rattled his ability to be the habitually rational creature he knew himself to be.

"Yes, you ought to be kissed, you know," she responded sagely. "Then you would not be so peevish most of the time, always hurrying to find fault. I begin to remember now why it was you and I brangled so much. You know, Robert, you should have had a wife long before this. You would have been a much more reasonable creature had you married, although I daresay you would have plagued the life out of her!"

"Much you know about it," he retorted hotly. He realized vaguely she had hooked him into another fruitless argument, yet he felt powerless to resist engaging the battle. "There is not a lady of my acquaintance who would not be an impossible burden to bear were we to wed. 'Why are we not in London this season? Why do I not have more jewels? Why cannot we purchase a townhouse in Brighton, Bath, Cheltenham, and . . . and York, for God's sake!' "

"York? Of all the absurd starts!" she exclaimed, smiling broadly. "And may I inquire if this is a mimicry of your stepmama?" She also folded her arms across her chest.

"I was not referring to Lady Sandifort," he said. He released his arms but could not keep his hands from clenching into fists. "I was merely referring to the vast array of those ladies with whom I am acquainted."

"Then I am very sorry for you if you truly believe what you say."

"You are no different."

These words served to drop the smile from her lips. Her arms fell to her sides as well and she, too, made a neat pair of fists. "I beg your pardon?"

"How many times have I heard you proclaim that you intend to marry a very wealthy man for only such a man could make you happy."

"Oh, yes, just so," she admitted, but she began to smile again, and her hands relaxed. "Oh, Robert, what a ridiculous fellow you are. I was very young when I said such things, and besides, I did not know precisely the nature of my own fortune at that time. But here, the day is too fine to be brangling and that so early, for it is not even ten o'clock! Instead, let me cheer you up." With that, she took sudden hold of the front of his coat, pulled him down to her, and quite brazenly kissed him full on the lips. "Better?" she asked, drawing back.

He could not help himself. Something about Lucy always brought the challenging beast out of him. The kiss had been a rather wonderful greeting, but he could not say as much. Instead, he lifted a cool brow. "I have had better kisses from my pointer, Tess, but I thank you anyway."

She rose to the bait. Her blue eyes flashed wildly once more and with her intentions sublimely clear, she untied the ribbons of her bonnet, removed the silly creation from her head, and dropped it to the weed-ridden grass below. She then took a stronger hold of his coat and even slung her other arm about his neck. She kissed him hard on the lips for a very long moment and he found himself a little more than intrigued.

When she drew back, she cried, "There! You cannot possibly complain about that!"

She released his coat and was sliding her arm away from his neck, but he caught her firmly about the waist and did not let her disengage. At the same time, he tossed his own hat on the ground. "This is a very interesting game you have chosen to begin this morning, *Cousin,* only I wonder how deeply you are willing to play?"

She gasped. "Let me go," she commanded. For the first time since he had known her, she appeared out of her depth.

He did not, however, release her but instead kissed her, intent on proving that he was not hers to do with as she pleased.

Lucy was as mad as fire. How dare he hold her captive! She struggled against him for a very long time, realizing she had erred, that she had begun a wicked game she ought not to have and now she was suffering for it. She knew Robert as well as she knew her own thoughts and feelings. He was as stubborn as she but far less temperate in any of his thoughts or actions. She should not have kissed him even if her initial reasons had been quite harmless. Now, as she pushed against his arms trying to disengage herself from his strong hold about her waist, she could not conceive what had prompted her to so reckless a course.

The more she struggled, however, the tighter his hold became. At last she wearied, and realizing she had lost the battle she surrendered, allowing him to seek her mouth and give her the kiss she had been evading.

His lips were surprisingly tender, even though his arms were still a vice about her waist. As his tongue touched her lips, sending a shiver down her neck, she realized he was not going to be content with a simple kiss. No, his intentions became quickly obvious and she regretted anew that she had so brazenly kissed him in the first place.

She allowed him what he sought, parting her lips and allowing him to touch the deepest recesses of her mouth. How very wicked he was! She counted the seconds waiting for him to desist and leave her in peace, but he was clearly in no hurry to release her. She wanted to protest but she knew such protest was useless. There was only one thing to be done— she put her arm about his neck and returned his kiss, pretending to enjoy his horrid assault.

Robert felt so sweet a sensation of satisfaction and victory at the feel of her arm about his neck that he knew the moment had arrived in which he could end the silly charade, except that suddenly, and for no comprehensible reason, he did not desire to end the absurd tug of wills. He was holding a beautiful young woman in his arms. She was kissing him warmly, even passionately, and for this moment all his cares seemed to vanish like chaff in the wind, swept away forever. What a tender peace filled him, something he had not experienced in a very long time, not for years.

He did not realize until this moment just how harried he felt. For a long time, extending at least two years before his father's death, he had watched the estate decline without the smallest power to prevent its disintegration. Lady Sandifort had ruled his father and she had spent the Sandifort fortune, having collected a fine array of jewels while at the same time letting the estate take on the appearance of a neglected ruin. Though he now held the purse strings, every spare groat went not into his own house but rather into the estate farms, for repairs and improvements that the rent rolls might be enlarged. And still Lady Sandifort remained!

How glad he was that Lucy had come for all her games, trickery, and mischief. How happy he was to be kissing her!

Lucy had thought he would let her go but he did not, though she felt his arm about her waist slacken considerably. She could, then, withdraw, but some deviltry was working within her, and the knowledge that he had somehow become engaged in the kiss in a way that rather shocked her, spurred her on.

Only . . . she began to enjoy kissing Robert as well! So much so that she forgot just how much she was used to quarrel with the man kissing her so . . . well, passionately.

Her mind became fixed on the softness of his lips as he drifted them over hers. She thought of nothing else except perhaps that she had begun to feel warm all the way to her toes! How was it she had never known how pleasant Robert's lips could be? The same lips that released so many sardonic words now seemed to be enchanting her heart. But how was that possible when Robert had no heart?

Awareness that she ought not to be kissing Robert dawned quite suddenly and she flew back from him as though he had just breathed fire. She gasped and did not close her mouth for staring at him. He did not speak either, for he was staring at her in return, his mouth equally agape.

"Lucy," he whispered suddenly, reaching for her.

She recoiled. "Good God!" she cried. "What on earth was that?"

His expression altered instantly and once more he was the arrogant creature she had known since she was a little girl. She did not want to hear what he might next say to her so she whirled about, caught up her bonnet quickly in hand, and ran in the direction of the maze. She had not gone far when she caught sight of Henry approaching from the direction of the stables, to the east.

"Lucy!" he called after her. "Whatever is the matter? You appear as though you have seen a ghost! Lucy, is anything wrong?"

She could not answer him. Everything in this moment seemed wrong. Her thoughts were so jumbled that her brain felt as though a whirlwind had taken up residence in the middle of it.

You are in love with him. Her mind began to betray her with such thoughts and she had only one fixed intention of the moment: to escape.

She shook her head at Henry and turned the other direction, moving into the tangled depths of the maze.

"Lucy, wait!" he called after her. "There is something I would say to you. It is of very great importance!"

She did not stop to give him answer but continued wending her way through one uneven path of yew branches after another.

CHAPTER
TWO

Some time later, after she had calmed her mind, Lucy emerged from the maze only to find Henry sitting on a patch of uneven lawn not twenty feet away.

"Oh, dear," she murmured, moving quickly in his direction as she made a loop of her ribbons and slung her bonnet over her arm. "Were you waiting for me?"

"Of course." He smiled crookedly as he rose to his feet. "I saw Robert walking quite briskly in the direction of the house, his expression severe, so I knew that something had gone amiss. Shall I escort you back to the house?"

"If it pleases you."

"Very much, only do tell me what has my wretched brother done this time to so overset you, although I must say I am not in the least surprised?"

"It is not worth mentioning," she responded, happily taking the arm he proffered and moving with him in the direction of the terrace. She had spent at least half an hour composing her thoughts and had concluded that the bizarre and quite shockingly passionate kiss she had just shared with Robert had evolved because of her own foolish conduct. She was resolved, therefore, never again to engage him in such a manner. To Henry she added, "So, let us not speak of Robert. Instead, tell me how you go on? You always were one of my favorites, you know."

"I am glad to hear you say so," he said, giving her arm a friendly squeeze. "And I must say that since you have come I have every confidence I shall go on very well, indeed!"

She giggled. "I see you have not changed. I will always remember Henry Sandifort as the most charming, the most *beautiful* of the Sandifort brothers." She looked up at him wondering how he would receive such compliments.

He pressed a hand to his chest, feigning deep regard. "How you warm my heart with such words. You have no notion!"

She could only laugh again. Henry was indeed an exceedingly charming gentleman who was, as Robert had said, one and thirty, just two years Robert's junior. He was, just as she had said, quite beautiful but so opposite from Robert in coloring that it seemed impossible the two men could actually be brothers. While Robert favored his mother's dark looks, Henry, and George as well, resembled their father. Henry's hair was blond and wavy and his eyes the most unusual green. His features were perfection, large eyes, arched brows, a straight nose, and lips that she knew had kissed a score of damsels, perhaps more. Presently he was dressed in riding gear and with a lean athletic body appeared quite to advantage. He may not have settled on a profession, but he certainly knew how to do the pretty in a drawing room, or in an unkempt garden for that matter, as he was now.

She realized his gentle demeanor and calm society were precisely what she needed after her most recent encounter with Robert. She had always been at ease in Henry's company. "Well, I must say," she began, swinging her bonnet, "you have not changed one whit in three years and how happy I am to see you again. Robert tells me you were to have taken holy orders in May, only you did not."

"That is because, my dear Lucy, I was waiting for you."

"What a very sweet thing to say," she remarked. "Do you mean to do so now?"

"Not yet," he mused. "I believe there is something wanting, but I hope by the end of the summer that lack shall be rectified."

"I have every confidence it will be," she stated reassuringly, though she did not have the faintest idea to what he referred. "So tell me, are you still writing poetry?"

She saw the surprised look in his eyes when he glanced down at her. "A little," he responded.

"I remember enjoying your poems very much. I recall one line in particular, *a garden beauteous where dreams abound, life's pleasure dawns a rose clustered crown. I believe that to be true.*"

"Good God," he murmured. "You have quoted it exactly. How did you recall it so perfectly to mind?"

She shrugged. "I cannot say. I just thought it exquisite. I always thought your poems exquisite."

"Lucy, my dear Lucinda! I am so happy you have come to Aldershaw."

"So you have said," she cried. Remembering, however, the recent sad events at Aldershaw, she said very softly, "So much has changed here. You must miss your father exceedingly."

He nodded. "And as usual, you seem to know my thoughts as well. Yes, I miss him very much."

"I cannot believe an entire year has passed, can you?" She stopped swinging her bonnet.

He shook his head.

"I remember when I last saw your father. I believe he already knew he was ill. I can recall him to mind so perfectly

Newsweek

SUBSCRIBER SAVINGS VOUCHER

Newsweek's Cover Price	Your Cost*	You Save
$133.65	$21.33	$112.32

Just use this card to get Newsweek for 84% off the cover price. That's only 79¢ an issue. (Order two years for just 69¢ per issue and save even more!)

Check one:

I'LL TAKE THE BEST DEAL!
☐ 24 months (106 issues) just 69¢ per issue.

☐ 12 months (53 issues) just 79¢ per issue.

☐ 6 months (27 issues) just 79¢ per issue.

Mr./Mrs./Ms. (circle one) _____ please print

Street _____ Apt No. _____

City _____ State _____ Zip _____

Check one:
○ Payment enclosed.
○ Bill me later.
○ Renewal (attach label).

J0832DC

*27 issues. Residents of DC and GA add applicable sales tax. Offer good in U.S. only and subject to change. Newsweek publishes weekly, except when combined issues are published that count as two issues, and when an additional special issue may be published.

BUSINESS REPLY MAIL

FIRST-CLASS MAIL   PERMIT NO. 309   HARLAN IA

POSTAGE WILL BE PAID BY ADDRESSEE

Newsweek

PO BOX 5551
HARLAN IA   51593-3051

NO POSTAGE
NECESSARY
IF MAILED
IN THE
UNITED STATES

in this moment. He squeezed my fingers and there were tears in his eyes. I thought he meant it as affection, but now I believe he knew he was not well. I am sorry for you, Henry, sorry for you all, that you had to suffer, that he suffered for so many years and long, long months until the end."

"What of your father? Did he linger long?"

"No, not really, I suppose. He had an inflammation of the lungs in July following the riding accident. He could not walk, you see, and the doctor said his immobility made the illness worse for him. He succumbed in a very short time, far too short." She sighed heavily but then gave herself a shake. It would not do in the least to dwell overly much on her sadness. "I buried him in the churchyard next to mama."

"I wish I could have been there for you."

"And I for you, for all of you. It seems so odd to think that our fathers, as good friends as they were, passed within such a short time of each other, scarcely a fortnight."

"Almost as though it had been destined."

"Yes," she murmured.

On this sad note, conversation dimmed and nothing further was said until together they mounted the stone steps of the terrace. "I was hoping to speak with George. Do you know where he might be at this hour?"

Crossing the terrace, Henry reached the large carved wooden door that led into the back entrance hall and held it wide for her. Lucy passed through, then moved into an adjoining chamber, a very fine, long room called the armory, completely paneled in wood. The walls were mounted with centuries of weaponry, from shields to crossbows to even a collection of firearms. A suit of armor stood like a sentinel in the far west corner. She had always been fascinated with this chamber, for in addition to the antiquities were several portraits of Sandifort ancestors all glaring down upon the chamber in Elizabethan splendor, their expressions haughty and proud. A doorway at the end of the chamber led to an antechamber and after that to the west wing of the ground floor. Two northern windows overlooked the terrace and what had been in more glorious days a beautiful garden.

Lucy moved to the window nearest the door and looked out. The vista, regardless of the unhappy state of the garden, was quite magnificent, for the land sloped gently upward from the terrace to the maze nearly a hundred and fifty yards from the house and rose to the home wood of fully leafed beeches.

Henry drew near. "I believe you may find George and Rosamunde in the small sitting room on the first floor. Rosamunde takes to her *chaise longue* most every day, you see. Eugenia has been with her aunts and uncle in the schoolroom since her arrival two years past."

At that, Lucy laughed. "So Eugenia is ten but were she pressed she would be required to address five-year-old Violet as 'Aunt Sandifort.' "

Henry chuckled. "It is very amusing. Of course they are like siblings now and Eugenia is very attentive to all three of the younger children, behaving just as an elder sister ought." He glanced at the mantel upon which a clock was stationed. "However, I see by the time that I must leave you now. I am promised elsewhere for nuncheon, but I shall certainly see you at dinner."

When she turned toward him and again expressed her happiness at seeing him, he took her hand in his and kissed her fingers quite sweetly. Yes, Henry was, indeed, a most charming gentleman.

As he turned to go, she cried out, "But Henry, stay a moment! I nearly forgot. What was it you wished to say to me?"

He shook his head. "Nothing to signify."

"But you said it was of great importance."

He laughed in an odd manner as though he were laughing at himself. "Not so important as a great many other things, like your seeking out George and seeing if you are able to coax at least one pleasant greeting from him, though I promise you it will be a difficult task, indeed!"

"Very well."

She smiled warmly upon him. "You have made me feel exceedingly welcome, Henry, and for that I thank you. Until dinner, then."

She watched him quit the armory and a second later he was walking swiftly across the terrace, down the steps, and traversing the weedy, dry lawn, clearly heading for the stables.

Desiring to greet the third Sandifort brother, she left the armory, returning to the back entrance hall and traversing a quite long hall to the front entrance hall, and set about climbing the wide bank of stairs leading to the first floor. Reaching the first floor she heard shouting not far distant, and glancing to the right she saw a girl whom she presumed to be Eugenia clinging to the wall next to an open doorway. She wore a white muslin gown caught up high about the high waist with a pink ribbon. She was clearly eavesdropping.

Lucy settled her bonnet once more over her curls and moved in the direction of the squabble.

"Eugenia," she called softly as she drew near.

The girl whirled around, panic in her green eyes. She was very much in the mold of the two younger Sandifort brothers and would no doubt blossom into a considerable beauty. Her hair was a very light red, almost blond, and pulled into a knot atop her head with another pink ribbon. Her mouth was agape as she stared at Lucy.

"I am Miss Stiles, Lucy Stiles," she murmured softly. The shouting within grew louder and a deep blush quickly suffused Eugenia's cheeks.

"I remember you," the young girl said, approaching her on tiptoe.

"You have grown so very pretty and I would know you for

a Sandifort at once, for you have the look of your father." She found she was whispering, for the bickering had not ceased. When a thump resounded, Eugenia whirled back to the doorway.

"They have been arguing this half hour and more," she explained.

"Trouble?" Lucy inquired, moving to stand beside her.

Eugenia sighed heavily. "Of late they quarrel nearly every day and usually just at this hour, before noon. Mama wishes to go home, you see, even though papa insists the repairs at Baddesley are not yet complete, but mama no longer cares. She wishes to be in her home more than anything."

"I can understand her feelings perfectly."

"She misses her garden most of all, and it has now been two years, but . . ." Her brow split into furrows.

"What is it?"

Eugenia shook her head. " 'Twould be disloyal for me to say more. I know my parents love each other. Indeed, they do."

Lucy could see that Eugenia was worried more than any child ought to be. She therefore changed the subject completely. "Would you do me a very great favor?"

"Of course," Eugenia responded sincerely.

"Well," Lucy began smiling, "would you be so kind as to fetch Hyacinth, William, and Violet for me? I have brought gifts for all of you and I do believe they need to be removed *immediately* from my trunks."

At that, Eugenia beamed. "At this hour, they are in the schoolroom with Miss Gunville. Where shall I bring them?"

"To my bedchamber. Though I have not yet been there, Finkley said I would be residing in my usual room which has always been the green and rose chamber on the second floor in the east wing."

"Next door to mine!" she finished with a smile.

"How wonderful," Lucy responded.

"I shan't be but a few minutes."

"I will come to you as soon as I greet your parents."

She lifted a finger as though to say something, glanced nervously at the doorway from which angry low voices could be heard, shook her head in something very near to despair, and took off on a run.

Lucy drew in a deep breath and without hesitation entered what proved to be a very pleasant sitting room. As soon as George Sandifort saw her, he whirled around and faced the windows that overlooked the avenue, his complexion high. Rosamunde, reclining on a lavender *chaise longue,* began to weep into her kerchief all the while gesturing for Lucy to approach her.

"Lucy," she called out in faint accents at last. "You have come to us. How we have needed you!"

For some reason George took umbrage at these words and faced Lucy abruptly. Running a hand wildly through his blond hair, he cried, "Fine house you have come to, although I do hope you may have some effect on my wife. At the very least I wish you would persuade her to stop her caterwauling and weeping!" He bowed once curtly and marched from the room.

Lucy turned in much astonishment to watch him go. He was a big man, quite broad-shouldered with heavy, muscular thighs. He was in most respects a larger version of Henry, but not in possession of Henry's intelligence, wit, or ease of manner. Yet Lucy had always had the impression that she was never safer than with George nearby. After all, he had once lifted a carriage off Henry, saving his life. In this moment, however, he had all the appearance of a man who had lost complete control of his life.

She turned to Rosamunde, however, and smiled. "I saw Eugenia a few minutes ago. How pretty she is become. She will break a great many hearts in the coming years. She is ten now, is she not?"

"Though I am her mother, I fear I must agree with you,

she is as pretty a child as I have ever seen." A frown descended over her brow. Rosamunde was quite lovely with an almost bluish hue to her exceedingly fair skin. Her eyes were the color of the sky and her elegant red hair, when released from its careful braids, hung to her waist. For the barest moment Lucy wondered if she had begun to fear that George had strayed in his affections.

That seemed impossible, for there had never been but one lady for George Sandifort. He had tumbled in love with Rosamunde when he was eighteen and married her before his next birthday. Eugenia had been the result of the wedding night, for her birth had been nine months to the day. It had been believed and hoped that their home, Baddesley, would soon be full of young Sandiforts ready to spar with the world, but none had followed, not one. The subject had never been raised within her hearing, but she believed the disappointment between them was severe.

"You look as beautiful as ever," Lucy stated. She drew close and Rosamunde extended her arms to her. Lucy embraced her gently and kissed her cheek, taking care not to bump her forehead with the brim of her bonnet. She smelled of lemon. She was very thin. Holding her bird-like arms she began to wonder if Rosamunde was ill. "I trust you are well?"

Rosamunde released a very deep sigh. "You have no notion how I suffer from the spasms and pains in my side. And there are times when my heart races and I cannot breathe." She laid a theatrical hand across her brow and suddenly Lucy laughed.

"I vow you should have performed in the theatre."

For an instant, Rosamunde appeared offended, but then a quick, secretive smile overtook her features. "You always understood me." She giggled and a great deal of light flowed into her pale complexion. What a strange enigmatic person she was.

Lucy remained with her conversing for several minutes, all the while knowing that the children were probably awaiting her in her bedchamber. Rosamunde talked in one quick, long streak, wrapping and unwrapping her lace kerchief in and around her fingers. "The entire house is in uproar. *Her ladyship* rules every inch of the manor and speaks in such vulgar ways, embarrassing all of us and dominating the men with her sly looks. I despise her more than I can say. She makes no secret of detesting me as well as Hetty. I wish I had never come to Aldershaw. I wish George had never forced me to leave my home. I long to return to Baddesley. Oh, Lucy, I long for it more than I can say!"

Lucy listened attentively, trying to understand with as much clarity as she could why it would seem Rosamunde had taken to her *chaise longue*. She remained for a few minutes longer, expressed her hope that they might become better acquainted in the coming weeks, and at last quit the sitting room.

Once in the hall beyond, and out of view of Rosamunde, she drew in a deep breath. She had been at Aldershaw less than three hours and already it seemed the roof hung too low over her head.

She made her way to the formal and slightly spiraled staircase that connected the first and second floors at the east end of the Elizabethan mansion. She was about to climb the stairs when she heard Robert call her name.

With a hand on the banister, she turned to face him. He was coming from the direction of the main staircase and seemed quite serious in expression. Her heart skipped a beat as memories of the several kisses they had so recently shared rushed back to her like a quick breeze. Her breath caught in her throat. He had changed into riding gear and strode toward her in his purposeful manner.

In these few seconds, time slowed. Her gaze drifted over his fine figure, the breadth of his shoulders, the buckskin of his breeches defining lean, athletic legs. And what was there in a glossy pair of boots and well-tied neckcloth that became a gentleman so very well?

Her heart was racing by the time he reached her and covered her hand with his own. "I am glad I found you. I am so very sorry. I must apologize for what happened earlier. I should never have kissed you as I did. The entire event was wholly unwise and completely unforgivable. I do most earnestly and humbly beg your pardon."

How sincere he seems, she thought, but a whisper of rage whipped through her mind. How could he refer to a kiss they had shared in such a manner, as though he needed to have the sin of it expunged from his soul.

"I kissed you first," she stated softly, withdrawing her hand from beneath his.

"Well, yes, but . . ."

"Am I now to apologize to you because what I did was so *unforgivable* in your eyes?"

He frowned. "I did not mean to imply . . . Oh, Lucy, why do you turn this about? I only meant that I was sorry for my conduct, that the whole thing got so wildly out of hand."

What was it in Robert that so set up her back? She ought to be grateful that he was apologizing. Instead, she was offended, rather deeply, perhaps because for a particle of a second she had begun to think he actually cared for her. "Well, God forbid that a little passion steal between us!" she cried. She did not wait for him to offer his apologies again, but rather began mounting the stairs quickly.

"Lucy!" he called after her.

"The children are awaiting me," she retorted over her shoulder. "I brought them presents and I do not desire to keep them waiting any longer."

"Lucy," he muttered, his voice a growl.

Lucy reached the top of the stairs and felt compelled to look back, even perhaps to beg pardon for becoming the crab as she had just now. She opened her mouth to speak, but Robert was gone.

Just as well, she thought. Venturing down the hall that led to her rooms, she felt intensely frustrated, yet she was not certain why. She ought to have appreciated his apology, his attempt to make peace with her, and yet she felt it was a complete insult to call any of the kisses they had shared *unforgivable*. Oh, but what did it matter? Why was she even up in the boughs? She would never comprehend Robert and he certainly did not understand her in the least. How could he ever know, for instance, how deeply wounded she felt when he offered his criticisms or gave her hints on just how she should conduct herself?

When she reached her rooms, she heard a great deal of childish laughter and squealing coming from her bedchamber. She passed through her sitting room and peeked around the edge of the open door to see what had brought such merriment. A game of tag was in progress and of such a lively nature that she was tempted to join the four young bodies racing around the room, over her bed, and through her several trunks.

After a few minutes of delighting in their antics, she finally made her presence known. "Hallo," she called out, walking in as though she had just arrived.

The children all stopped playing, freezing in position for a moment then gathering shyly about Eugenia. Three years had passed since she had last seen Hyacinth, William, and Violet. How very much each had grown!

She approached the eldest first. "You must be Hyacinth. I see we have the same hair."

Hyacinth smiled. "We do. Is yours always curly? Mine is."

Lucy untied the ribbons of her bonnet and removed the feather-laden creation from her head. She then withdrew several hairpins that had been keeping her coiffure in place and shook out her curls. How good it felt to be freed after hours of traveling. She turned around and let Hyacinth observe for herself. Her hair was very long though not so long as Rosamunde's. "A little wet weather and my whole head appears as though it exploded."

Hyacinth clapped. "It is just like mine!" she cried.

William apparently liked her description, for he laughed heartily.

Lucy turned around and faced the children once more. "You must be William." He was a sturdy lad with black hair and gray eyes, not at all in the mold of his elder half brothers and sisters. His chin was pointed, his nose rather aquiline in appearance, and his expression bold. He was the sort of boy one expected to grow into a rather forceful man.

She approached him and offered her hand to him. He assumed a more formal position as a young gentleman ought and took her hand, giving it a proper squeeze. "How do you do, Cousin Lucy?" he asked, bowing just as he ought.

"Very well, I thank you."

"Are you really our cousin?" Violet asked.

Lucy turned to the smallest and youngest of the Sandiforts. "No, not really, I'm 'fraid. But I have known your family for so long, for my father and your father were exceedingly good friends, that I often feel as though I am related to all the Sandiforts."

"I like you," she stated with childlike simplicity.

"And I like you very much, but my, how big you are. When I last saw you, you were barely as tall as my knee, for that was fully three years past."

She straightened her shoulders. "I am nearly as tall as William."

"You are not," William retorted hotly, as was only proper since his younger sister had so violently offended his masculine dignity.

"Well, at least I come to your shoulder." Lucy was a trifle stunned by Violet's appearance. When she had last seen her she was so young that she had but wisps of hair. At five years old, her pretty locks were a shocking red color and her eyes a very pale blue. Save for a faint resemblance to her mother, whose hair was dark brown, there was nothing of the Sandifort look about her.

Oh dear, she thought, awareness dawning sharply. She had always heard rumors of Lady Sandifort's conduct but she believed that in both William and Violet she saw the truth returning her gaze innocently.

Lucy knelt before her largest trunk. "I brought presents for you, as I am sure Eugenia has already told you."

Violet drew close. "But if you are not our cousin, what do we call you? Must we call you Miss Stiles?"

"That sounds far too formal when I do feel like your cousin. Please call me Lucy, or Cousin Lucy if you like. I shall be here until the end of September and I do hope that I will be treated like one of the family."

Violet smiled so sweetly and the next moment dropped down to sit close beside her. "I like you," she whispered.

Lucy's heart melted at the tender expression on the child's face. "I like you very much, too. Now, shall we open the trunk?" She glanced around the bank of faces.

A resounding "Yes" returned to her quite in unison.

When the trunk was wide open, she dispersed a box to Hyacinth containing a colorful variety of embroidery threads, a new riding crop to William, and a doll to Violet that she had made herself. To Eugenia she presented a parcel of white muslin embroidered with strawberries.

"This will make the most lovely gown," she cried.

Lucy was delighted to see Eugenia's eyes sparkle, since she could still recall being ten years of age and growing in awareness almost daily as to how important fashion was to any lady of quality.

A rapping sounded on the door and Hetty appeared suddenly. "Lucy!" she cried. "Oh, do but look at you sitting on the floor, with Violet almost on your lap. Hyacinth, what have you there? What a lovely array of colors."

"I cannot wait to begin a new sampler," Hyacinth said in her sweet voice.

Hetty sat down on the bed beside her niece. "Ginny, did Lucy bring you this muslin? How very pretty!"

Eugenia beamed her delight.

"She gave me a riding crop," William announced, slapping it against his thigh several times. "I must show Henry at once!" He ran from the room and a moment later appeared in the doorway again. "Thank you, Cousin Lucy!" Then he was gone.

Lucy lifted her hand to call after him, realizing Henry was presently from home, but she could hear in the distance his running feet pounding down the stairs. If nothing more, he could show his new acquisition to either of his remaining elder brothers, if he could find them.

"I can see you have made everyone very happy," Hetty said, her arm about Eugenia's waist. "And look at all these trunks! One, two, three . . . good heavens, there are seven in all!"

Lucy shrugged. "I thought I might as well have my wardrobe with me as not. I no longer live at Littleton and though I have a great deal of my mother's furniture, which I put in storage, I could not bring myself to place everything there as well."

"The gowns might mildew if not properly attended to."

"As well I know."

"And now, my darlings," Hetty said, addressing the girls, "I fear I must spirit Lucy away and you must return to your lessons."

Lucy slid Violet from her lap and rose to her feet.

Eugenia slipped from the bed and immediately took Violet's hand. "Pray do not pout," she said to her youngest aunt, "for it makes you look quite ugly."

"I don't give a fig for that. I want to stay and I do not want

Lucy to leave!" Tears brimmed in her young eyes and her lip began to quiver.

"Here's your doll, now make your curtsy." Eugenia clearly had her well in hand.

Violet wrapped her doll tightly up in her arms and curtsied, if unsmilingly, to Lucy and Hetty. Hyacinth rolled her eyes and thanked her for the embroidery floss, and the children quit the room.

"Now, come with me," Hetty ordered her. "I have tea prepared for you in my rooms."

Hetty, having long since given way to her stepmother, also had rooms on the second floor, on the other side of Lucy's room. Eugenia had the room facing south and Hetty the room facing north. Lucy was in between.

Lucy walked into her sitting room and smiled. "I had forgotten, but you were just having your rooms refurbished when I was here last. Hetty, this is a beautiful blue and gold. And do I detect an interest in horticulture? For I vow I have never seen so many potted ivies in one chamber."

Hetty moved to examine one of the pots. "I need to water this one. As for your question, I certainly lay no claim to expertise, but I believe I have developed a strong interest in plants. Well, at least in ivy. Do sit down." She gestured to a large, comfortable *chaise longue* in a cornflower blue silk.

Lucy sat down and sank into the feathered cushions, shifting her feet to stretch out before her. "This is quite delightful." She glanced at Hetty and marveled at how much she resembled Robert in both coloring and feature. Her hair was as black as Robert's and her eyes as beautifully brown. She was tall, elegant in demeanor, and quick-witted. She was also kind, generous, and considerate and tea was waiting, just as she had promised. A polished silver pot was flanked by simple white cups and saucers but of very fine, delicate china. Embossed along the rim of both were ivy leaves.

Hetty bid her rest as she served her. "Are you exhausted?"

Lucy took a cup of tea and stirred to dissolve the sugar, milk, and lemon. "Not terribly so. I traveled post so that I was spared the difficulties of trying to use the mail coach, and the roads seem to improve each year. Also, my carriage was particularly well sprung. The inns at which I rested last night and the night before were clean, the sheets properly aired, and the food quite good, though I must confess I still do not care for eel and I was offered it twice!"

Hetty laughed. "I quite agree. Dreadful!" She smiled and her smile softened as she took up a seat nearby. "You appear quite content, as always, but you must not have been so these many months and more."

Lucy shook her head. "When Papa first died, I vow I nearly perished from grief. He was always so robust but I watched in complete despair as the loss of the use of his legs robbed him of his strength. When he took sick, he did not have the will to live."

"I wish that I could have come to you."

"And I to you."

"It is still so odd that we lost our fathers in the same year."

Lucy nodded and stirred her tea a little more. "Quite odd, indeed, but the very reason I have always thought of you not as just a friend or even a cousin but as a sister. Our families always knew a great rapport."

"Indeed." Her smile was warm and genuine.

"But what of you, Hetty? These must be sad times for you as well."

She shrugged faintly and sipped her tea. "I loved Papa, of course. Who did not, for he was such a jolly man. But I do not think I ever enjoyed so easy a relationship with him as you enjoyed with your father. Only George seems to have had that camaraderie with Papa. Certainly none of us, George included, comprehended his choice of second wife."

"I do not think he could have chosen a prettier bride."

"She is beautiful, I will allow her that." She then smiled. "I am so glad you have come, you have no notion. How I have longed for you."

Lucy shook her head. "Hetty, I have received half a dozen letters from you in the past twelvemonth. Why did you not tell me what was going forward here? I was never more shocked by the state of the gardens, and half the house is in Holland covers."

Hetty sighed and sipped her tea. "As for that, I believe I was far too depressed in spirit to mention it. I love Aldershaw. You cannot imagine my own grief and despair that the estate has gone to rack and ruin."

"Is it merely a lack of funds, as Robert has suggested?"

A cloud descended over Hetty's face. "For the greater part, yes."

Lucy sniffed suddenly, for a very strong bouquet of roses had just greeted her senses. She wondered if flowers were blooming somewhere on the estate and the perfume had found its way up to Hetty's sitting room. She turned her head to look at the window to see if it was open but instead saw in the reflection of a small mirror at her elbow a woman standing in the doorway, clinging to the shadows.

Lucy was so shocked by what otherwise could have been an apparition that she nearly spilled her tea. Whirling back to look at the door she called out, "Lady Sandifort, are you there?"

A soft scratching sounded. "Do I intrude, dear ones?"

CHAPTER
THREE

Hetty stiffened perceptibly as Lady Sandifort floated into the room.

Lucy nearly spilled her tea again at the sight before her. She had forgotten completely just how lovely, indeed exquisite, Lady Sandifort was. She had large, thickly fringed blue eyes, and a beautiful chestnut-colored hair, which she wore to advantage in the Greek style so that much of it cascaded down her neck in banded waves. Her complexion was absolute perfection. Her brows were arched undoubtedly by design, her chin faintly cleft, her cheekbones marked, and her expression rather devouring. She gave the impression of a creature from mythology, one that could be both angelic and devilish at the same time. She wore purple silk and appeared as though she studied carefully the pages of *La Belle Assemblée*. For a house that was suffering the effects of strict economies, there was no such evidence in the lady before her.

"How do you go on, Miss Stiles? I have not seen you in an age." Her gaze never wavered from Lucy's face but rather searched her eyes as though attempting to peer into her soul.

Lucy set aside her cup and saucer and slipped her feet over the edge of the *chaise longue*. She rose and bowed slightly as she offered a small curtsy. "Tolerably well, as can be expected in these sad times. I am very sorry for your loss, my lady."

Lady Sandifort grunted faintly in response but said nothing more. Instead, she turned to Hetty and lifted a brow.

Hetty, still stiff with disapprobation, rose from her seat and gestured for her stepmother, who was of an age with her, to take her place. "Do sit down."

Lady Sandifort nodded as one who had power over a slave. "Tea, if you please, Hetty, dearest."

"Of course, but I shall have to fetch another cup and saucer."

"There is a good girl. Do go at once. I cannot abide awaiting one of the servants when you have two perfectly good feet of your own, and that will give Lucy and me a chance to have a little *tête-a-tête* before you return."

"Of course." Hetty turned on her heel and quit the room, her gait as stiff as a palace guard at attention.

Lucy also turned to regard Lady Sandifort in complete astonishment. "I see you are still mistress of Aldershaw," she stated, smiling.

"I recall you as a young lady who always speaks her mind."

"And you were always quite direct as well. I remember liking it very much, but Sir Henry was alive in those days."

"Yes," Lady Sandifort said, smiling happily. "So he was."

Lucy remembered something her papa was always used to say. *When you approach the enemy, do so without a particle of feeling that you might always have the upper hand.* She was surprised that these words came back to her now, not just because they embodied a fine piece of sage advice but because she had in this moment identified Lady Sandifort as the enemy. There could be no two opinions on that score.

So it was that she took up her seat once more, stretching out her legs quite comfortably on the *chaise longue,* determined to come to know just what manner of person held sway in Robert's home. Of course she had known Lady Sandifort for a long time, but she had not been in her company in recent years. She began, "I was surprised to find that you were still here. I should have thought you would have long since left for London, for you always spoke of the metropolis as your favorite place in the entire world."

Lady Sandifort admired one of several rings on her fingers. "I have my reasons for staying, although I must say I adore London."

"As do I," Lucy responded without the smallest pause. "One of my greatest regrets in being situated in Somerset all of my life was the unfortunate distance from London. Papa was never one to travel for the sake of amusement. He always said he could ride fifty miles a day on horseback in pursuit of the French but not one in pursuit of pleasure."

A very sly smile overtook Lady Sandifort's features. "I always enjoy the military mind but I think such men must be more interesting on the eve of battle than hanging about a ballroom floor."

"I believe you may be right. Did you never see Sir Henry in his regimentals?"

"On occasion he wore them for me. In his case, however, I humored him in permitting it, although somewhere in his parading about and pretending to be a great warrior I saw a little of his youth."

"I believe Sir Henry in a red coat would have charmed all the ladies. His manners were quite engaging, a little like his namesake in that respect, I think. How I loved him. I knew him from the time I was a child. He was used to take me for rides around his estate several times on the back of Dragoon."

"Ridiculous name for a horse," she said impatiently.

"He always loved horses. You did not?"

"I cannot abide the beasts. At best they are stupid and at worst, the meanest animals in all creation. A horse bit me once." She rubbed her arm in recollection.

Lucy noted that her ladyship's shoulders were not so squared to her seat as they had been and that she had slipped down a little in her chair.

Lucy immediately picked up her tea and began to sip anew. She understood that something about their discourse had taken Lady Sandifort off her guard. "Henry loves horses as well," she stated.

"That he does." Lady Sandifort giggled. "Poor Henry. I never knew such a foolish man. He could have whatever he wants, instead he scratches out poetic lines in that book of his and waits for God knows what here at Aldershaw. Of all the Sandifort men, he is the greatest mystery and completely impervious to any attempt to gain his confidence." She seemed to be speaking to herself.

Lucy glanced at her, meeting her gaze once more. "Do you know I have the very same impression of him? I cannot make him out and I do not understand his delay in taking orders."

"My dear Miss Stiles, I beg you will not play the simpleton. Henry has not taken Holy Orders because he would be miserable as a priest. I have seen it in his eyes. He longs for something greater than preaching to the poor in spirit and offering succor to the poor in pocket." She then smiled quite warmly and in this moment was more beautiful than any lady Lucy had ever seen before. "You know, I generally do not like women overly much, but I could like you. Indeed, I do believe we could be very great friends."

"I am of a similar mind," Lucy said. How odd it was to tell whiskers so easily to Lady Sandifort.

The aging beauty again trilled her laughter just as Hetty entered the chamber, winded from her long run to the dining room and bearing a cup and saucer in hand. Upon seeing

Hetty, Lady Sandifort rose and shrugged slightly. "I do believe I have lost my interest in your tea, but I thank you for making such a sweet effort on my behalf. I shall retire now to prepare for nuncheon."

"Of course," Hetty said, dropping a curtsy.

Lucy had a dozen questions for Hetty, but refrained on the simple premise that she knew quite well Lady Sandifort would be waiting in the hall just beyond the doorway in order to hear what would be said next. She made a decision in that moment never to say a disparaging word about Lady Sandifort unless she knew for absolute certain her conversation could not be overheard. Presently, she had but one object: to endear Lady Sandifort to her.

"How I despise her," Hetty said vehemently, moving into the chamber and dropping onto the seat Lady Sandifort had just vacated. Lucy turned to look into the small mirror and saw that what she suspected was true. Lady Sandifort was still listening, and having heard Hetty wore an expression of complete satisfaction.

"I do not know why you should," Lucy said. "I have always found her quite charming."

Hetty's expression was wholly shocked, as though Lucy had just slapped her across the face. Lucy gave her a meaningful look and swept a finger over her mouth by way of indicating she should remain quiet. Hetty understood at once, glancing toward the door, her expression suddenly full of chagrin.

Lucy continued easily, "I am come to believe your stepmama is one of those rare creatures which is frequently and completely misunderstood."

"Indeed?" Hetty queried, this time with a frown pinched between her brows.

"Indeed, very much so, only I must ask, Hetty, where are the twins? I have not yet seen Anne and Alice. You have written of them so often, of how wonderfully they have grown into beautiful young ladies, that I find myself agog to see them for myself."

Hetty glanced at the small clock on her bedside table. "At this hour, Miss Gunville permits the twins to take the children for a very long walk." She rose and moved to the window. "Yes, there they are, at the outskirts of the orchard, for I see the tip of Alice's walking stick. She has a very tall one, you know."

"Is she as bookish as ever?" Lucy asked, moving to the window as well. In the distance she could see the bouncing tip of what must have been a very tall stick, indeed.

"Oh, yes," Hetty responded, sighing deeply. "Of late she has been saying that when she gains her majority she intends to take up a cottage in Cornwall and reside there permanently, that she might study the effect of the ocean tides on the seashore."

"That sounds rather ambitious."

"So it does," Hetty said cheerfully. "Alice has a very firm mind of her own and I predict will never live an ordinary life, at least so long as she has command of her future."

"Shall we go in pursuit?"

"Yes, of course."

By the time Lucy and Hetty reached the orchard, the entire group, seven in number, which included the youngest Sandifort children, Eugenia, the twins, and Miss Gunville, had already circled behind what was a dense undergrowth beneath a variety of apple, cherry, peach, and apricot trees. Lucy noted that a great number of dead branches needed to be removed along with young thickets of encroaching shrubs and even a few seedlings of beech and blackthorn.

"So tell me, Lucy," Hetty said, before they had reached the group, "was Lady Sandifort eavesdropping? I can only presume she was hidden behind the door by the manner in which you spoke and indicated I must remain silent."

"She was. I saw her reflection in the mirror on the table next to me."

"Oh, dear," she murmured. "Do I also apprehend that you did not mean all that you said about her?"

Lucy whirled in a circle all the while pretending to look at the hapless garden. In truth, she was searching for the smallest sign of Lady Sandifort. Satisfied that she would not be overheard, still she whispered, "Of course not, but I am come to believe it would be best were I to appear to befriend her."

At that, Hetty chuckled. "You always were notorious for getting up schemes. I suppose you have something in mind already, although when you were younger they were designed to overset Robert."

"Indeed, they were," Lucy cried, laughing with her. "However, now that I am a little older and hopefully have grown up a trifle, I generally extend my peculiar taste for intrigue to more exalted objectives."

"You have your father's military mind."

Lucy giggled. "I suppose I do!"

"Oh, Lucy, you must miss him dreadfully."

She was so caught off guard by the remark that her throat began to ache quite without warning. Tears bit her eyes. "More than I can ever say. He was my best and dearest friend."

Hetty slipped an arm about her waist, gave her a quick hug, and walked with her in that manner until they finally came upon the adventurers.

The group had collected by a stream. The children huddled together just at the muddy bank.

"Got it!" William cried.

His younger sisters drew close. Lucy noted that Violet held her new doll tightly beneath her arm. "I think it horrid!" Violet cried.

Hyacinth wrinkled her nose.

Anne also grimaced. "You do not mean to keep it, do you? Pray, William, put it back. It will not survive in the house."

"If it dies I shall feed it to Tess."

The youngest Sandifort girls shrieked in despair that William would do something so truly wretched, but Lucy watched in some amusement as Eugenia and Alice exchanged despairing shrugs as if to say, *how horrid little boys can be.*

Eugenia, having turned, caught sight of them. "Hetty! Lucy!" With that the magic of the frog disappeared, William even lost his grip, and the little creature plopped back into the water.

Anne approached Lucy immediately and offered her a hand. "We are so glad you are come, Miss Stiles."

"Pray, call me Lucy." Hetty was right. Anne had grown into a considerable beauty. She was in Henry's mold and had lovely wavy blond hair and large green eyes. Her face was the shape of a perfect heart, her teeth very white and even, her smile perfection. She then addressed the younger twin. "And you must be Alice."

Alice took her outstretched hand. "How do you do, Lucy?"

"Very well, indeed." Were there never twins so less alike? Lucy wondered. Alice more nearly resembled both Hetty and Robert, for her hair was very straight and black and her eyes were brown. The family was a great curiosity, that some of the children resembled so nearly their father while the others took after the first Lady Sandifort. She glanced at Alice's tall, crooked walking stick. "I have never seen anything so fascinating. You must have found it in the woods."

"Yes," Alice said, moving the stick in a small upright circle. "We had been walking in the home wood, nearly two years past now, and I came across a fallen limb and this was one of the smaller branches. I particularly loved its shape, going off first in one direction and then another but always returning to form a straightly line. Mr. Quarley fashioned it into a proper stick, stained it, then rubbed it thoroughly with beeswax."

Hetty said, "Lucy, do you recall Miss Gunville?"

"Yes, of course. How do you do?"

Miss Gunville, a very thin woman perhaps somewhere betwixt forty and fifty in years, dropped a slight curtsy. Her peppered brown hair was smoothed into a tight knot on top of her head. "Very well, I thank you," she responded in a crisp manner.

"I see the children are prospering beneath your wing."

She nodded in acknowledgement at this compliment but said nothing more.

Eugenia drew close. "We were taking a tour about the western reaches of Aldershaw before nuncheon. Will you come with us?"

"I should like nothing better."

For the next half hour, Lucy traveled with the educational group, which received instruction from Miss Gunville about the trees and shrubs. Alice told anecdotes about how their father, for all his jollity, knew the names of all the plants on his estate.

"We know, we know," Anne groaned. "Alice, must you be so tedious?"

A sharp glance from Miss Gunville silenced Anne. Until the twins' birthday in late August, they were still beneath her strict tutelage as well.

In the short half hour, as the party began the last leg of the journey which brought them near to the edge of the home wood and northwest of the maze, Lucy had begun to see how disparate the twins were in interest and temperament. Anne, even on a walk in nature, was constantly patting her blond hair and smoothing the skirts of her pink muslin gown. Though twigs collected at the hem of Alice's gown, she scarcely seemed to notice. She was quite a scholarly young lady and bore little resemblance to her sister.

The large party walked the small footpath next to the stream that had its origin in a spring on the estate. William, having removed his shoes and stockings, plunged happily along his way in the very middle of the stream.

"So tell me, Hetty," Lucy said. "Is there anyone else living at Aldershaw at present?"

Hetty laughed. "No, you have spoken with all of us now."

"Look!" Hyacinth called out.

The stream had rounded a small bend, and where the deep, thick woodland of beech, bluebells, and ferns met the stream a colorful caravan was planted in a clearing of green grass. An old man was bent over a black pot. Smoke rose from a fire beneath. Robert was standing over him. He was conversing with the man but at such a distance neither could be understood.

Lucy drew close to Hetty. "Who is this? A Gypsy, though I must say he does not have the look of one. I thought you said I had met everyone."

Hetty shook her head. "I have never seen him before. I wonder if Robert is acquainted with him."

"We shall soon know."

The party drew close and Lucy began to feel uneasy. Recalling her last brief encounter with Robert, she felt embarrassed by her pricklish conduct. When he met her gaze, he did not smile, not in the least. He introduced the party to the old gentleman, who proved to be Mr. Jeremy Frome, an itinerant woodcarver by trade. The grass at his feet was littered with wood shavings.

"I have given him permission to remain on my lands for the summer," he said.

Violet slipped her hand in Lucy's as she watched the gentleman carefully. Lucy knew that the child was nervous at meeting the stranger, but she sensed there was nothing to fear in Mr. Frome. He was quite old, his hands gnarled but active in expression, his pate completely bare, though a silver rim of hair, cropped short, encircled his head like a laurel wreath. His eyes were gray and in them so wise an expression that she found herself completely intrigued.

"My brother owns this land," William said, speaking in a

forthright manner. Apparently he felt it necessary to make Robert's circumstances clear to the old man.

"No one owns the land," Mr. Frome said affably, giving his head a shake and clucking his tongue. "Though many like to think they do. No, the land belongs to all that were here before and all that will come after and, to my way of thinking, any who work and even walk on it. Only think who might have been here two thousand years ago."

"You are mistaken," William argued. "My brother does own this land. He is a baronet."

Robert moved to place a hand on William's shoulder. "That will do," he said gently. "Particularly since I tend to agree with Mr. Frome. In many ways I am but a steward of what has been given to me."

William frowned up at his eldest brother. Lucy could see that he did not understand but to his credit remained politely silent.

Mr. Frome cast his gaze about the group. "This is a very merry party. Do you often ramble about these exquisite grounds?"

"You call them exquisite?" Anne cried, snickering.

"Why, yes, I do, for I am able to see them as they very soon will be."

Lucy wondered what he meant by speaking in such a mysterious manner.

"I can as well," Alice cried, shifting her tall walking stick to her other hand. "Why, if a few weeds were pulled here and there—" she paused dramatically.

Mr. Frome continued with a smile, "A few dead branches chopped to bits—"

Alice added, "A few plants replaced—"

"The lawn watered—"

"Flowers encouraged to bloom—"

"And a garden you have."

"Indeed," Alice stated with a firm nod of her head.

Anne glanced at her eldest brother. "Nothing could be simpler, Robert, do you not think so? And there is our ball to consider. Could not something be done with our gardens before our come-out ball?"

Robert cleared his throat and replaced his hat on his head. "Mr. Quarley, I fear, has only sufficient time to keep the drive in order. I am sorry, Anne. But your come-out ball will be held exclusively in the ballroom, so you need not worry that any of our guests will be offended by the sight of our gardens."

Lucy watched Anne's shoulders droop. Alice in turn patted her shoulder. When silence fell, Miss Gunville spoke. "I fear I must return the children to their lessons now." Addressing her brood, she said, "Pray, bid Mr. Frome 'good day.' "

Eugenia, Hyacinth, William, and Violet all politely took their leave, offering young curtsies and one proper bow before racing away to the stream. Anne and Alice followed. Hetty appeared to desire to comfort Anne as well, for she hurried to catch up with her and, having done so, slipped her arm about her waist.

Lucy felt the strongest desire to remain with Mr. Frome, though she could not say precisely why. He seemed to be a very interesting sort of man with intriguing ideas, but Robert turned to her rather abruptly and offered his arm. "May I escort you back to the house?"

Though she wished to refuse him she felt it would be unwise to do, since she had come the crab with him at their last encounter. At the very least, it was her turn to offer an apology. "Yes, of course," she murmured, taking his arm. She could not resist, however, glancing back at Mr. Frome. He held her gaze for a long moment. There was something very odd yet very pleasing about him. She felt as though she had met him before yet she had no recollection of him. His smile broadened. She could not help it. For reasons she was loath to explain, she liked Jeremy Frome. She liked him very much. She offered him an answering smile, waved with her free hand, and turned back to walk with Robert to the stream.

"I trust you will leave him in peace," Robert said, once they were out of range of Mr. Frome's hearing.

"I do not take your meaning," she stated, not liking the tone of his voice.

"Only that I believe I know you quite well."

"Who is he?" she asked, ignoring his disapprobation. "Do you know him?"

"Not in the least."

"He is a stranger then and you have permitted him to remain on your lands? Why? I wonder."

He seemed uncomfortable and even cleared his throat. "There can be no harm in it."

"What a hypocrite you are, Robert! You pretend such indifference but the goodness of your heart shows at every turn."

He cast her a scathing glance. "Much you know of the matter. I cannot comprehend in the least why you think you understand everyone so perfectly, what is best for them, and how each of us should go on."

Lucy wanted to reply that she had always had just such a gift, especially since in saying so she would instantly set up his back, but the angry look in his eye quelled her tongue. Instead, she responded, "You are attempting to shift the subject, but I shan't permit you to. I think it an excellent thing that you have extended your charity to Mr. Frome and I mean to know him better."

At that he stopped. They had reached the edge of the stream where several steppingstones had been carefully placed to allow even the feeblest person to cross safely. "I am most serious," he began quite firmly. "I will not have you interfering in the business here at Aldershaw. You will only make matters worse."

What matters? she wanted to ask. "Yes, Robert," she responded flatly.

He narrowed his eyes. "Lucy," he stated, cocking his head. "You will leave well enough alone, including Mr. Frome."

"Yes, Robert."

"The deuce take it, stop saying that! I know very well you are mocking me."

"Yes, Robert," she said breezily. But turning from him quickly, she picked up her skirts and crossed the stones on several light leaps. Once on the other side, she walked briskly in pursuit of the others.

Robert caught up with her. "You are angry that I kissed you and now you mean to punish me."

This time she stopped and whirled on him. "How could I ever be angry that you kissed me?" she cried. She blinked at him and realized she should not have said such a thing. She continued, "I will say only this. I do not understand you, that much is quite true, for I will never comprehend how you have allowed things at Aldershaw to come to such a pass as they have when so much can be done and that without a great deal of effort!"

"I wish you had never come here!" he cried. "I knew how it would be, but indeed, you do not know with what fire you are playing and you do not have the wisdom to manage things. You are still such a child in that regard, a ridiculous, vulgar, interfering child! Why, you are not even wearing your bonnet and your hair is hanging almost to your knees!"

With that, he moved quickly away from her.

Lucy stared after him. How his words stung, becoming a whirlwind in her mind, *ridiculous, vulgar, interfering*. He wanted her anywhere but at Aldershaw and in this moment she wished she could leave as well. After all, she was hardly here by choice. An outdated requirement in her father's will had brought her to Robert's home.

She did not follow him. Indeed, she was far too overset to put her feet in motion. She felt as though the wind had suddenly left her full, billowing, happy sails.

"Come, child."

Lucy turned abruptly to find that Mr. Frome had stolen upon her, and so quietly that her heart began to pound. "Mr. Frome!" she cried. "You have given me such a fright."

"I never meant to do so," he said in his gentle way.

He extended his hand to her. She looked at it, realizing that he meant for her to accompany him to his camp. Without needing to ponder the situation overly much, she put her hand in his. Together they walked as old companions back to his caravan.

As she drew near his camp she smelled the delicate aroma of a very fine coffee. A smaller pot with a lip for pouring was hanging over his fire. He must have prepared the coffee while she and Robert were brangling. "Would you care for a cup?" he asked, directing her to take up a seat on a stool he set out for her.

"Yes, thank you, I would."

When the coffee was served and he was sitting on his stool as well, he addressed her. "So, tell me, Miss Stiles, what is causing you such grievous distress?"

Lucy regarded him in some astonishment. After all, she hardly knew him. "I would not wish to burden you," she said tactfully.

He sipped his coffee. "My wife was used to tell me that I always pushed where I ought not to. I suppose she was right, but I must say you seem quite unhappy and I have always believed that talking about a matter, even if it proves insignificant, can be of great benefit."

Lucy did not know how it was, but she said, "I am thinking that I am not wanted here."

"I saw something very different a few minutes ago. The youngest child in particular seems to have need of you."

"Violet is a very dear little girl," she responded, feeling as though her heart would break. Robert's unkind words had pierced her heart.

"I hope you will not think me officious," he said, his voice gentle and kind, "but I believe there is much for you to do at Aldershaw."

"A few minutes ago I would have agreed with you completely," she said. Her heart grew heavy thinking again of Robert's harsh words. She leaned over, settling her elbows on her knees and lifting the cup to her lips. So unladylike! Perhaps Robert was right. Perhaps she was horridly vulgar. "But there are those who would think my involvement somewhat *interfering.*"

"And who would think that?" he asked pointedly.

She glanced at Mr. Frome and saw nothing but a very great kindness, even understanding, in his aged gray eyes. "Sir Robert."

"And his opinion is so important, then?"

His opinion is everything! The thought was so quick to enter her mind that she caught her breath, for it was as absurd a notion as it was wretchedly true! "I have never thought of it before, but yes, I believe his opinion is very important, indeed, perhaps too much so."

"What sort of man is he?"

"Odious, beyond permission!" she responded heatedly, but for some reason her heart was fluttering wildly in her breast. "On that subject there can be no two opinions."

"But he is very handsome. I can see it in your eyes." Mr. Frome was smiling.

"Wretchedly handsome and well he knows it." She felt irritated of a sudden. "And quite arrogant. He is a handsome, arrogant, and quite useless fellow."

Mr. Frome nodded sagely. "A blackguard?"

"No," she drawled, frowning. "At least not to my knowledge and I certainly hope not."

"Good. His faults are not a matter of his deepest character, then."

She sighed. "I do not think so, but he is horridly ill-tempered."

"Perhaps he has a reason to be."

His words gave her pause. Did Robert have a reason to be on his high ropes most of the time? She recalled quite swiftly to mind just how many of his family inhabited Aldershaw and she rather thought she had her answer.

"I fear his family is become a trying lot. All live beneath his roof, including his stepmama. I believe my arrival may have been the last straw."

"He has great responsibilities, then?"

"Innumerable. However, I do not give a fig whether he should have one or a thousand! A gentleman ought to be polite regardless of his mood."

"Indeed he should," Mr. Frome agreed readily. He looked about him. "Whatever do you mean to do with this orchard? I have not seen anything so ill-kempt in many a year." His camp overlooked the northern reaches of the orchard.

"You are very right." She sipped the excellent, mild coffee again. "From nearly the moment I arrived, I had the most outrageous notion of taking the gardens in hand, but would not that be wholly impertinent? For I am merely Sir Robert's ward. I am not even a real cousin, though they call me 'cousin' nonetheless. I have no right to interfere in the least."

"Yet there is a sparkle in your eye," he said teasingly, leveling his cup at her.

"That is the difficulty, I suppose. I never could resist a challenge."

"What fault is there in that?" he asked.

"I see we take a similar view of things." She regarded him carefully. She was smiling now. What was there not to like in this old man? She glanced at his domicile, noting that the caravan was painted with an idyllic scene and quite realistic:

ewes and lambs, fields enclosed by dry stone walls, the roll of the downs, a stand of trees, even a brook.

"Did you paint this yourself?" she inquired.

"Yes."

"The sky is so real. It is almost as though I can see through your wagon. And you live here?"

"I have for forty years."

She was quite surprised. "Since you were a young man, then? But you spoke of your wife—" She regretted her words.

"You cannot offend me by asking of her or of my dear children. Yes, I had a family once. How I loved them, but the pox took them from me."

"I am so sorry."

Lucy glanced about, becoming more and more intrigued by the old man. She noted his chair, the old cups, the small stone ring he used for his fires, the stones as black as ink. She could only wonder of all the places he had lived and seen.

"So, tell me of your relationship with Sir Robert."

She sighed heavily, for the very nature of the question brought many pressing aspects of her life to the forefront of her mind. "He is my guardian."

Mr. Frome seemed greatly surprised. "A young lady your age hardly needs a guardian."

"I told Papa as much, but he was insistent."

"I see," he murmured softly. "He was a stubborn man, your father?"

"Nearly as stubborn as myself."

"He is recently passed?"

She nodded and sipped her coffee again, for a very large and painful lump had formed in her throat. "A year ago, but it seems little more than a day."

"I understand. Completely. And you have no other family?"

"No. That is, I have an aunt who resides in London, but I

have never seen her, although I was told she held me once just after I was born. Sir Robert's father and mine were great friends. That is how we know one another. Our fathers had hoped we would make a match of it one day, but how could they have known just how ill-suited we are?"

"Fathers generally have the best of intentions, but they certainly cannot predict the path of the heart. Do I take it then that you are in love with someone else?"

Lucy shook her head and sighed. "Not at present. I did love once, but his father did not approve of me and my betrothed, Mr. Goodworth, married another lady."

"And his father approved of her?"

At that Lucy burst out laughing, yet her heart hurt all over again at the memory of it. "Therein lies the rub. After telling me countless times all the ways his father disapproved of me, I finally broke off our engagement, after which Mr. Goodworth took to wife the most worthless creature! She was the daughter of a farmer and his father was a viscount!"

"That is a very sad tale," he cried, "but it sounds as though he was determined to punish his father for having been unkind to you."

"I suppose he was."

"It is not a bad thing, however, to have known love," he said softly, sipping his coffee, "even when nothing comes of it."

"I have many tender memories of Mr. Goodworth."

"As you should."

Lucy let her gaze drift over the gardens, at least as much as was visible from the edge of the home wood. Because the wood was on a rise, she could see the tips of many shrubs and hedges that delineated various parts of the garden.

Ridiculous, vulgar, interfering. Robert's words came back to her with the force of a blade to her heart.

"I would not rely overly much on Sir Robert's manners at present," Mr. Frome said, as though reading her mind. "If his house is as crowded as you say, then I daresay he is not entirely himself."

Lucy found that Mr. Frome's conversation had soothed her wounded sensibilities exceedingly.

"Lucy!"

Lucy lifted her head and could see that Alice was calling to her from across the stream.

"Nuncheon is served!"

"Oh, dear," she said, rising swiftly from her stool. "I believe I may have kept everyone waiting." She handed her cup to Mr. Frome, thanking him for his many kindnesses. She then hurried to return to the house.

CHAPTER
FOUR

Nuncheon was a difficult affair in which only the eldest of Aldershaw's inmates were permitted to partake. Eugenia, Hyacinth, William, and Violet all took their meals with Miss Gunville in the schoolroom. Anne and Alice, nearly out, were required to dine with the family.

Henry was absent as he said he would be, George appeared to be sunk in a fit of the megrims, and Robert's expression could only be described as one of painful forbearance.

Lucy's mind was taken up primarily with her conversation with Mr. Frome and so it was that she made her inward peace with Robert, though she said nothing to him, setting down his unhappy conduct as having its source in the various difficulties at Aldershaw.

She ate her cold chicken, beef, and salad slowly. Conversation languished. Lady Sandifort sat at the foot of the table, undoubtedly having retained the position even after her husband's death, and ate heartily of her meal. She drank a great deal of champagne, which Lucy thought quite odd and which was served exclusively to her. She watched everyone with careful eyes but generally seemed to be enjoying herself hugely. Hetty, being the eldest, sat in the center of the table opposite Rosamunde. The latter pushed her food about on her plate. She appeared as one who had the headache. George, seated next to her, ignored her entirely.

The twins, nearest to Lady Sandifort, flanked her and were fairly silent throughout the entire meal, except when addressed by their stepmother. Their responses remained monosyllabic.

Hetty, at least, made an attempt to converse and asked Lucy many things about Somerset. Lucy was happy to talk about the county she had called home for the entirety of her life and spoke at length.

"Hetty," Lady Sandifort called out. "I see you at least have the proper manners to entertain our new guest as ought to be done. What a sad lack of civility in the rest of you!" She trilled her laughter and swilled her champagne.

Lucy, having taken her measure, was not especially surprised. George, however, shot dagger glances in her direction while Hetty stiffened instantly and speared her chicken more forcefully than necessary.

"My head hurts," Rosamunde said.

"Your head always pains you," Lady Sandifort said.

"It was not used to pain me. I never suffered in this way at Baddesley."

"Why must you always be praising Baddesley to the skies? You sound as though you are not grateful to Sir Robert for providing a home for you."

"I have a home," she answered dully.

"Lady Sandifort," Hetty called out suddenly, "Anne and Alice were wondering if you had finally decided on the date for their come-out ball. Will it be in late August or early September?"

Lucy saw a darkness descend over Lady Sandifort's exquisite features, her gaze shifting strangely to Robert for the barest moment. She lifted an imperious brow. How much her beauty seemed to fade in these few seconds. Only after meeting Robert's gaze did she turn to address Hetty. "I have decided, given the general lack of maturity in your full-blood sisters, that they ought to wait another year for their ball. Look at them. Both as silent as the grave! They are not ready to be in company."

Hetty gasped.

George cried, "What the deuce!"

Robert frowned at his stepmother. "But this is absurd," he said. "And all because . . . but this is absurd!"

Lady Sandifort merely smiled as one impervious to their complaints.

Lucy glanced at Anne, whose complexion first turned a pretty shade of chalk and then a violent crimson. At the same time, she rose abruptly from her seat, and the chair fell backward with a loud cracking sound on the planked wood floor. "You would not do this to me!" she cried. "How could you be so cruel when you must know how much I have been waiting, indeed, longing for my come-out ball?"

Lady Sandifort gestured to the chair on the floor as if to say that Anne had just proven her point. "Sit down," she stated firmly.

Lucy watched Anne debate within her mind just what she ought to do. For a moment, she thought Anne would do as she was bid, but finally she lifted her chin and said, "I do not like you, Lady Sandifort, I never have. You are very mean, perhaps one of the meanest females I have ever known. Were it not for my youngest brother and sisters, I should have detested that my father ever married you!"

"Anne!" Robert called out, obviously horrified.

But Anne was beyond reason. She burst into tears and fled the room. Alice rose as well. "You know I do not give a fig if there is a come-out ball, but I do not understand how you could hurt Anne so much as you just have. What did she ever do to you?"

"Well, for one thing, Alice, if you may recall, she put three large spiders in my bed when I first came to Aldershaw."

George snorted his laughter and received a glare from Lady Sandifort in return.

Alice continued. "But she was ten years old then. She was a child."

"She did it again just last year, so pray do not try to defend her. As for you, do not even think I shall permit you to take your trip to Cornwall in the fall. Perhaps next year, if your conduct toward me has improved as well, or did you think I believed the nasty letters I received all last year were not of your hand? You have a very specific manner of drawing your Ts, unlike anyone I've ever known."

Alice's face blanched. There was nothing more she could say. With some great effort at dignity, she lifted her chin. "You deserved every word."

"Neither you nor Anne may sit down to dinner for the next fortnight or I shall have you locked up in one of the attic bedchambers."

Alice walked away.

Lucy glanced at Robert to see what he meant, if anything, to do about the situation, but he had grown very quiet. He frowned heavily, staring at the silver epergne in the middle of the table.

"A delightful meal as always," George announced as Lady Sandifort finished her third glass of champagne.

Rosamunde addressed her husband. "I wish to see Baddesley. Please take me there, George. I do not care in the least if the repairs are not yet completed."

This sudden turn of conversation brought all eyes trained upon George. He grew uneasy. "You know I cannot do so. The last time I was there part of the roof was open to the sky. It is not fit to be inhabited."

Lady Sandifort laughed heartily. "How you do tell your whiskers, George!"

George's face turned bright red and he ground his teeth.

Rosamunde began to weep loudly.

Lucy found she could eat nothing more.

George rose and fairly threw back his chair so that now two of them were reclining on the floor. He stomped from the chamber and was gone.

Hetty moved to console Rosamunde, taking her arm and lifting her from her chair. "Come, dearest, let me take you back to your room. I shall have some tea brought to you."

"Thank you."

"Yes, please do take her away," Lady Sandifort said, laughing. "She is always a watering pot and I cannot bear sniveling creatures that weep and pout incessantly."

Hetty cast a hate-filled glance at her, but Lady Sandifort merely laughed anew.

She addressed Lucy. "See what a happy house you have come to? Charming, is it not? But do not think, Miss Stiles, that I have not made a push to improve things. I have. I have recommended to Robert a score of times to be rid of his brothers and certainly Hetty could find employment as a governess or something since she has no intention of marrying. But he refuses to take my suggestions."

Lucy glanced at Robert to see how he received her comments, but he remained silent, meeting her ladyship's gaze but briefly, and directed Finkley to right the fallen chairs.

Lady Sandifort, made content by her champagne, however, did not seem to require anyone to speak. Sipping at her fourth glass of bubbling wine, she began to enumerate all the ways she had attempted to be of use at Aldershaw, but how all her efforts went completely unappreciated. She knew she was right about forcing the twins to wait another year for a come-out ball, for did Lucy not notice their behavior even today? How could such improperly behaved young ladies be set loose upon the world?

At last, after another glass of champagne and perhaps a

thousand words more on the subject of how ill-used she had been, Lady Sandifort rose unsteadily to her feet. The butler, seeing she was about to capsize, caught her by the elbow and set her upright.

A moment later, Lucy found herself alone with Robert. She might have attempted to converse with him, but he rose suddenly to his feet. "You will excuse me, Lucy, but I have a great deal of estate business to attend to this afternoon. I will stay, however, if you wish for it."

She could see that he was greatly overset. "Pray do not concern yourself," she said briskly. "Of course you must tend to business. There can be nothing more important at present, after all."

He glanced at her and hesitated. Finally, he said, "I hope you are not too discouraged by what you have witnessed today. All will be well, I am certain of it."

"How?" she inquired simply. "How will all be well?"

"There are matters that must be . . . resolved."

"What matters?" She felt certain he had not a single solution in mind for the troubles at Aldershaw.

"I wish you would trust me but a little," he snapped.

"And I wish you would trust me," she cried.

He ground his teeth as George had, offered her a polite bow, then quit the room.

She was alone now. She looked down at her partially consumed meal, cut a slice of beef, and began to eat. She had the strong impression that she would be in great need of such sustenance over the coming weeks.

After nuncheon, Lucy went to her bedchamber and remained there for a very long time. The sole and quite overworked upper maid had unpacked her trunks in an understandably hasty manner. She therefore set about to rearrange the wardrobe and the highboy more to her liking but with the stronger purpose of letting her hands be busy while she engaged her heart and her mind in trying to determine just what, if anything, she could do about the disaster that was Aldershaw.

More than once she moved to the window of her bed-chamber and looked out over the sad garden, thinking how difficult and long was the climb to create something of beauty but how swiftly any endeavor could be destroyed. Plants themselves were a mystery that they did not seem to know proper boundaries all by themselves, so that left to grow wild many trees and shrubs would be positively mangled by late season winds and storms.

The garden appeared as though each plant had been at war with its neighbor from the time of taking root in the soil.

With such thoughts she moved from wardrobe to window to chest of drawers and back, her mind trying to find its way through the tangle of feelings, conduct, and relationships that existed beneath Aldershaw's ancient roof. She glanced about her chamber and chuckled, wondering just how many people had lived, laughed, perhaps even died in this very room over the two centuries the house had been in existence. Were there any ghosts present to laugh or scorn her current thoughts and even intentions?

Only what were her intentions, she wondered as she rolled up a pair of silk stockings and placed them in a drawer with a dozen other such mates. She had an equal number of garters. She particularly enjoyed embroidering small strips of fabric to create her garters. For the barest moment she wished that the embroidering of garters was her only concern.

Only what to do about Aldershaw? Poor Anne and Alice and their dreams, and what of Rosamunde and her need to return to her home, and what of George's pricklish, even moody, conduct? And above all, what was to be done about Lady Sandifort? What *could* be done about her? That was the true conundrum. Lady Sandifort held sway, but how could one dethrone her without injuring Anne and Alice further? Given all the circumstances of the house, she understood now that hurting the young ladies was her primary weapon in any given situation. She wondered what had occurred that might have caused Lady Sandifort to refuse the come-out ball. Now there was the real question, for she doubted her ladyship did anything without either believing herself provoked or without a purpose in mind. She recalled the manner in which Lady Sandifort had given Robert a rather profound look, the haughty lifting of her brow. There had been a message in that glance, but what had it meant? She could not imagine.

Later that evening she sought out Robert in the library, where she found him alone reading a book. She wanted to ask him if what she suspected about Lady Sandifort was true, that something had happened to prompt her refusal. "I know the day has been long and full of trials, but there is something I would ask you."

He seemed very tired. She knew he had been on horseback for most of the afternoon. "What would that be?"

"Only this. Did Lady Sandifort's sudden cancellation of the come-out ball have its root in some injury she believed she had received, I mean other than spiders and anonymous letters?"

He sighed heavily and impatiently. "I told you not to concern yourself."

"Very well." She was unwilling to overset him further. Besides, she knew that time would bring an answer even if Robert would not. "I shall bid you good night. I do not mean to trouble you."

She moved as if to go, but he called after her. "And yet you do trouble me, exceedingly."

She turned back to him. "I beg your pardon?"

"You trouble me, Lucy. I fear you mean to involve yourself and I wish you would not."

She stared at him for a long moment. So many things came to mind that she wanted to say, most of which for the purpose of defending her position, but she could see in his fatigue there would be no point in a discussion. They would merely fall to brangling again. Therefore, she smiled. "Good night, Robert."

She whirled about. This time he did not call to her until she had reached the door. "Lucy!" She turned back again and he added, "The answer to your query is yes, retaliation was involved, but on that subject I will say no more."

With that, she nodded and passed from the library. She was surprised that he had given her an answer, nonetheless one that confirmed her suspicions. Only against what had Lady Sandifort been retaliating?

By the next morning, Lucy was still undecided as to what she ought to do. After all, Lady Sandifort had made her pronouncement: there was to be no come-out ball. So how was she supposed to make her ladyship rescind her decision? The case seemed quite difficult. However, the day was new and full of every promise.

She entered the morning room where breakfast was served and saw that none of the gentlemen were present. As for the ladies, a depressed air hung over the chamber. As befitted the mood, a surprising clap of thunder rumbled over the distant hills.

"I suppose it will rain," Rosamunde murmured. She held a cup of tea in one hand and a slice of toast in another. She leaned back in her chair and sighed as she glanced out the window.

"Hallo, Lucy," Hetty called to her. She was standing at the sideboard ladling eggs onto her plate. "I trust you slept well?"

"Very well, thank you." Having noticed her, each of the ladies greeted her in turn, Lady Sandifort merely nodding, for her mouth was full.

The morning room was situated opposite the armory and next to the ballroom. Colorful chintz draperies and walls painted a vivid yellow should have enlivened any party, but the present company, as Lucy could well see, was quite blue-devilled, and not without reason. Rosamunde was homesick for Baddesley, Anne had been refused her come-out ball, Alice was told a life in Cornwall was not to be considered, and Hetty could scarcely contain her dislike of Lady Sandifort. In actuality, the only person present enjoying even a particle of her surroundings was Lady Sandifort, who gulped her tea and all but smacked her lips. On her plate were a cherry tart, scrambled eggs, bacon, ham, a slice of toast, and a large dollop of strawberry jam. Lucy did not know how she kept her figure when her appetite was so enormous. If Lady Sandifort was nothing else, she was a woman of great appetites, and not just for that which would fill a dish.

Lucy moved to the sideboard and began filling her plate. Afterward, she chose to take up a chair between Anne and Lady Sandifort, causing that woman to raise a surprised brow.

When her ladyship finished chewing and swallowing, she said, "You are a welcome guest, Miss Stiles, as I have said before."

"Lady Sandifort, I hope I am not being presumptuous, but since the rest of the family addresses me as Lucy I hope you will do the same. It would mean a great deal to me."

The remaining ladies all turned to stare at Lucy.

"I take it very kindly in you, *Lucy*," Lady Sandifort said. "There, you see Anne. You could learn a great deal from our dear Lucy. Now here is a young lady who knows how to behave properly."

Anne merely lifted her chin, her continued hostility quite obvious.

"Do you mean to keep pouting?" she asked.

Lucy glanced at the elder of the twins and watched as she compressed her lips and as two spots of color appeared on her cheeks. She desired more than anything to intervene but did not know how. Suddenly, inspiration struck in the most extraordinary way. Without questioning in the slightest whether she ought to proceed down the path that now filled her mind, she turned slightly toward Lady Sandifort. "My lady, are you per chance acquainted with Lord Valmaston?"

Even Hetty glanced at her rather sharply. The Earl of Valmaston had a shocking reputation.

"No, I am not," she said, laying down her fork and knife. "But of course I am well versed in his escapades. What lady who has ever been to London is not? Why do you ask?"

"Well, as it happens, I am in a bit of a quandary. You see, I do believe I have erred quite greatly and I am hoping you might advise me."

"I should be happy to, but how does this concern the Earl of Valmaston?"

"Perhaps you are not aware, but I am very well acquainted with his lordship—"

"You are?" she asked, obviously stunned. "How is that possible when you seem to be such a good sort of girl, Miss St—I mean, Lucy. That is, do go on."

"I can understand why you are so surprised. The whole world knows of his reputation. As it happens, he was one of our neighbors in Somerset and a great friend of my father."

"Oh, I see. Well. Well, that puts a very different light on the matter, indeed."

"At any rate, I knew that Anne and Alice were to have a come-out ball this summer, for Hetty wrote of it in one of her letters, but I fear that I may have led Valmaston to believe he was invited to the ball."

"*What?*" Lady Sandifort cried.

"Is this so?" Hetty asked.

Lucy did not dare look at her, but rather continued to address Lady Sandifort. "I see I have given you a shock and I do beg your pardon. Allow me to explain. In my many conversations with him, I spoke of all of you very much, so much that I believe he came to see you as part of his family in the same way I have always felt Aldershaw was a second home to me. For if you must know, Valmaston was of great use to me after father died." At least this latter portion of her story was true, the earl had been an enormous comfort to her. However, Lucy rather thought that, were she to be judged in this moment by an angelic court, she would not be allowed to step one foot in heaven for all the whiskers she was presently telling. "I have quite overstepped the bounds of propriety, and certainly including Lord Valmaston in a come-out ball is nothing but foolishness, yet he was so kind to me, you can have no notion! The truth is, ma'am, that I fear I *suggested* he might wish to come to Hampshire in August, perhaps even to stay several days at Aldershaw. He agreed, of course, for he promised my father that he would tend to me. I know it was impertinent of me and horribly imprudent but, Lady Sandifort, what should I do? I fear offending him by writing and saying that there is to be no ball and that he cannot come. Do you not think he will be grossly offended?"

Lady Sandifort forgot all about her meal. She appeared as one struck by lightning. "To think you are so intimately known to a man who, well, never mind that!" She glanced at Anne and Alice. She bit her lip. She looked up at the ceiling. Her cheeks grew flushed. "He is worth ten thousand a year," she murmured. "Valmaston, here!" Her eyes glittered. Her lips twitched. She gulped her tea, then clattered the cup and saucer on the table.

"I do not know what to tell him," Lucy muttered. "How will I ever tell him there is to be no ball? Perhaps you can help me compose my letter."

"Lucy, I must say you have behaved abominably in extending an invitation you had no right to extend. But I simply cannot bear the thought of offending in any manner the Earl of Valmaston." She drummed her fingers on the table. She shifted in her seat. She plucked at her chestnut brown curls.

Lucy stole a glance at Hetty. Her expression was one of such vast amusement that Lucy quickly looked away.

And so it begins, Lucy thought. Her decision to involve herself in the affairs at Aldershaw was made the moment it occurred to her that the mere speaking of Valmaston's name would change everything for Anne and Alice.

Lady Sandifort slapped her hand on the table. "There is nothing for it now, I suppose," she cried, appearing incensed, but her blue eyes were alive with excitement. "Good God, Lucy, I hope you do not mean to keep us at sixes and sevens with such wretched conduct as this, for I can think of only one recourse—if Valmaston has been invited to a ball at Aldershaw, then a ball there must be!"

"Oh!" Anne cried out with shocked delight, but Lucy quickly caught her arm and gave her a gentle pinch. She instantly silenced herself.

"As for you, Miss Anne!" Lady Sandifort exclaimed. "I hope you mean to improve your manners, for if you are to meet so famous and exalted a gentleman as the Earl of Valmaston, your conduct must be impeccable!"

"Yes, ma'am," she murmured and lowered her head obsequiously.

Lucy chanced to meet Alice's gaze. The more studious of the twins was watching her with great curiosity and not a little respect in her brown eyes. A small smile of understanding played over her lips.

Lady Sandifort glanced from Anne to Alice. "Well, well. So you will have your ball after all."

"I do not see how you have any other choice," Alice said,

and that so somberly that Lucy began to wonder about her as well. "Indeed, Stepmama, I will try to do better."

"I hope you will. And you may take Miss Lucy for an example. It seems to me she is the only lady in this house, other than myself, who knows how to conduct herself properly." She turned to Anne. "And I suppose you will be floating about the manor now, Miss Anne?"

Anne wisely refrained from saying anything but instead cut a piece of ham very slowly and kept her head down.

"And, Miss Alice, you must listen to me very carefully. The time has come for you to begin thinking seriously of matrimony."

"I do not desire to be a wife," Alice said firmly, meeting Lady Sandifort's gaze quite forcefully. "Love does not interest me in the least."

"Who is speaking of love? You will marry. It is your duty to your eldest brother. He will desire that you marry in order to enhance the fortunes of the family. And you need not glare at me, for I am doing you a great service. You must begin to understand your obligations in this situation and you will save yourself a great deal of sadness by not setting your heart on Cornwall."

Alice lowered her gaze to her plate just as Anne did, and began spreading jam on her toast. Lucy was afraid that she might be overset but her expression was surprisingly sanguine. Again she wondered about her.

"I suppose there is but one more thing," Lady Sandifort said, clearing her throat and picking up her cup of tea. "If Valmaston is to be at Aldershaw, and if the pair of you girls are to learn to conduct yourself as proper ladies, then I suppose I must allow you to dine with the family."

"Yes, Stepmama," the twins said in unison.

Rosamunde stood up slowly and in faint accents said, "I fear I am not feeling well. I simply . . . must . . ." She placed the back of her hand against her forehead and tottered in the direction of the door but quite close to Lady Sandifort. The next moment she stumbled, jostling her arm and therefore the cup of tea quite forcefully. The amber liquid sloshed over her plate of food.

Lucy gasped, as did the other ladies at the table.

"You have ruined my cherry tart! Good God, Rosamunde, if you are not well I wish you would remain in your bed-chamber!"

"I do beg your pardon," Rosamunde said in weak accents. "I am feeling very faint indeed. Pray excuse me."

So commanding was her performance that Lucy was truly not certain if she had purposely bumped Lady Sandifort or not. She paused in the doorway, however, then turned back to wink at Lucy before disappearing into the hall. Lady Sandifort was too busy removing the sopping tart to have seen her. Lucy bit her lip.

Lady Sandifort cried, "What an absurd female! A complete ninnyhammer!"

"What the deuce do you mean by telling Lady Sandifort that you invited Lord Valmaston—*Lord Valmaston*—to a come-out ball for my sisters? What maggot got into your head, Lucinda Stiles?"

"The one that should have got into yours!" she countered hotly.

She closed the door behind her and approached Robert on a quick firm tread. He was in his office going over a great many books and rose from his desk when she entered. He had summoned her and it was clear he was very angry.

When she spoke, however, she kept her voice low. "I do not know how it has happened that Lady Sandifort is still be-having as though she is mistress at Aldershaw, but of one thing I am utterly certain—you have managed your step-mother quite badly."

"Why the devil are you whispering?"

Lucy held her tongue for a very long moment then glanced at the door and afterward back to Robert, staring at him in a meaningful manner. When he continued frowning and shaking his head, she cried, "You were never so stupid as this! Have your wits gone a-begging?"

She watched as enlightenment dawned. He pointed at the door. "You cannot mean that you suspect that she—" Lucy knew what he was going to say so she rushed up to him and quickly put her fingers against his mouth.

"Hush," she murmured. In a more normal tone of voice she said, "I came here to speak with you about Valmaston, to explain what happened. My father was well acquainted with him. He was with me much of the time when Papa passed away and I did not mention it earlier but I fear I already invited him to Anne and Alice's ball. He has only been awaiting word from me as to just when he should come into Hampshire."

He frowned more heavily still as he searched her eyes. He then glanced about the chamber uncertainly. After a long moment, he said, "I fear yet again I must beg your pardon. I do not know how I came to be so uncivil. Of course, if Valmaston is a friend of yours and, more particularly, of your father, I suppose he must be invited to the ball."

"There is more. I fear I also promised him that he could stay for a full sennight."

The color on his cheeks rose so quickly that Lucy instinctively took a step backward.

"What?" he thundered. "Under my roof? Here? At Aldershaw? For an entire week?"

Lucy narrowed her eyes and tried to imprint his mind with the direction of her thoughts but he seemed completely

obtuse. "Of course at Aldershaw. I am persuaded his lordship would not at all be comfortable at the inn at Bickfield,
which leads me to say that, now that a ball is forthcoming, I
was hoping to speak to you about some improvements I feel
would be necessary. Will you take a turn about the gardens
with me?"

Robert was fairly shaking with rage. There was so much
in this impudent, impertinent speech to cause his ire to ex-
plode in his head that he scarcely knew where to begin. He
was about to give her the dressing down she so richly deserved when suddenly she smiled and spoke, "Yes, yes, I
know you wish to feed me to the dogs, but indeed, if you will
only listen to me I believe you will not find my purposes
quite so abhorrent." She dropped her voice to a whisper, but
still she smiled, "Besides, if you ring a peal over my head,
there is a good chance that the children will hear us quarreling and I strongly suspect they have heard enough of that to
last a lifetime."

How much he despised her warm smiles, especially when
they were coupled with rational thought and precise truth.
"Very well," he said between clenched teeth. "To the garden
we shall go . . . at once!"

CHAPTER FIVE

Robert followed Lucy out of doors and in a low voice began, "I have never known a lady so presumptuous as to have extended an invitation she had no right to give, and that to a man of, of, of—" He could not complete his thought, for to speak of Valmaston's reputation to a complete innocent was unthinkable.

"Do save your breath to cool your porridge, Robert. I can see that you are overset but let us retire to the maze that we might brangle in private." She cast a meaningful glance up at the windows.

Once more he clenched his teeth but refrained from speaking, at least until they had reached the depths of the horridly overgrown maze. His face was stinging from at least two branches of yew Lucy had let flip back into his face. Finally at a clearing, when he threw up his arm to ward off the striking of yet another branch, he took strong hold of her arm. "Is that necessary?" he cried.

Lucy began to laugh. "Of course it is, for I know very well you mean to come the crab with me. However, we are now free to speak, so let me understand you. In your office you were play-acting when you said that of course I must invite Lord Valmaston?"

"Yes, I was following your lead! Lucy, I ask again, how could you—"

"But what possible harm can come of inviting Valmaston to stay for a few days beneath your roof?"

He stared at her utterly aghast. "And you accused me of stupidity!" he cried. How was it possible she could imagine it would be at all acceptable for a rogue of Valmaston's stamp to be welcome in his house? He could think of only one thing that would give satisfaction in this moment: to box Lucy Stiles's ears! Unfortunately, he was a gentleman of some conscience and regardless of how much he knew he would be justified in doing so he showed great strength of character in restraining himself.

"I see you have at last taken command of yourself," she said, smiling in that maddening fashion of hers.

He growled. "Valmaston! Of all the wretched things to have done, I cannot believe you would have invited him to my house! Have you gone mad?"

"Of course not," she responded, lacing her fingers in front of her. "Quite the opposite. As I was saying before, I believe I have shown great good sense, and if you had a little yourself you would have done something similar any time this twelvemonth past."

He took deep breaths. He forced his rage to diminish, for it would do no good at all to simply keep arguing with her. She seemed to believe she had acted rightly, perhaps even prudently. "Do you have any comprehension at all just what sort of man Valmaston is?"

At that she grew very somber. "The best of friends," she stated firmly, and so sincerely that he was taken aback. She continued, "He was always a perfect gentleman with me and over the years he grew very dear to my father, I assure you.

Our estates marched beside one another in Somerset, but surely you knew as much."

He shook his head. "I did not know you accounted him as a friend."

"He called often, at least once a fortnight when he was in the West Country, and he was especially attentive to me when my father died. So you see, whatever his reputation may at one time have been and perhaps even still is, I will always consider him and call him my friend."

Robert narrowed his eyes. There was no dissimulation in her expression. She meant what she said. A terrible suspicion pierced his heart. What if Valmaston had worked his wiles on Lucy? What if she had already lost her heart to him?

"Tell me you are not in love with him," he cried, unable to keep quiet on the subject.

"I shall not rise to that fly," she returned, this time folding her arms over her chest.

"You ought not to allow yourself to be swayed in any manner by that man. If you only knew half—"

"I do not give a fig for gossip," she cried, cutting him off, "whether based in truth or not! He is my friend and I will stand by that."

"But he has not invaded your heart, at least tell me that much!"

She seemed rather shocked and lowered her arms. "Nothing of the sort."

He breathed much easier. "You are such an innocent."

"I am not a chit just out of the schoolroom, Robert. You do not need to protect me, if that is what you are thinking. And let me say this, that if my heart did lean in his direction, I would let it lean all the way! He is a great man. You do not do him justice in these opinions."

"I will grant that he does serve well in Parliament, but we are not speaking of such things."

"Robert, pray be at ease. He is needed here and I would trust him with my life. I promise you that if I thought for a moment any of your sisters would be endangered by his attendance at Anne and Alice's come-out ball, or a brief stay beneath your roof, believe me I would not have invited him."

He fell silent, pondering all that she had said. Finally he asked, "Why is he *needed* here? You said he was needed here. To what purpose?"

She shook her head as though trying to make him out. "You truly do not see in which direction my purposes tend?" she asked.

"Only that you seem to want Valmaston here with you," he said. Again he feared that, regardless of what she had said, her heart was not indifferent to the earl.

"Then let us just say that my sole object was to make certain that Anne and Alice had their ball—or are you not amazed at how reasonable Lady Sandifort became once she learned that I had invited the earl?"

He opened his mouth to speak and then he understood. "Oh," he murmured. "I begin to see." He sincerely doubted, however, that Lucy had guessed at the entire truth as to why Valmaston's presence would so greatly appeal to Lady Sandifort. Of course she would have designs on the earl, but he saw something more, something that had provoked her into refusing the ball in the first place. In truth, Lady Sandifort had been angry with him, but this he could not say to Lucy, certainly not without receiving a host of questions on the subject, which he had no desire to answer.

"Robert, I suppose I am asking you to trust me. Can you?"

He was surprised by the question. "A little, I suppose," he responded, but there was an odd voice from deep within his mind that said, *you trust her a great deal more than that.* He found himself shocked.

She smiled. "I suppose *a little* will have to do then. Let

me just say that I have a profound reason for requiring Valmaston's presence here at Aldershaw."

"So I have apprehended but I do not believe you understand everything."

"Perhaps not," she said, "but of one thing I am certain. There will now be a ball whereas yesterday there would not."

At that he smiled. "To argue that point would be fruitless."

"So it would," she said cheerfully.

"Then a ball there will be and Valmaston shall reside beneath my roof. Good God!"

"Then all that remains is to settle the date for the ball. I shall consult with Lady Sandifort. Will that be agreeable to you?"

He shook his head. "As much as any of this can be!"

Lucy returned to the house and discovered that Lady Sandifort had already spoken with Cook, and the date of the ball, which would of course include a supper for which Cook would be responsible, had been set for the third Tuesday in August. Armed with this information, Lucy retired to her bedchamber and opened her writing desk. She penned a long letter to Lord Valmaston explaining her need of him at Aldershaw, something she knew would come as a complete surprise to him, for she had indeed told more than one whisker about having invited him to Anne and Alice's come-out ball. How her conscience prickled her! But there was nothing for it—a woman of Lady Sandifort's unhappy character required measures of the most extreme!

Instead of seeing the letter posted by the mails, however, she walked to the village and hired a man to ride to London and deliver the message personally to the earl's townhouse in London. She knew he was fixed in the metropolis for several weeks and she only hoped that, after all her machinations, he would be able to attend a ball about which he had not even the smallest awareness. She instructed the rider to await an answer, even giving him sufficient funds for several nights' lodging should he be required to stay in town until such time as he could receive the response.

Afterward, she went to the local pub and discussed the hiring of laborers with the innkeeper who, by the nature of his profession, was able to direct her to the proper men. Though she did not have her entire fortune at her command, her quarterly allowance was quite generous so that in the end she was able to hire several house servants as well.

Later that evening, in the armory where the family gathered as was the tradition, Lucy informed not Robert but Lady Sandifort as to precisely what she had done, that she had hired laborers and servants to put the house and gardens in order so that the family could be comfortable. She had not dared to look at Robert as she spoke. "I know it was presumptuous of me and impertinent, but it is my gift to Anne and Alice that they might enjoy a proper come-out ball. Of course, had I not already invited Lord Valmaston, I would not have done so."

Lady Sandifort lifted an approving brow. "You did very right, though I daresay had Robert managed his affairs better he could have long since seen things mended at Aldershaw. But you have done what was right and good."

"Thank you, ma'am." Only then did she dare to look at Robert to see how he received her news. As she suspected, he was not in the least content with her. His complexion was ruddy, his eyes seemed to bulge a little in their sockets, and the glare he settled upon her face sent a severe shiver down her spine. *In for a penny, in for a pound*, she thought.

Lucy glanced at the others. Henry appeared completely stunned, Hetty not less so. George, however, merely frowned rather heavily.

"We are to have a proper number of upper maids?" Rosamunde asked, glancing around in strong disbelief.

"Yes," Lucy responded.

"I shall have a bath every night," she murmured ecstatically. "In rose water."

Her husband glanced at her, clearly surprised that she would say such a thing. As for the others, several throats were cleared.

Robert rose solemnly to his feet.

Lady Sandifort called out sharply. "Now, Robert, I can see that you mean to give our darling Lucy a dressing down but I wish you will not, for she has meant only what was best for all of us. I take it kindly in her that she has acted on behalf of your sisters and why should she not be of use while she remains here?" She turned to Lucy and offered a beaming smile.

Lucy said, "You have spoken my thoughts precisely. I ought to be of use and I will be."

Anne regarded Robert anxiously. "Do you mean to forbid our ball? Is that what you were going to say before Lady Sandifort interrupted you?"

Lucy watched a great deal of indecision pass back and forth across his face. "I was," he said.

"No," Anne whispered, tears filling her eyes.

Robert turned to Lucy and cast her a scathing look. "I suppose if I refuse now I will be harassed by all the ladies of the house."

"Yes, you will," Hetty said, but she was laughing and hurriedly gained her feet to slip her arm through his. "All will be well," she said. "You must trust that Lucy is doing what ought to be done. Do not worry. We will find some way to repay her for this great kindness."

"Yes, we will," Henry cried, also rising to his feet. He crossed the room to quickly possess himself of Lucy's hands. "You are an angel. I am convinced of it."

George, seated in a chair near his wife, shook his head. "But these expenses will be very great, indeed! Are you certain, Lucy? I only wish that I could be of use as well, but all my funds are fixed at Baddesley."

"Do not distress yourself, George. I believe my father would have wished for me to be of use to your family. He loved you all so very much, and you in particular, for he always thought you would have made a very fine officer had your inclination tended in that direction."

George glanced at his wife and appeared to grow uncomfortable. "Very kind of you to say so. Colonel Stiles was a favorite here at Aldershaw, as you very well know, Cousin."

"Am I to have no say in this?" Robert inquired strongly.

"No, Brother," Hetty stated softly. "Lucy is doing what she believes is right and following the dictates of one's heart is always a proper thing."

Lucy watched Robert's shoulders fall and she realized for the first time that he was obviously bearing a rather heavy burden, perhaps heavier than she had yet come to understand.

Two days later, the rider returned with word from Valmaston. He would be delighted to attend the come-out ball as well as to pass several days at Aldershaw. With this portion of her scheme in motion, Lucy turned her attention to the manor and surrounding grounds.

The next fortnight at Aldershaw saw rapid changes. Three upper maids entered into service and Mr. Quarley was assigned six stout laborers, fine young men used to hard work, to remove years of debris from the orchards, portions of the home wood, and all the areas of the formal gardens both in the front of the house and the back. No part of the estate was left unattended, so that as each morning dawned, Lucy saw improvements that warmed her heart.

Her primary interest was in shaping the leggy shrubs,

trees, and overgrown flowerbeds into a reasonable state but not so severely that they would require months of recovery before appearing pretty again. To this end, part of the job of the laborers was to bring water to the garden, a task that required primarily the work of their shoulders as they hauled brimming buckets from the stream by the home wood.

The effect of sufficient water applied beneath a vibrant summer sun was evident day by day and week by week. The lawn recovered quickly and even the bare patches filled in speedily. The entire expanse, both front and back, was kept properly scythed by a seventh man that Robert decided to hire permanently as undergardener to Mr. Quarley. Fortunately for the lawns and the flower beds, summer showers became sufficiently frequent so that within a month Aldershaw had the beginnings of recovery.

Lucy had the children help supervise the trimming of the maze yews. Of course, their involvement added greatly to the amount of time the task required, but she believed all four of them benefited from the parts they played. Where the yews were too thin and the walls not established clearly, Miss Gunville had the children collect long reeds and taught them how to weave them into loose lattices, which Mr. Quarley in turn used to shore up the maze walls.

The final addition to the maze was a surprise that Lucy had prepared for the children. Miss Gunville had kept them in the schoolroom until Lucy sent for them. Once at the center of the maze, they were astonished to discover a fort made of fallen logs from the home wood, supplemented with lumber prepared by the laborers.

Eugenia and Hyacinth gasped in wonder. "We have a proper place for our tea parties," the latter cried.

"Tea parties!" William called out in disgust, racing toward the door of the fort. "We will have nothing so absurd in this outpost. Who would serve tea to soldiers doing battle with Indians?"

Violet, carrying the doll Lucy had given her on the first day, entered after William then slowly emerged, her expression beatific. "There is a table and chairs inside just my size. I am going to bring Tom in here as well."

"He won't stay," William cried. "No cat will."

"Tom will," Violet said, scowling up at her older brother.

"A table and chairs?" Eugenia cried. "Then we can indeed have tea parties."

"No tea!" William cried.

"What about lemon cake, Will?" Hyacinth asked, coaxingly. " 'Tis your favorite."

"Well, lemon cake might be all right, and if we did have cake I suppose you could have your tea, but you shan't make me put on a bonnet like you did last year!"

Lucy bit her lip to keep from laughing. Her heart swelled at the sight of their happiness. The fort even had a short staircase leading to a tower, a place William claimed as his own a moment later.

"Lucy has certainly made great strides in the past month," Lady Sandifort said.

Robert was standing by the open window of his library and looking down into the garden below. Mr. Quarley was directing three of his laborers in the planting of a great many shrubs and flowers that he had apparently been nursing to maturity for the past two years. In the center of the lawn, Lucy had a kerchief tied about her eyes and was leaping and lunging in the direction of four squealing, laughing children playing at blindman's buff. He vowed he had not heard so much laughter in years at Aldershaw and she had done this. His heart swelled in gratitude and something more he was reluctant to put a name to. A month past he had told her he wished she had never come, but how foolish such a statement seemed now.

To Lady Sandifort he said, "Indeed, you are quite right. I am beginning to think Lucy could heal a blind man if she set her mind to it." He turned away from the window.

Lady Sandifort was gowned exquisitely as always. She wore dark blue silk that accented her brown hair and warm complexion quite perfectly. Her hair was gathered in a knot of curls atop her head. She was almost beautiful save for the hawk-like expression of her eyes, something all her beauty could not dispel.

"I wonder," Lady Sandifort said softly, in just that tone of voice all too familiar to his ears, "if she could work a small miracle for me."

He shot a reproving glance, then asked briskly, "So, have all the invitations been sent for the come-out ball?"

She smiled, also in a manner too familiar. "You do not mean to ask me what miracle I would wish for Lucy to perform for me?" She was advancing on him slowly, drifting the tip of her finger over the table that separated them.

He tried again. "Hetty said there were no less than one hundred invitations and that we should expect twice that number in guests, even if many cannot come."

She began to pout but continued to move toward him. "Do you mean to be tiresome this afternoon?"

"I mean to be sensible. My feelings have not changed and I would not wish to encourage you."

"Encourage me? What a ridiculous thing to say." Still she moved in her languid manner toward him. She looked as hungry as a cat eyeing a bowl of cream. "You speak as though I desire something *proper* between us."

He drew in a deep breath, wishing she would not press him in this manner. She held all the cards and he could hardly give her a set-down lest she take a pet and once more refuse to allow the ball. "You are my father's widow and because of my love for my father I would never disgrace you in any manner, nor his memory."

"I do not think a kiss would disgrace your father's memory. One little kiss?"

"No, Lady Sandifort. It is improper and I do not want you to think, that is to hope for more from me, as I have said a score of times before."

"I do not hope for anything save one little kiss," she said. Her eyes were very wide and, for all their innocent shape, held so cunning and devouring a look that he wished himself a thousand miles away. "A single, quite harmless kiss, nothing more."

The day Lady Sandifort wanted *nothing more* would be the day she drew her last breath.

"Enough," he said sharply.

She pouted in her flirtatious manner and continued to advance on him.

A scratching sounded on the door. "Come," he called out, greatly relieved.

Henry strode in. "Rosamunde has already left on her weekly pilgrimage to Chaleford, and Hetty cannot be found at all. It would seem a very large parcel has arrived from the dressmaker's and one of the needlewomen begs a word.

"I will go," Lady Sandifort said.

She swished by Robert, her current purpose forgotten in the exhilarating prospect of seeing the new gowns that had been ordered not just for the come-out ball but for daily use as well. Lucy had been beyond generous in every way and in this moment he was particularly grateful to her since Lady Sandifort's attentions had been diverted away from him. He wondered just how he would ever be able to repay her and that for so many things!

"What is all the laughter I am hearing?" Henry asked, moving toward the window. Robert followed him. "Ah, it is Lucy, of course. What a darling she is. Are you not glad she has come?"

"Yes, for I have never seen Hyacinth smile so much, nor Violet."

"I do not believe they have been happier," Henry observed.

"I quite agree. Hetty told me only last week that Lucy has finally persuaded Lady Sandifort that she ought only to be a mother to her children in those ways that pleased her else the children would be, how did she put it, 'distressed by her own evident unhappiness.' "

"Do I take that to mean our beloved stepmother has ceased torturing her children by insisting they be brought to her each morning?"

"Precisely."

"So that is why we have not heard Lady Sandifort shrieking so much of late."

Robert shook his head. "There are some women who should not have children. She is one of them."

"By all accounts, then, Lucy ought to have a dozen." Henry sighed deeply. "I am come to believe she is a very great lady and she is certainly the first person I have known who could manage Lady Sandifort."

"I think you may be right." He paused for a moment, then asked, "So tell me, are you prepared to take holy orders yet?"

Henry immediately grew uneasy. "Not yet. I beg you will forgive me but I have decided to wait to make my decision until the autumn."

Robert glanced down into the yard, clapping him on the shoulder. "You could not do better," he said, watching Lucy reach for William and miss him entirely.

"Then you know?"

"Of course. A sapscull could see you are in love with her and I begin to think you well suited. She is never so calm as when you are about."

"As opposed to you, Robert? It has not escaped my notice that you set up her back with the speed of lightning. Sometimes I have even wondered—"

"What?"

"Well, you do not seem to appreciate her as I think you ought. You rarely compliment her on the progress of the grounds and the house! Good God, all the rooms have been made so pleasant, there are fresh flowers everywhere, and the smell of lavender and beeswax in every chamber. Would it hurt you terribly to thank her?"

Robert rolled his eyes. "I fear thanking her," he stated firmly. "I fear what such a statement will cause her to think. I fear she will dig a canal!"

Henry threw his head back and laughed so loudly that the children called to him from below.

"What is so amusing?" William shouted.

"Your eldest brother said something absurd!"

"What?"

"He said he is afraid Lucy means to dig a canal on his property!"

William thought this a great joke as well, as did the other children. So it was that Lucy removed her kerchief and called back. "What an excellent notion! If we dug a canal— just a small one, mind—the children could have fun helping, and we could bring water more easily to the gardens!"

"Is she joking?" Robert asked, horrified.

Henry turned back to him. "I do not think so."

"I shall have your head for this!" he cried.

Henry backed away but lifted his fists in a boxing stance.

"What, ho!" Robert cried. "You know I am the better man!"

"We shall see. I spent last spring at Jackson's."

The brothers sparred for a quarter of an hour, removing their coats and quitting only when both were sadly out of breath.

Between gasps, Henry said, "You see, brother, we are all happier now that Lucy is come."

Lucy sat with the family that evening in the armory. Anne and Alice scrutinized a copy of *La Belle Assemblée,* Henry and Robert were engaged in a game of chess, George reclined in a chair and snored contentedly by a cold hearth, Rosamunde wove her kerchief in and about her fingers but otherwise refrained from useful employ, Hetty worked on her embroidery, and Lady Sandifort oversaw the chess game.

"Why do you play with such small pieces?" she asked. "Were I to play chess, each piece would be quite large and made entirely of gold."

"They would be very heavy," Robert responded pragmatically.

"But beautiful," Henry said, smiling at Lady Sandifort.

"I never could abide this game. Far too complicated. Checkers can be fun, but really I would much rather play at billiards. George, play at billiards with me?"

George, hearing his name in his dreams, woke up drowsily. "What? What?" He shifted slightly, folded his hands over his stomach, and resumed his snoring.

"What a useless creature!" Lady Sandifort cried. She turned to Lucy. "What are you reading, pray tell?"

"A novel. A very good novel."

"What is the name of it?"

She consulted the cover. "*Pride and Prejudice.* A curious title, do you not think so?"

"Is it a book of sermons?"

Lucy laughed. "No, it is a romance, I think. Quite good. You might like it. You may read it when I am done."

"I am not a great reader."

Lucy was not surprised. She resumed reading and had not finished that very page when a servant appeared in the doorway and called to her. She closed her novel, an interesting story about five sisters, and set it on the chair. Speaking with the servant, she soon discovered that the children had a surprise for her.

She made her way to Hyacinth's bedchamber and found them all gathered there.

"We each made something for you!" Violet cried.

"Violet!" Hyacinth reproved. "I was to tell her. We each made you something, Lucy. Come see."

She approached the bed and sat down on the edge. Violet offered her present first. It was a small sampler that had the word "friend" spelled out in a simple cross-stitch. "How lovely, Violet, and do look how your work has improved. Thank you." She kissed the youngest Sandifort on the cheek.

William presented his, a dagger carved out of wood. "Mr. Frome helped me."

"How very kind of him and what an excellent job you did!"

"Now you may protect yourself."

"How very thoughtful. Sometimes at night, particularly after I have watched all of you playing at pirates in your fort, I blow out my candle and wish for this very thing. From now on, I shall keep it beneath my pillow."

"In case of pirates?" Violet asked, excitedly.

"Precisely."

Hyacinth shuddered. "But there are no pirates in Hampshire, are there, Lucy?"

"Even if there were," she said, "how could they possibly vanquish Robert, Henry, and George? Why, there would have to be an army of pirates to defeat three such strong men and I have never heard of such a thing, especially not at a place so far from the sea as Aldershaw."

Hyacinth seemed relieved. Shyly she presented her small gift, which was wrapped in silver paper. "This feels very soft. I wonder what it might be." She unfolded the paper and found a lovely kerchief within, bordered in crochet lace. "It is perfection. Did Miss Gunville teach you to crochet so beautifully?"

"No, Rosamunde did."

Lucy glanced at Eugenia. "Your mother did this for Hyacinth? How very sweet of her."

Eugenia nodded. She was as shy as Hyacinth and presented her gift as well. A pair of gloves with the letter L embroidered on each in a soft yellow. "The color of your hair," she said.

"Oh, Ginny, this is just lovely and so thoughtful. Thank you. Oh, look, you have made me cry."

"You may use Hyacinth's kerchief," Violet offered helpfully.

Lucy dabbed at her eyes and began giving hugs and kisses all round. She then suggested that unless they wished for Miss Gunville to ring a peal over their heads they would immediately withdraw to their beds.

The children squealed then clapped their hands over their mouths. William slipped into an adjoining bedchamber and Hyacinth and Violet climbed eagerly into bed. Eugenia reached the doorway but the hall was dark beyond.

"If you will wait, Ginny, I should like a little company at least as far as your room."

"I should like that." Her uneasiness was obvious, especially after talk of pirates.

Lucy walked swiftly into William's bedchamber and did not hesitate to tuck him in tightly and to blow out the candle. She thanked him again for the useful dagger, then returned to give both Violet and Hyacinth another kiss good night.

Blowing out their candles as well, and with her gifts in hand, she ventured into the hall with Eugenia. She was a little surprised that the older girl slipped her hand in hers. She gave it a comforting squeeze.

"I am not frightened," Eugenia stated firmly. "Not in the least."

"Well I am," Lucy said. "These long dark halls at Aldershaw have frightened me since I was a child. But you give me courage, Ginny, indeed you do!"

"Well, maybe I am a little frightened, too."

"Who would not be?"

After seeing Eugenia safely to bed and saying good night, Lucy turned in the direction of her room intent on retiring to the quiet of her bedchamber. After reaching her door, however, she remembered the interesting novel she had been reading and decided to return to the armory to retrieve it. With all her gifts in hand, she made her way down the east staircase and afterward the central stairs to the ground floor.

As she entered the hall leading to the armory, she was surprised to find that most of the candles had been extinguished. She wondered what was going forward.

CHAPTER
SIX

Upon reaching the back entrance hall, Lucy heard in the distance the sound of a lovely melody plucked on the harp, a Bach piece perhaps. Lady Sandifort, it would seem, had decided to relieve her boredom with a little music.

She listened for a minute or so. The performance was quite perfect and not an unhappy way to enjoy the last remnants of an evening. She thought it one of the most intriguing things in the world that someone of Lady Sandifort's unfortunate temper could also play the harp like an angel. Mr. Frome, with whom she conversed often, would offer the circumstance as an example of one of the great paradoxes of human nature, that not even the vilest creature was wholly bad.

With a sigh of something very near to contentment, she entered the armory, surprised to find that but a handful of candles remained lit and that Robert was quite alone in the chamber. He sat where she had left him, in the corner before the chessboard, the pieces still in play. Apparently he was contemplating his next move.

"I did not expect everyone to be retired," she said. She

drew close to the board, staring down at it. The pieces from above combined with the black and white squares to form an unusual pattern. "Though I know where at least one member of the party is, for I believe I am hearing Lady Sandifort at the harp."

He glanced up at her. "Yes. She grew fatigued watching my game with Henry."

"She plays exquisitely."

He leaned back and glanced at the empty doorway. Faint strains could still be heard. "Indeed, she does. I believe her musical expertise to be her finest quality." He shook his head and lowered his voice. "Perhaps her only quality."

"And the others? Was everyone fatigued from watching you play chess?"

At that he smiled. "Hetty had reasons of her own for seeking her bedchamber. She said she had a letter to write. George awoke, after which he and Rosamunde began to quarrel. I suggested to my brother that he might be more comfortable elsewhere."

"Oh, dear."

"Precisely so. He was as mad as fire when he left and Rosamunde dabbed at her cheeks for a full minute before running from the room as well."

"The twins?"

At that he smiled. "I believe they felt it absolutely necessary to examine once more the gowns that the dressmaker sent today."

"A necessity, indeed! And what of Henry?"

"He is being the best of brothers and is presently searching the cellars for a bottle of very old brandy." His gaze fell to her hands. "What do you have there?"

"Your youngest siblings and your niece each made a present for me. Would you like to see them?"

"Of course." He smiled and slung an arm about the back of the chair, turning more fully toward her.

"Violet embroidered this sampler for me. Is it not precious?"

He fingered the letters and looked up at her. "I believe she has grown very fond of you. All the children have."

"And I am fond of them. They are darlings and I must say Miss Gunville has cared for them exceedingly well. What a treasure she is to serve as both nurse and governess."

"Indeed, she is. We are very fortunate."

"Now, this handsomely carved dagger is a gift from a young man who, I believe, will one day see a very fine military career, if I do not mistake the matter. He says he likes the notion of the army, but if he were to join the navy he could go aboard a ship next year."

Robert chuckled, turning the dagger over in his hands. "Well, perhaps not next year, though I must say he does seem to be full of ambition, even for one so young, but then his father—" he broke off and cleared his throat.

"You need not think you will embarrass me," she said, keeping her voice very low. "Only a simpleton could fail to see that his features belong to a different fold entirely."

He sighed.

"Did your father know about his wife? Did he ever have any understanding of her character?"

He shrugged. "He would never have admitted as much. He loved her quite to the end, you know."

"I would have supposed no less of him. He had his faults as we all do, but disloyalty was not among them."

A speculative light entered his eye. "That is very kindly said."

She met his gaze and, of all the absurd starts, felt her heart give pause. She had been so busy of late that she had rarely been alone with Robert, as she was in this moment. And though the last kisses they had exchanged—more than a month past now—had fallen deeply into her memory, for some reason she was put forcefully in mind of them. She found it difficult to breathe and quite stupidly could think of nothing to say. A strange sort of dizziness descended over her.

"You look very pretty tonight," he said quietly, his gaze holding hers strongly. He seemed to give himself a shake and looked back at the gifts in her hands. "What else do you have there?"

Lucy looked down at the remaining two gifts and blinked at least twice before saying, "Hyacinth made this kerchief. Is it not beautiful? Look at the workmanship. Rosamunde has been teaching her to crochet."

He settled the dagger and the sampler on the table beside the chessboard, then took the kerchief in hand. "Rosamunde, indeed! What an oddity she is, for she rarely makes a push to do anything, but I can see she must have taken some pains with Hyacinth." He ran his fingers over the lacy edging. "Hyacinth takes after Hetty in her skill, I believe."

"And your mother?"

"Yes," he smiled suddenly and his smile did more to brighten her heart than anything. "Mama was used to enjoy all forms of needlework. She always had her sewing bag beside her chair. As a child I would play with her scissors, beneath her strict supervision, of course. She had several pair, one with handles like peacocks. How odd to remember such a thing. Hetty has them now, I believe."

"You are fortunate to have such memories. I was too young to recall anything of my mother."

"Then I am very sorry for you, Lucy."

There was such genuine compassion in his eyes that again her heart paused. She felt suddenly in danger, but of what she was not certain. Swallowing very hard, she showed him the last gift, the pair of soft gloves. "Eugenia embroidered the Ls. She said she chose yellow because of the color of my hair."

He looked at her hair and reached up to touch a ringlet

that dangled to her shoulder. "*Like golden wheat of summer's light, her hair danced round in moonbeams bright.*"

"Robert, do not tell me you wrote these words!"

"No, of course not," he returned, laughing, releasing the lock of hair. "Henry showed me his latest poems, of which there are quite enough for a volume or two. He has been writing and writing in recent weeks."

"Robert!" Henry's voice called suddenly from the doorway. "Do you know where the key to the buttery is? So you have returned, Lucy. Will you have some brandy with Robert and me?"

"I should like that."

"Is the key not on the hook just inside Finkley's door?" Robert called back.

"Of course! What was I thinking?" Henry whirled around. His footsteps could be heard echoing down the hall.

"I think he is an excellent poet," Lucy said.

"He has some talent, yes. But just how much is not so easily ascertained."

"But he should be encouraged, do you not think so?"

He fingered the gloves Eugenia had embroidered and placed both the kerchief and the gloves beside the dagger and the sampler. He chuckled. "I think that were you to encourage him, he could be very successful, indeed, perhaps at anything he chose to pursue."

"What an odd thing to say, Robert," she cried, tilting her head. "But very sweet."

"There is something I would say to you, Lucy," he said, rising to his feet. "I wished to thank you for the interest you have taken in the children. You have been very attentive and gentle with them. They have all blossomed since your arrival. We all speak of it."

Lucy did not know what to say at first. She found herself rather dumbfounded. "If this is truly how you feel, then I am flattered and rather pleased, although I do not know that I agree with you entirely. It has not escaped my notice that you are quite involved in their lives as well. I admire that very much. They have need of you and you do not withhold yourself from them. Yes, Robert, I admire this very much in you." He was now staring at her so strangely that she could not imagine what he was thinking.

Robert looked down at her and felt each of the words she spoke sink into his mind and fill him with the most extraordinary and wholly unforeseen pleasure. Yes, he did pay a fair amount of attention to his youngest siblings, but he had never done so in order to gain anyone's praise. That Lucy chose in this moment to express her admiration of him worked strongly on his heart. The very deep, passionate kisses they had shared more than a month past seemed to steal into his awareness with the force of a sudden gunshot. The desire he had felt for her at that time fairly swept over him as he continued to look into her eyes. "Lucy," he murmured.

Was she aware that she had just taken a step toward him and now stood so close to him that she was barely a breath away? And what was that light in her eye, barely visible in the dim candlelight? And how did his arm find her waist so easily, so quickly?

He touched her cheek with his hand. "Darling Lucy," he murmured. "You have made my home bearable these past several weeks."

"Robert," she whispered, turning her face to his so that her lips were within a few inches' reach. He slid his hand behind her neck and very softly settled his lips on hers.

Time stilled and then stopped. He found himself lost in another place entirely, one made up of faint light, mist, and wonder. He was enchanted. How had this happened to him, that a woman with whom he frequently quarreled should suddenly feel heavenly in his arms?

He deepened the kiss and, as before, she responded, parting her lips and moaning so softly that her voice sounded just like a dove's coo. He drew her tightly to him that he might feel the length of her pressed to him. He wondered what sort of wife Lucy would make and whether or not she would take delight in his bed. He kissed her fiercely and another coo and yet another warbled from her throat. What was she feeling? he wondered. Was she as lost in faint light, mist, and wonder as he?

Lucy could not credit Robert was kissing her again. A month had passed, but was it really a month or perhaps only a fleeting second since he had last embraced her so passionately? In all her long acquaintance with him, this is what surprised her about Robert: that he was capable of such powerful feeling and expression.

Somewhere in her mind she knew she should not be allowing him to kiss her, yet not for the world would she willingly or purposefully end such a kiss, not when she could no longer feel her feet or even her legs. She was floating blissfully in a state of perfection and desire so wondrous that she wished Robert would go on kissing her forever.

He drew back and looked into her eyes. "Lucy," he whispered, but he was frowning.

"Robert!" Henry's voice called from the depths of the house.

"Good God. Henry," he said, closing his eyes and releasing her at the same time. In a loud voice he called back, "What is it, Brother?" He seemed to be pained.

Lucy backed away and picked up the gifts that Robert had settled on the table by the chessboard. She turned away from him and moved to her chair where she had been reading her novel. She sat down almost blindly.

Henry appeared in the doorway holding a bottle in hand. "You will not credit what I have found! I believe it may be thirty years old."

Lucy glanced at him. "That is very old indeed."

"Yes, indeed!" he returned gleefully. "And now we are to discover whether it is any good."

Lucy stood up suddenly. "I beg you will forgive me, Henry, but I fear I have the headache. You must excuse me, but I believe I should retire."

He frowned and appeared quite concerned. "Of course. I am very sorry you must go. Do you need a doctor?"

She shook her head and smiled. "No, 'tis only the headache. It will pass."

"What is this?" Lady Sandifort called out, addressing Henry. "Did I hear you say thirty-year-old brandy?"

"Yes, my lady. Will you join us?"

"With pleasure. I am sorry you are feeling unwell, Lucy. I hope your head is better in the morning." She approached Lucy and gave her a kiss on the cheek, then swept past her.

Lucy's nostrils were filled with the scent of roses, which Lady Sandifort wore heavily. She bid good night to Robert, then walked quickly from the armory. Just as she reached the stairs, however, she heard running steps behind her. Robert caught her arm.

"I am so sorry. I have made you uncomfortable and all because you offered me a very sweet compliment. I vow I do not know how I could have lost my head. I should never have kissed you. It will not happen again."

Lucy's throat felt very tight. Why did he not wish it to happen again? "Good night," she said, her throat beginning to ache. She turned and walked slowly up the stairs. She felt rather than saw that he remained at the bottom step watching her go. When she was halfway, she heard his footsteps fading down the hall as he returned to the armory.

Later, Lucy lay in bed. She had never known her heart to feel so heavy. She did not understand what had just happened, how it was she had let Robert kiss her again. Worse, however, was how wonderful the kiss had been, how utterly transported she had felt, as though kissing Robert had the ability to make her feel that she was no longer at Aldershaw but in some magical place that belonged only to them, almost like the sweetest of dreams from which she never wanted to awaken.

She had found it utterly impossible to remain in the drawing room once Henry returned. She was feeling far too much, her senses were completely overwhelmed, and she did not know how she could have sustained a meaningful conversation with anyone under such circumstances. Yet so much was left unsaid that surely needed to be said, only why did Robert follow her and make such a hurtful statement? Why should he not have kissed her? Why? Why did he not desire to kiss her again?

Another question, perhaps more critical, rose within her mind. Why had he kissed her? What was it that had prompted him this evening to so gently take her in his arms? Was he perhaps feeling something for her of a truly romantic nature, something he wished to deny? And what of her own conduct, was it possible that she was actually tumbling in love with Robert Sandifort?

She covered her face with her pillow. Was she in love with him, and if not, why then did she let him kiss her? Except that he was being so tender and so sweet, and his eyes, oh the expression in his eyes had been so passionate! How could she have resisted such a kiss?

At the same time, she needed to know what his thoughts had truly been when he kissed her. Was it possible he was coming to love her?

The next day, Lucy found herself arguing the subject with Robert.

"But you kissed me!" Lucy argued. "I wish to know why. I do not think I ask too much."

Robert would not face her but stared out the window of

the library, his hands clasped behind his back. "Why must you press me when I have already told you that I erred in doing so, that it was but an inexplicable impulse of the moment, that you were merely looking very pretty and that I should not have kissed you? Why will this not satisfy you?"

"But why was it so wrong of you, that is what I wish to know? Perhaps we all have impulses, but why do you insist that you erred?"

"For a dozen reasons. I am your guardian, for one. You are residing beneath my roof, for another. I have no serious intentions toward you. I am not courting you with the intention of marriage." He turned back. "Kissing you last night was wholly improper and imprudent."

Lucy had not slept well. She had rolled about on her bed, turning this way and that nearly the entire night, trying to determine just what had happened last night. She could make no sense of it. "You and I quarrel nearly every time we are together. So how did you come to kiss me?"

He stared at her. "In one sense, that is the most ridiculous question you could ask. You might rather ask how I keep from kissing you one minute out of two, or do you not know how beautiful you are or how desirable?"

Lucy listened to his words and thought she had never heard anything so absurd in her life. "You truly kissed me merely because I am pretty?"

"Yes," he stated flatly.

"Nothing more?"

"What more could there be?"

"A great deal more. Perhaps that you hold me in some affection."

"I suppose I do," he responded rationally. "However, nothing to signify. You have too many flaws for me to have any serious feelings toward you."

"Too many flaws?" she retorted, appalled.

"Oh, now do not get on your high ropes, Lucy. I am certain any other gentleman would not mind that you are willful and stubborn, that you are officious and interfering, but I think these faults quite serious, indeed."

"Your list has slipped from your tongue so swiftly that I begin to think you ponder my flaws quite frequently."

"Well, yes, I suppose I do. Naturally, I remain silent most of the time because it serves no purpose to say something which I know will set up your back."

She lifted a brow. "I wonder you can bear to speak to me at all."

"Now, Lucy, do not be dramatic."

Having heard enough, Lucy turned on her heel and quit the room. She had tossed on her bed all night for this, to hear Robert say he had only kissed her because she was pretty? Good God, he was scarcely better than Valmaston!

For a moment, Robert thought she might slam the door, but she did not. He had let her go, feeling an enormous twinge of guilt, yet he did not comprehend why, precisely. Certainly he had already apologized *again* for kissing her and that should be an end of it. Yet for some reason he felt incomprehensibly uneasy about the situation. Well, perhaps not incomprehensibly, since he had, after all, kissed the young woman with whom his own brother had already confessed to being quite deeply in love.

He sank into his favorite chair and put his head in his hands. Whatever concerns he had about Lucy's heart, they were not nearly so significant compared to how badly he knew he had used his own brother! He understood Henry's sentiments quite well. Henry doted on Lucy. Whenever she but entered a room, he had eyes for no one else. He was always the first to offer her a chair, the first to speak with her, the first to tend to her comforts. But worse, however, were the poems! Good God, the poems! By the score he had writ-

ten them to his beloved Lucy. He even suspected that Henry
was intending to have them published, the whole work dedi-
cated to her.

The promise therefore that he had made to Lucy last night
not to kiss her again had been proffered more for Henry's sake
than for hers or even for his own.

As these thoughts went round and round his head, he realized how little he was considering Lucy's feelings. She
was the one he had importuned and therefore she ought to be
the one for whom he felt the greatest dismay, not Henry.

Very well, he had used them both quite ill. There was no
justifying what he had done, and to some degree no compre-
hending what he had done either, and worse still no denying
that kissing her again had been one of the most extraordinary moments of his life. He lifted his head from his hands
and let this thought dwell in him for a long moment. How
could he describe what it had been like to hold her in his
arms, to kiss her? He had wanted her and something more.
He had wanted to take her to his bed. He had wanted to love
her as he would love a wife and he had wanted her desperately.

There had been nothing weak in the desire he had felt for
her last night, so that in all his consternation at having kissed
her, these feelings confounded him the most. Was it merely
that Lucy was living in his house and caring for his home as
well as his youngest siblings that he must desire her in this
way, or was it possible . . . ?

No, he would not let such thoughts enter his mind, even
in the smallest sense. His feelings, even his desires were not
to be considered in this situation, not when he had betrayed
his brother by kissing Lucy. His conduct had been wholly
dishonorable, but none of this could he have said to her, so
he had told a whisker—that the only reason he had kissed
her was because she was pretty.

* * *

Over the next several days Robert found his attention wandering to Lucy more often than he wished. For all his careful reasoning he often found that in the course of his activities, if she but came within his view, everything else was forgotten. Of course, it did not help at all that, though her taste in fashion was not always reasonable, she was always the picture of glowing beauty. There was something about the way she chose to live that lit her complexion from within. Her smile was quite infectious. She had but to enter a room and very soon everyone was laughing. He found he was most often drawn to her when she was engaged in playing with Hyacinth and Violet, Eugenia, and even William. She had a natural rapport with the children that warmed his heart, however ill his opinions might be of her otherwise.

He had spoken his mind frankly about her flaws and he had not regretted doing so. For one thing, she seemed less inclined to engage him in conversation afterward and that was a good thing, especially where her blossoming romance with Henry was concerned. For another, Lucy ought to be informed about the ways that she needed to be improved. How else would she mature into a proper sort of young woman if all her friends remained silent?

He knew he had offended her by speaking so plainly. From that time forth she had avoided him. At first he had been grateful, since he desired nothing more than to keep her at a distance. After a sennight, however, of being favored with brief responses to his questions, with restraint in her blue eyes whenever she would meet his gaze, and indifference to any subject he put forward, he found himself growing restless, even irritable. He did not like to be on unhappy terms with anyone, and especially not the young woman who had brought so much peace and even joy to his home.

He strove therefore over the next several days to speak

more kindly to her, to listen with greater consideration and politeness to all her conversations, and certainly to withhold any biting observations of her character. Though he believed himself in the right, he did not like that she was so withdrawn in his presence. She began to relax in his company and to be more talkative and lively, as was her custom, so he knew he was making progress.

"Lucy, I must ask you," Hetty began quietly. "Why have you been so remote in your discourse with Robert?"

Lucy glanced at her friend and could not help but smile. They were on another long walk with Eugenia and the youngest Sandiforts, this time paying a visit to the stables before returning to the garden through an entrance near the home wood. Mr. Frome was their object. She carried a basket of treats for him that the children had collected from Cook. An excursion to pay a call on Jeremy Frome had become a daily event not to be missed.

"If you must know, nearly a sennight past now, your brother offended me quite sorely. Of late he has been behaving more kindly toward me so I may forgive him."

"In what way did my brother offend you?"

"He read me a very long list of all my faults."

"He did not!" she gasped.

"Yes, I am afraid he did."

"What a sapscull."

"The odd thing is," Lucy said, slowing her walk so that the children might be out of hearing range, "I do not recall him always being so stuffy and critical. I mean, we always tended to quarrel, but when we were younger it was the natural cause of my being a child and quite provoking and his that he was older and unwilling to tolerate such provoking conduct. I also recall a time when I was seventeen or eighteen in which he was perfectly amiable and we never quarreled and he certainly was not uncivil to me. But it is even worse than incivility now, though I cannot explain how that is."

"I believe I understand. He seems determined to search out your faults so that he does not grow too close to you. I think he fears loving anyone too much."

Lucy turned to stare at her. Such a reason had not occurred to her before. "Do you truly think it possible?" she asked.

Hetty smiled. "Robert is not easily known. Do hold a moment." She called out loudly, "William, be sure to ask permission of the head groom before entering the stables. Pooksgreen will not want you disturbing the horses."

"Yes, Hetty." William disappeared inside the stables.

The younger girls, however, did not have the same interest, so it was that they ran in the direction of a nearby pasture in which there were a great many sheep and lambs half grown.

Lucy nudged Hetty playfully. "And now there is something I have been wanting to know for ages. May I ask a very personal question?"

Hetty smiled. "I imagine I can guess. You wish to know why I have never married."

"Well, yes." Lucy noted that a soft smile settled quite quickly upon Hetty's lips as well as in her soft brown eyes. She was a very pretty young woman but this sudden glow made her absolutely beautiful. She knew the truth without having to hear the words. "You are in love with someone," she whispered.

Hetty turned shocked eyes upon her. "Why would you say that?" A blush swept over her fine complexion. "Of course I am not!"

Her protests startled Lucy. She could see that Hetty was deeply mortified but she also knew that she was telling a whisker by saying that she was not in love. She therefore spoke quickly, "I can see that I was mistaken. I do beg your pardon. It was a very impertinent remark."

"Well, I am not in love and to answer your question, I have never married because there was no one I wished to marry, no one who truly captured my heart." She held her head very high.

Lucy let her gaze drop to the gravel at her feet. The gravel ended and a grassy path commenced leading toward the dry-stone wall over which all three young girls were leaning and calling to the sheep. She had seen the truth though Hetty had denied it, yet what mystery was this? It would appear Hetty was indeed in love with someone, but with whom and for how long a time?

Lucy called to the girls, "Do be careful not to lean so far forward. You would not wish to tumble into the pasture where the sheep have been grazing."

Hyacinth leaned back, then pulled Violet back as well. The younger girl complained but Eugenia quickly pointed out that the sheep left quite a mess behind them wherever they grazed and Violet quickly became more tractable.

Hetty chuckled. "You treat them all as your own," she said.

"That is what Henry says. I suppose I am a little protective, though I cannot say why. Perhaps because on my first day here I heard a great deal of shrieking."

"Oh, that. I must thank you, Lucy, for putting an end to it. We, none of us knew what to do and Lady Sandifort would insist upon having the children brought to her when it was clear it brought her little pleasure."

"She is something of a riddle, I think. Sometimes, when she is not deliberately taunting one or the other of us, I have seen an odd, almost hurt expression in her eyes. In fact, there are times when she has the appearance of a very young child."

Hetty elbowed her gently. "You are a very odd creature as well, Lucinda Stiles."

Lucy chuckled. "I suppose I am. I admit as much. On another subject entirely, however, there is something I wish to put to you. What would you think of taking Anne and Alice to the next assemblies in Bickfield? I am persuaded they would each benefit from the experience, but what are your thoughts?"

Hetty seemed surprised. "I begin to think it an excellent notion and we would have at least three weeks to prepare since the assemblies are not until the first Tuesday in August. Though I must say, Lady Sandifort will not like to take them."

"Well," Lucy drawled, "she will if she believes it is her idea."

"Oh, Lucy! What a devil you are. I begin to see what you are at."

"Never mind that and pray be discreet. I have already told you far too much and if you ever expose me to your stepmother I shall be in the basket, indeed! Only tell me, do you think it a reasonable idea, indeed? I believe it would do both of them a great deal of good to be dancing in society before they are expected to perform at a very large ball."

"I must agree with you. Goodness, I have not been to the assemblies in years. I always enjoyed dancing."

Again there was a secretive smile on Hetty's lips and Lucy was intrigued once more, but she dared say nothing further.

"It is settled, then, only I beg you will say nothing until I have spoken with Lady Sandifort."

"I only hope you will be able to persuade her."

"As do I."

"And now I wonder whether Mr. Frome will be serving coffee or tea today."

CHAPTER
SEVEN

Once arrived at Mr. Frome's caravan, Hyacinth called out, "Look! There is Tom! I begin to think he prefers your home to ours!"

" 'Tis my fault," Mr. Frome called back, smiling. "I give him pieces of ham."

"You are a very nice man," Violet said, drawing close to him and looking up into his face intently.

He was brewing a pot of tea, which he served to Hetty and Lucy.

"I do not know which I prefer, your coffee or your tea," Lucy said. "Both are wonderful." She took a sip. "How do you manage it? What is your secret?"

"Indeed, yes, Mr. Frome, " Hetty said. "You must tell us, for no matter how well Cook prepares either I vow yours excels hers by a mile!"

"It is very simple," he said, smiling. "Anything brewed or cooked in the open air has tenfold the flavor."

Hetty nodded. "I believe you must be right, which reminds me, the children have brought you something."

"Indeed?" He glanced at the girls, who were seated on the

grass and playing with Tom. His black tail swished back and forth quickly as Eugenia dragged a long duck feather in front of him.

Hyacinth looked up at him. "Yes, we have." She rose swiftly and took the basket from Lucy. "We thought you might like something different," she said.

"These arrived only this morning," Hetty added. "Muscadel raisins, Portugal plums, and Jordan almonds. Oh, and a little of Cook's best spice cake."

He smiled at Hyacinth, who was at his eye level since he was seated on the stool. He pinched her cheek very gently. "How you spoil me. Thank you, my dears, all of you."

Violet suddenly drew Tom into her lap, then clutched him to her chest. "You cannot have Tom for your own, Mr. Frome, even if you want him very badly. He is our cat."

"My darling Violet, I would no more think of keeping Tom than I would of cutting off my chin."

He appeared so serious that Violet's eyes got very big. "And you would never cut off your chin," she stated firmly.

"I should think not. Would I not look a queer sight without a chin?" He covered his chin with his hand. "I would look like this."

Her eyes got even bigger. Hetty laughed and reassured Violet that Tom was theirs to keep forever. She then relinquished the cat, which sped away into the home wood after having been confined so tightly in Violet's arms. She in turn forgot all about Tom and asked if she might have some of the raisins.

Hetty would have protested, but Mr. Frome lifted a quieting hand. "Of course you may. Raisins come in a box ready for sharing. You shall have the first, if you like."

Lucy smiled warmly upon Mr. Frome. She had grown very fond of him over the past several weeks. They had enjoyed many long talks together and he had been able to give her much helpful advice, particularly where Lady Sandifort was concerned. Most particularly, however, he was always kind and generous with the children.

At last the children were ready to continue their walk. Hyacinth called for Hetty to help her over the stones crossing the stream. Though Mr. Frome's caravan was now situated closer to the maze, though a considerable distance north the stream still meandered through the upper reaches of the garden. Eugenia led the way. William nearly pushed her off the last stone so that Hetty felt obliged to call sharply to him. Violet was not far behind William.

So it was that Lucy had one last word with Mr. Frome.

He asked, "What is to become of Lady Sandifort, Miss Lucy? Have you given any thought to her future?"

Lucy chuckled. "I think about such matters every day, as you already know. Although I am hoping that once Lord Valmaston arrives I will know better what next to do."

Mr. Frome frowned.

"You do not approve?"

"It is not a matter of approval, but are you certain Valmaston is the one to accomplish the necessary task where her ladyship is concerned?"

She shrugged a little. "I hope he is and his reputation certainly indicates he ought to be able to pique her interest."

"I have no doubt of his abilities on that score because of all that you have told me of him, but I wonder . . ."

"What?" she inquired, exceedingly curious as to the exact nature of his thoughts.

"Well, it is possible that the years have brought a new wisdom to the earl. He may prove to no longer have his former interests."

At that Lucy chortled loudly. "Oh, Mr. Frome. If you only knew of whom we speak you would not express so much doubt." She had been in Valmaston's company a great many times over the past five years and he was as he had always been, quite wild in his pursuits. To think that such a man had relinquished his roguish ways was akin to slashing at the borders of probability with a long sword! Valmaston was and always would be a confirmed rake.

She heard Violet calling to her, and turning, saw her standing on the other side of the stream.

"You are being summoned," he said.

"I must go to her then. Thank you for the tea."

"You are most welcome."

The occasion did not arise that day in which Lucy felt she could properly present to Lady Sandifort her scheme of taking Anne and Alice to the assemblies at Bickfield. Her ladyship seemed particularly out of spirits and not for the world would she choose to overset her with any novel idea, nonetheless one that was likely to set up her back. She did, however, spend much of her time trying to determine in just what manner she could broach the subject once the time was right. However, no brilliant inspiration struck and she retired to bed that night without knowing just how to go on.

She could not sleep. So much did she wrestle with her bedcovers in an attempt to solve the dilemma that finally she rose from the torturous bed and donned her robe, intent on walking the halls a little to see if she might wear out her mind by moving her feet.

She had just reached the bottom of the east staircase when the sound of voices in argument struck her ears. Outside the billiard room, located across from the library, she saw that Eugenia was once more listening secretively to her parents squabbling.

Lucy waved to her and approached her quickly. "What is going forward?" she asked quietly.

"Oh, Lucy, it is quite terrible. Papa has accused mama of being foxed and of something else I do not understand. What is a *tryst*?

Oh, dear, Lucy thought. However was she to explain this to a ten-year-old girl? "I cannot begin to think what your father might mean by it," she responded truthfully. "Dear Ginny, do go to bed. Never fear. I shall discover what is amiss."

"Yes, please do, Lucy. I . . . I rely upon you."

When Eugenia made no move to leave her post, Lucy twirled her in the opposite direction. "Go to bed," she commanded softly, then gave her a little push. Eugenia sighed but picked up the skirts of her nightdress and ran down the hall to disappear up the east staircase.

As Lucy stood listening to the quarrel, she did not know what to do. Should she scratch on the door to announce her presence? Should she march in? Perhaps she should start humming a tune to warn them that someone was coming?

In the end, she chose a stealthy course and stole quietly up to the half-open door. Goodness, in this moment she was scarcely better than Lady Sandifort, listening in hallways to conversations behind private doors! Though her conscience smote her, still she took a quick peek inside, then hid herself. In that time she took in the entire scene; George stood over his wife, lecturing her severely about her conduct, about how inappropriate it was for her to return to Aldershaw in such a disgraceful state and how it was perfectly clear to him that she had been doing something other than visiting and comforting an infirmed friend. Secondly, Rosamunde was not taking him in the least seriously. She grinned at him rather sloppily while lounging in a most unladylike manner in one of the chairs that flanked the wide chamber, having slung one of her legs over the arm of the chair. Her gown of royal blue silk was trapped about her legs, exposing her ankles most improperly. One of her silk stockings was torn.

Lucy heard her say, "I forgot how adorable you are. Oh, George, I always loved you so!"

Lucy was about to retreat, thinking that the quarrel would soon take a happier turn, but George shouted, "Who is he,

Rosy? Tell me at once! Who the devil have you been kissing tonight?"

Lucy could not have been more shocked if someone had thrown ice water on her face. She had never heard George address his wife so cruelly. From the time of her arrival at Aldershaw she had known that George and Rosamunde's relationship was quite troubled, but never would she have supposed that George would accuse his wife of unfaithfulness.

To Lucy's surprise, Rosamunde began to laugh. She was clearly in her altitudes. "I . . . only wish . . . you could see . . . 'my beloved'," she said between chortles.

"Then it is true?" George asked in a quiet voice.

For some reason, this made Rosamunde laugh harder still. "If . . . only you could . . . see your face!"

"You would say such a thing to me when, when it is obvious you have all this time been engaged in—"

There was a loud thumping sound. Lucy peeked again, then hid herself, but barely kept from bursting out laughing.

"Rosamunde! Are you all right?" George cried.

Rosamunde's laughter rose to the ceiling once more. "I fell off my chair!" she squealed, laughing harder still. "No, no, George! Do not go."

"Would you please release my leg?"

"I shan't, my darling. I love this leg! I do! I do!"

"Rosamunde! For heaven's sake! Do stop kissing my knee. What are you doing? Good God, I believe you must be very foxed, indeed!"

"Only a very little." Her giggles were nearly incessant. "Oh, please do not scowl at me. Oh . . . oh, dear. The room is moving about in a circle."

"There, there. Sit very quietly. No, do not try to stand."

Lucy thought the moment opportune. She scratched on the door and entered. "I wonder if I might be of some use." The scene before her was both endearing and pathetic at the same time. Rosamunde sat on the floor with one arm hooked about her husband's leg. She weaved to and fro and blinked ever so slowly.

"I do not feel well," Rosamunde stated.

"I should think not," Lucy said. "Were you drinking sherry all evening?"

Rosamunde shook her head. "Ratafia. Peach ratafia. Glass after glass. I was never so amused."

"So it would seem."

George waved her forward. "Will you help me, Lucy?"

"Of course." Lucy took an arm and in a slow, careful movement helped George to assist Rosamunde to her feet.

The next several minutes were spent in seeing a quite vocal Rosamunde to her bedchamber, which was thankfully located on the same floor. Even Lady Sandifort, whose room was not far from the billiard room, appeared in her doorway quite sleepy-eyed as they paraded by. "What is wrong with Rosamunde?" she asked, blinking and tugging at her mob-cap.

"Ratafia!" Rosamunde called to her quite gaily.

"Well, I hope you have a wretched headache tomorrow for having awakened me tonight!" The door slammed behind her.

All the way to her room, Rosamunde either giggled or sighed heavily and begged George to take her back to Baddesley. "I want my home," she moaned pitifully. Then she would begin giggling again.

George did not attempt to address his wife except to say "Yes, dear" and "of course, dear," as was required of him. He remained in her bedchamber only until one of the upper maids arrived. He was about to leave when Lucy called to him, "I should like to speak with you, George. Will you allow me a few minutes?"

"Of course." There was a great deal of mistrust in his eyes and in his voice. Of all the inmates of Aldershaw, she con-versed the least with George. Though he never spoke unkindly to her, she sensed he would prefer not to speak at all. She did not understand what was troubling him so deeply.

Some time later, with Rosamunde settled between the sheets, Lucy went in search of George and found him once more in the billiard room. He was hitting the balls hard with his cue stick, his large frame jostling the table when his abrupt thrust would cause his hip to lurch forward.

She entered the room and felt instinctively that she ought to be straightforward. "Is there anything I can do to be of use to you?" she asked.

"I do not see how," he returned flatly, once more slinging his cue and hurtling a ball across the table.

"You cannot possibly believe she had an assignation this evening."

"What am I supposed to believe?" He turned sharply toward her and stood the cue upright. "She returns to her home at a very late hour and in a condition that I find quite appalling. And she was supposed to be visiting an infirmed elderly woman in the village of Chaleford! Do you suppose the invalid actually desired her friend to get foxed on ratafia? Doing it up too brown, Lucy, too brown by half!"

Lucy was not certain what next to say. George did have the right of it in the sense that if Rosamunde was paying her weekly visit upon an invalid, she ought not to have come home in her altitudes. She supposed he had a right to be suspicious.

"Perhaps there is another explanation."

"It hardly matters what it might be. Besides, this is none of your concern."

"You are very right. It is none of my concern save that I found your daughter listening to the entire exchange and asking me what a *tryst* was."

At that George's complexion paled. He sat down in a chair against the wall, his cue stick still in hand. His shoulders sagged. "Good God. I never meant for things to come to such a pass as this."

Lucy sat down in a chair near him.

"Rosamunde longs to go home," she said quietly. "She misses her gardens and the life she knew before all the repairs began."

He shot an angry glance at her. "I have told her and everyone, I will not remove my family from Aldershaw until the repairs are complete." He looked away from her, his complexion now very high.

Lucy watched him closely, trying to understand him. She knew he had just stated his case again but something disturbed her about the way he looked, or perhaps in the way he refused to look at her. She knew then that something more was amiss than just a delay in the work at his home in Sussex.

When he continued staring at the wall opposite, his chin set mulishly, she sensed there was little to be done and rose to her feet. "I shall bid you good night, George. I did not mean to overset you."

He glanced up at her. "I say, Lucy, I do beg your pardon. I know your interference is meant for good, but I wish you would not. I . . . I prefer to manage my family in my own way."

Lucy felt her cheeks grow warm. He had spoken of her conduct as Robert did, that she was involved where she was not wanted. She had meant only to offer her help but George saw it as interference. She nodded in response and quit the chamber.

She returned slowly to her own room, pondering what he had just said to her. Was she being officious and interfering without truly having either cause or the capacity to offer real help? Was she overstepping the bounds? Was Robert right in his criticisms of her?

She did not know. She believed that she had been of some use to the household, in particular where Lady Sandifort and the children were concerned, and even more practically in the refurbishing of the gardens. However, was she going too far in attempting to become involved in the difficulties between George and Rosamunde?

On the following morning, Lucy rose early to pay a solitary call upon Mr. Frome. She was greatly concerned about what George had said and she wished to know his opinions.

He welcomed her as he always did, quite warmly and with a twinkle in his eye. "Good morning. Had you arrived a few minutes earlier, you would have seen Sir Robert. He is looking very well these days, as sun-bronzed as he is from riding about the estate so much."

"Yes, I suppose he is."

"You seem a trifle distracted."

"A little," she confessed. He handed her a cup of coffee, which she took without hesitation. "Thank you."

"You are most welcome. Sir Robert tells me you were, how did he phrase it, 'meddling in George's affairs last night.' "

The sip Lucy had been taking spurted from her lips in a strong spray, even reaching the fire and creating a snake-like hissing sound.

Mr. Frome laughed.

"How is that possible?" she cried. "It was but a few hours past when I spoke with George."

"So you were interfering?"

Lucy felt quite ill-used in a way she could not easily explain. "His wife was feeling very poorly last night. I thought I was being of use to both of them."

"You speak of Rosamunde?"

"Yes. She returned from her weekly trip to Chaleford, but in a slightly, shall we say, indiscreet state—she had imbibed a great deal too much peach ratafia."

"Ah," he murmured.

"But then if Robert has already spoken to you on the subject, you must already know as much."

He shook his head. "Nay. Sir Robert merely said that he had learned from his brother that you were involved again where you were least wanted and he felt obliged to address the matter with you as soon as seemed appropriate to him."

"Why did he speak of this to you?" she asked, offended.

Mr. Frome sipped his own coffee and crossed one knee over the other. "I believe it helps him to speak with me."

There was laughter in his eyes and she knew he was poking fun at her, yet she was not offended. After all, she often spoke of Robert to Mr. Frome.

"Well, they may both call it interfering, but I should have liked to have seen Robert put Rosamunde to bed!"

"And that is what you did?"

"Of course. After that I, well, I spoke with George in the billiard room and asked him a few questions. He did not like my asking them nor did he care for my comments about his wife, which I felt were rather harmless. I merely said that Rosamunde wished to be home, a circumstance which everyone, even George, knows quite well, for she hardly restrains herself on that subject!"

Mr. Frome was silent for a long moment, his gaze fixed to the fire. "What ails these two, I wonder?" he offered without the smallest concern for the fact that such a discourse as might follow could be viewed as quite meddlesome.

Lucy sipped her coffee and sighed. "They love their daughter very much and I believe each other quite passionately. When I said to George, however, that Rosamunde wished to return to Baddesley, his face grew quite red, the color of a tomato."

"Indeed? Well, that is curious."

"I thought so as well," she said, meeting his gaze fully. She could see that he had an opinion on the subject. "Only tell me what you think."

"I am not certain except that I have heard of this dilemma now for I believe five weeks and yet the repairs have not been completed for a period of two years. Does not this seem odd to you?"

"Of course it does."

"The answer you seek might lie in the discovery of why the repairs are not yet complete."

"You know, Mr. Frome, I do not think Sir Robert would approve very much of our conversation just now."

Mr. Frome smiled. He picked up a stick lying beside his stool and poked at the fire. "I suppose not, but there is one question I would put to you, Miss Lucinda Stiles. What is really troubling you this morning, for if I do not mistake the matter you are not fretting merely about Rosamunde's troubles, are you now?"

She leaned forward on the stool. The caravan was settled near the home wood but had a view of the back of the yew maze, though some distance away, which had begun taking shape. Indeed, as she glanced about, in particular at the well-scythed lawn upon which her slippered feet rested, she rather thought much of the garden was coming into its peak of perfection. As to just how she was to answer Mr. Frome's question, she was not entirely certain.

"I think," she said slowly, "that it may have something to do with Robert and George, at least in their opinion that I am meddling. They both think I am too interfering and I suppose I have come to doubt myself. Am I in the wrong in this instance?"

"I cannot say," he responded, shaking his head and poking at the fire a little more. "What do your instincts tell you?"

"Only that if I can do so without distressing George, I should like to help Rosamunde. She is pitifully unhappy and last night George said some truly awful things to her. He accused her of, well, of having had an assignation last night!"

Mr. Frome frowned. "That is wretched, indeed. And though I do not mean to be cynical, is there reason he ought to be concerned on that score?"

"I would stake my life on it that she is wholly faithful to George. I have never seen a woman adore her husband more than Rosamunde. She was quite foxed last night and was holding his leg and kissing his knee!"

Mr. Frome threw his head back and laughed heartily. "She is a treasure. I only hope George has enough sense not to accuse her again."

"Rosamunde laughed and laughed at his accusations. She was quite foxed. I only wish George had not taken exception to my questions."

He nodded. "Some gentlemen cannot bear such scrutiny, particularly if there is some secret they are concealing."

She eyed Mr. Frome carefully. Over the weeks he had been living at the bottom of the garden, she had come to know him quite well. She understood to perfection that he was giving her a very powerful hint. "Do I apprehend from this conversation that you do not think I am so very flawed as Robert does?"

He chortled almost gleefully. "My dear, you have a heart of the purest gold. I would entrust my secrets with you. Just remember that it is always best to get over rough ground lightly."

She felt infinitely relieved until he turned to her and said, "However, there is one thing I would ask you, if you would permit it."

For some reason, her heart began beating very fast. "You may ask me anything."

"What do you think of Sir Robert's criticisms of you?"

"I despise them," she returned quickly, then regretted her words. She wished she had given a more measured, sensible response.

"But why? He seems to be a reasonable sort of man. Why do his opinions incense you?"

Lucy was taken aback by the penetrating question and felt rather reluctant to even ponder the subject. The fact that she never had, that when confronted with one of his wretched opinions she usually grew as mad as fire, was telling in itself. "I do not know," she said quietly, looking into the small fire at his feet. "That is, I suppose it is because of John Goodworth."

"And the worthy Mr. Goodworth to whom you were once betrothed."

"The only man I ever loved," she said softly.

"I recall your speaking of him. He was the unfortunate gentleman who tried to make you into a creature his father would accept."

Her heart began to hurt and she wished the subject had not been brought forward.

Mr. Frome spoke softly. "Do you wish now to tell me that I am the one who is interfering and that you wish I would stop?"

"Yes. I wish it very much. The subject causes me great distress." She could barely see him through the tears shimmering in her eyes.

"Then perhaps, my dear Lucy, you can now comprehend what George is possibly feeling about your questions."

She nodded. "You think I may have touched upon a very tender spot with him."

"I have every confidence that you unwittingly did just that, but will you now honor our friendship, trust me but a very little, and tell me more of your Mr. Goodworth, despite how you feel at present?"

Lucy did not answer him right away. Memories of John surged over her mind and with it waves of pain. She did not want to speak of him and yet at the very same moment she wanted nothing more. She sighed deeply and sat down again. "I have told no one, for at the time that I tumbled in love with him there was no one to tell of the troubles that followed, except of course for my father, but I would not have distressed him for the world. He was very protective of me, you see, and he would have become quite angry, not at John but at his father, Lord Holbury. I am sorry. This is all jumbled up in my head. John Goodworth, you see, was Lord Holbury's eldest son and heir, and even though I had a considerable fortune, I did not have the excellent connections that Lord Holbury expected for a future viscountess.

"He therefore made his displeasure in me known from the start. He did not wish us to marry but he did not refuse his son outright. Instead, his campaign was far more insidious. He was constantly speaking of my numerous flaws to John, that I had little social grace, my fashion sense was atrocious, I was silent at the table or I spoke too much at the table, I held my tea cup improperly, I was too friendly or too severe with the servants, I could do no right. John, in turn, drove me to distraction with lessons on how to behave, how to dress, how to speak, so much so that I began to feel as though I might go mad. John was equally as unhappy. Finally, I ended our betrothal and that is when he married the most vulgar young lady I had ever known. I believe he did so merely to torment his father, but oh, how he broke my heart!"

"My dear, Lucy, I am so sorry."

"It was a long time ago, Mr. Frome. I . . . I never think of it much anymore."

"Yet the hurt remains."

"I believe it always shall to some degree."

"Do you blame your Mr. Goodworth?"

"At the time I blamed his father, but in truth John should have stood by me against his father's railings. We were very young then, however, and Lord Holbury was a master at manipulating his children. I believe it was too much to expect that a man just twenty would be able to counter such vicious attacks."

"So, do you suppose this is why you are so unhappy with Sir Robert's hints, with his strong criticisms of you?"

Lucy stared at him for a long moment. "You may be right. It is possible that when he complains of my faults I may be afraid that were I to take him seriously I would once more be in danger of striving to be something I can never be."

"And are you in danger of doing so?"

Lucy smiled. "No, not in the least. I begin to understand myself a little. All this time it was Lord Holbury's opinions that have distressed me so, not Robert's. Besides, Hetty said something that makes a great deal of sense to me. She believes that Robert is determined to search out my faults so that he does not come to feel too great an affection for me."

Mr. Frome nodded. "How curious," he murmured.

"In what way?"

"That Sir Robert's greatest concern is that he restrain himself too much in his associations with you."

"I do not understand. What would he mean by that?"

"I am not quite certain. I believe he, too, was once disappointed in love."

"Robert?" she queried, much shocked. "Disappointed in love?"

"Is it so hard to believe that he might have loved once?"

"I suppose not, only how is it that I never heard a word of it."

At that he shrugged. "Well, I suppose to say more would be to *interfere* more than I ought. Oh, dear, do but look. There is Lady Sandifort waving to you and she appears quite distressed."

Lucy saw that Mr. Frome was right. Lady Sandifort was frowning quite severely. She thought she understood why.

"Oh, dear. I believe I may be in the basket now! You will excuse me, Mr. Frome?"

"Of course. Good luck, my dear."

CHAPTER
EIGHT

By the time Lucy crossed the stream, Lady Sandifort was upon her.

"I do not mean to deprive you of Mr. Frome's company," she said haughtily, "but I do believe there is something of import I must say to you."

Lucy turned with her to walk up the garden to the west of the maze and said, "And what would that be?"

"You are interfering where you ought not, as well you know!"

Lucy was greatly surprised and not a little dismayed at her choice of words. Had she somehow learned that George was overset by her interference of the night before? She knew better, however, than to reveal her hand, so she merely responded politely, "Indeed? In what way, ma'am?"

"I have learned that you mean to take Anne and Alice to the assemblies in Bickfield in three weeks. I do not hesitate to tell you, Lucy, that you have no right to do so and you certainly do not have my permission!"

So that is why she is in high dudgeon, she thought. Given

all that had happened during the night and even this morning, she had forgotten about her most recent scheme. She could only wonder, however, just how Lady Sandifort had learned of it.

Rounding the maze, however, she quickly discovered the truth, for at the far end of the garden, on the terrace, she saw Hetty, Anne, and Alice. Hetty was standing with her arm pressed to her stomach, Anne was covering her mouth with her hands, and Alice jumped about quite oddly. Their combined distress was obvious even at such a distance. She glanced at the lady next to her. "My dear ma'am, I know quite well that Anne and Alice cannot possibly go without your favor and permission. Robert has made that much clear to me in these few weeks that I have been here."

"Yes, yes," she returned impatiently.

Lucy frowned at her. She sensed something in particular was on her ladyship's mind. Lady Sandifort began pulling at the curls at her neck. She always pulled at the curls at her neck when something was teasing her brain.

"I wonder," Lucy suggested, "if there is something I might do for you that would persuade you to consider permitting the girls to attend the assemblies."

"There is nothing you can do for me," she retorted sharply. "I have all that I want and need at my command."

"As well I know," Lucy complimented her.

A considerable pause ensued.

Lady Sandifort cleared her throat. "And it is an absolute certainty that Valmaston is coming to the ball?"

"Yes. He is fixed in London at present, and as he said in his letter hopes to arrive at least by the Friday before the come-out ball."

She clucked her tongue. "I must confess, Lucy, and I would only say this to you, but I have been frightfully bored of late. I was used to be entertained by Sir Henry and even Robert for these many years and more, but now that my poor husband is dead and Robert is so ridiculously fixed on matters of business, well . . ."

Lucy turned these hints over in her mind. "It must be very hard for you living in the wilds of Hampshire away from proper civilization."

"How well you seem to understand me." She sighed very deeply. "If only a trifle of civilization might be brought here, then perhaps . . ."

Lucy understood her perfectly, only how on earth was she to get Lord Valmaston to come to Aldershaw beforetime, and that with Robert's acquiescence? Well, that was a problem requiring a solution at a later hour. For the present, she had but one object.

"If only Lord Valmaston could come earlier," she said. "He is such an amusing sort of man. He would undoubtedly enliven our evenings a vast deal. What do you think of the notion?"

"Valmaston, here, before the come-out ball?" she cried, tugging once more at the curls on her neck. "Why, I had not considered the possibility before. However, should he come I suppose we would have to make an effort to entertain him properly. Henry could take him out riding, for instance, for I understand Valmaston to be an excellent horseman. There is good trout fishing in the streams. And I suppose it would be amusing to take him to the local assemblies, that sort of thing, for I have always been given to understand that he is a man who quite depends upon society just as I do."

Lucy quailed at the thought of a renowned rakehell of Valmaston's stamp attending the local assemblies. She almost gave up her original scheme at the mere thought of the uproar his presence was likely to cause. As she drew near to Anne and Alice, however, she saw the misery on their poor faces and made her decision instantly.

"We have good news for you," she cried.

Take a Trip Back to the Romantic Regency Era of the Early 1800's

4 FREE BOOKS ARE YOURS!

4 FREE Zebra Regency Romances!
(A $19.96 VALUE!)

Plus You'll Save Every Month With Convenient Home Delivery!

We'd Like to Invite You to Subscribe to Zebra's Regency Romance Book Club and Send You 4 Free Books as Your Introduction! (Worth $19.96!)

If you're a Regency lover, imagine the joy of getting 4 FREE Zebra Regency Romances and then the chance to have these lovely stories delivered to your home each month at the lowest price available! Well, that's our offer to you and here's how you benefit by becoming a Regency Romance subscriber:

- *4 FREE Introductory Regency Romances are delivered to your doorstep (you only pay for shipping & handling)*
- *4 BRAND NEW Regencies are then delivered each month (usually before they're available in bookstores)*
- *Subscribers save almost $4.00 off the cover price every month*
- *You also receive a FREE monthly newsletter, which features author profiles, discounts, subscriber benefits, book previews and more*
- *There's no risks or obligations...in other words, you can cancel whenever you wish with no questions asked*

Join the thousands of readers who enjoy the savings and convenience offered to Regency Romance subscribers. After your initial introductory shipment, you'll receive 4 brand-new Zebra Regency Romances each month to examine for 10 days. Then, if you decide to keep the books, you pay the preferred subscriber's price, plus shipping and handling.

It's a no-lose proposition, so return the FREE BOOK CERTIFICATE today!

Lady Sandifort leaned close, all pretence at an end. "Then you will write to him?"

She turned and met Lady Sandifort's gaze fully. "I shall do better than that. I shall go to London on the instant."

"That would be most excellent," she whispered. "He should come, the sooner the better!" Aloud, she addressed her step-daughters. "You are to attend the assemblies in early August. Lucy has persuaded me, as she always does!"

As they mounted the terrace steps, Anne fairly flew into Lucy's arms. Lucy winked at Hetty, who in turn gave her a look that meant she wished to hear all about it.

A half hour later, Hetty was in her bedchamber, the door closed.

"I do apologize, Lucy," she said in a low tone. "It is my fault entirely that this situation came to pass. I was so excited about the notion of the twins going to the assemblies that I made the supreme error of actually telling Anne. She can no more keep a secret than she can refrain from seeing her hair properly dressed every morning. She most unwisely let the subject slip just after breakfast, and that within our stepmother's hearing."

"It hardly matters," Lucy responded, taking up a chair and gesturing for Hetty to do the same. "Do not give it another thought. As it was, I was having a very difficult time trying to determine just how I should broach the subject with Lady Sandifort, but all has turned out well."

"But Lucy, you cannot be serious about going to London?" Hetty remained standing.

"I must go. She requires Valmaston."

"You cannot have considered. You can hardly call upon a rake. And do you actually mean to bring him to Aldershaw before the come-out ball? Robert will not allow it, of that I am certain. Oh, how you put me in a quake!"

"And how you make me laugh! I vow, Hetty, I never knew you to be so hen-hearted!"

"I wish you would be more serious, for I am not in the least funning. Lucy, pray listen to me! To call upon a gentleman, nonetheless one of such a reputation, at his townhouse—!"

"But I have considered this situation. I will do whatever is required to make certain Anne and Alice have what they desire and what they need. They deserve no less and pray do not pay the smallest heed to my possible discomfiture. Besides, I shall take one of the maids with me, or two if such will set your mind at ease."

Hetty sat down on the bed, slinging her arm about the post. "You make me quite ashamed of myself, Lucinda Stiles. Indeed you do. I have not half your spirit and not a speck of your ability. The twins are my sisters but you have done more for them since your arrival than I have in the past two years."

"Hetty, pray do not distress yourself on that score. I am but a transient guest in this house. I do not live here, nor have I lived under the dominion of Sir Henry's second wife. I have no doubt that, had I been required to do so, my behavior would be quite different and certainly a great deal more docile generally. It is because I am a stranger that I can have a different view of everything."

Hetty did not appear to be in the least convinced. Indeed, she looked so very sad that Lucy could not help but leave her seat and take up one beside her on the bed. She put her arms about her. "Pray do not cry. I do not know what I have said that should have made you become a watering pot."

"It is not what you have said, Lucy," she responded in a small voice, sniffing all the while, "it is that you have shown me a part of myself about which I am suddenly and wholly disenchanted. You see, I have waited here forever and done nothing, in so many respects. While you merely *hear* that Lady Sandifort refuses to take the girls to the assemblies and so you instantly decide you must go to London!" She turned in Lucy's arms. "Do you not see how extraordinary that is?"

Lucy was baffled. "I suppose I do not," she said, rising from the bed as she spoke. "I am merely doing what I feel must be done. Now, dry your tears and no more recriminations. Indeed, I could use your assistance right now. Would you be so good as to help me pack my trunk?"

"Of course I will."

Lucy moved to her wardrobe and withdrew one of her trunks. Dragging it carefully across the carpet, she opened the lid.

"But where will you stay once you arrive in London?" Hetty asked.

"Well, I have an aunt in Cheapside. I suppose I could—"

"I did not know you had an aunt!" Hetty cried.

Lucy rolled her eyes. "My mother's sister, who was some twenty years older than mama. I have never before seen her, although I was told she held me once when I was an infant. Papa never liked her and she was always completely disinterested in me."

"That is very sad."

"But not unusual, I think. At any rate, she could hardly refuse a night's lodging to so near a relation."

"No, I suppose she could not."

"Unless, of course, I told her my true object—to call upon Valmaston."

Hetty laughed and shook her head. "What a dreadful thing to say. Would you actually tell her as much?"

"Only if she speaks ill of either Mama or Papa!"

Hetty laughed a little more, but tears continued to seep inexplicably from her eyes.

The following morning, Lucy was standing in the entrance hall pulling on her gloves of York tan when Robert stormed down the stairs, calling out at the top of his voice, "What the devil do you mean you are going to London? Why is this the first I have heard of your plans and where is it you mean to stay?"

Lucy turned sharply. She was quite startled by his address as well as by how quickly he descended the stairs. She could not help but take several steps backward. "I beg your pardon?"

"You are my ward until your birthday in two months' time. Do you not feel obligated to at least inform me of your intentions?"

" 'Tis only for two or three days."

"Oh," he responded. "Then you are not *removing* to London?"

"No, of course not. What made you think I was?"

"Hetty said you were going to London and somehow I supposed—then why the deuce are you going?"

"As it happens I have, er, business to attend to that cannot wait."

"What business?" he asked suspiciously. "I am fully informed of your inheritance and all other pertinent matters. To my knowledge there is nothing for you to transact in London and certainly nothing that could not be managed by means of pen, ink, and paper if you are set on speaking with your solicitor."

"Still, I must go."

"Then you do not intend to tell me."

Noting his stern expression, she found she had no desire at all to explain where she was going, or why, or with whom she meant most particularly to speak. She was reluctant, however, to withhold the truth from him. "I am going to see my aunt, my mother's elderly sister, who resides in Cheapside."

Robert narrowed his eyes. She could see his suspicion deepen. "I have known you for a very long time and I especially comprehend that particular expression of yours, one of complete innocence, and when you open your eyes that wide—Lucy, you might as well tell me precisely what it is you mean to do in London."

"I fear our darling Lucy," Henry said, as he sauntered into the entrance hall, "is intent on calling upon Lord Valmaston."

Lucy glanced at Henry, wondering both who had told him what she was doing and why he was so angry. Robert she could understand, for he was always displeased with something or other about her, but Henry rarely displayed even the smallest displeasure.

"Valmaston?" Robert cried. "You are going to London to call upon Valmaston? What the devil for?"

"You need not shout, Robert. I am standing but four feet from you."

"Tell me this is not true."

She was silent for a moment, then said, "It is true." She folded her hands, now neatly gloved in fine soft leather, in front of her. So much anger swept over Robert's face that she only barely refrained from taking two more steps backward.

He shook his head several times. "But why? To what purpose? He has already agreed to attend Anne and Alice's come-out ball and I have already said he may stay at Aldershaw for a few days. For what possible reason then could you have to travel to London and call upon him?"

How was Lucy to explain her purposes? Would Robert even understand them? "I . . . I have my reasons," she stated. "I beg you will not inquire further, but it is something I must do." Inspiration struck. "I can at least tell you this—I have a message to give him from my father that I should have delivered months ago but now I cannot wait another moment." This was partly true. Well, perhaps only a very little.

His eyes narrowed further still and she had the strong sense he did not believe her. He did not speak for a very long moment and the silence in the entrance hall grew louder and louder as each second passed. Finally his shoulders relaxed.

"You will have to stay your departure for at least an hour. I will need to change into traveling gear."

"You are not going with me!" Lucy cried, much horrified.

He smiled suddenly. "The devil I am not!" he exclaimed. With that he whirled on his heel and took the stairs by two. He was gone before she could think of even one excuse by which she might have gotten rid of him. She debated leaving on the instant but that would not work at all. Robert would merely follow after her and then she would be in the basket, indeed!

Henry approached her at that moment. "What are you thinking, Lucy? Valmaston has a terrible reputation, but you know that and yet you would go and that without protection?"

She turned to him and lifted her chin slightly. "Lord Valmaston has been a friend to me since I was quite young. Whatever his reputation, I trust him implicitly. If I have any concern it is that I will be importuning him with an unexpected visit."

"I would wish you a hundred miles from him," he stated darkly. "You are too innocent to know what sort of man he truly is."

Lucy straightened her shoulders. "I do know what he is. A good friend to my father and to me, and a gentleman I vow I have always admired. I know that his life has not been in the usual vein, but he has great generosity of spirit, a very penetrating wit, and a chivalry I have frequently found unmatched."

He seemed much taken aback. "Good God," he breathed, seeming rather shocked. "Are you in love with him?"

Lucy laughed. "Because I spoke highly of him you would reason that I am in love with him?"

He shook his head but still he scowled. "I do not think there could be a better reason. Only tell me, Lucy, do you love him?"

"No, as it happens I do not."

His scowl softened. "Perhaps I am being ridiculous." He moved close to her and took hold of one of her hands. "It is just that you have become quite precious to me and I abhor the thought that even the smallest danger could touch you."

"Truly, Henry, you need not be so worried, but I thank you for your concern."

"I believe I may be even a little jealous that you are seeking his society."

Lucy laughed. "Though I have known Valmaston for as long as I have known you, I will always think of you as a better friend."

He shook his head, appearing rather consternated. "With that, I suppose, I must for the present be content."

Lucy was surprised that he would say as much and she wondered suddenly if he fancied himself in love with her. This she dismissed as quite absurd, however. Henry had never shown any particular regard for her. He was as he had always been, attentive and kind. He was a true friend.

"Why do you not have a cup of tea while you wait for Robert?" he suggested.

"An excellent notion." He drew her into the armory and ordered tea. He remained with her, conversing as was usual on a variety of subjects until at last Robert was ready to leave.

The journey from Hampshire to London required the entire day. Discourse between them proved perfunctory. Robert seemed angry that he had been forced to accompany her and Lucy, in her irritation that he would be so high-handed, was unwilling to smooth his feathers.

Arriving at Robert's townhouse in Upper Brook Street, Lucy stretched her back and finally thanked him for his efforts. "You have made the journey quite comfortable for me and for that I thank you." She smiled, and added, "Besides, now that I think on it, I do not know what I would have said to my aunt who has never written to me once in four and twenty years!"

He shook his head. "Do you know, I believe you are the most incorrigible young lady of my acquaintance!"

Lucy laughed.

The London staff was quite surprised to see their master, but not displeased. Indeed, Lucy was rather impressed by the general affection with which the aged butler and equally aged housekeeper greeted him. She had never been to the London house, which was not a particularly large establishment but nicely appointed with elegant furniture—in part *a la chinoiserie* and in part the established prevailing mode with hints of Greek and Roman styling and embellishment. A royal blue dominated the receiving rooms, although the long dining room was decorated with a rich red silk on the walls.

Lucy retired to her bedchamber on the second floor and immediately sat down at the writing desk to compose her letter to Valmaston.

So it was that on the following morning he called upon her. Robert, in keeping with his deep mistrust of the rogue, insisted upon being present.

Lucy greeted him as she always had. She embraced him and he kissed her forehead. He was a tall man, quite broad-shouldered, with wavy brown hair and intriguing gray eyes. His smile was breathtaking.

"You are as beautiful as ever, *Lucia*."

"How long has it been? Oh, but that is a ridiculous question since we both know the answer."

He took her shoulders in hand. "You must tell me how you fare. I know how much you loved your father. I loved him, too. Tell me your heart is not still in pieces, and I shall be content."

Lucy smiled, if faintly. "At times, of course, but I am growing used to my life without him."

"I miss him as well," he said kindly.

"I know you do and it gives me great comfort to hear you speak of him." She turned slightly toward Robert. "I would like to make you known to my guardian. Sir Robert Sandifort, Lord Valmaston."

The gentlemen bowed formally to one another.

"Please sit down," Lucy said. Only as she took up her seat on the sofa near the front window did she become aware that the men were eyeing one another in a critical manner. She had the sense that were either of them to speak the wrong words a bout of fisticuffs would surely follow.

Finally, Sir Robert gestured for Lord Valmaston to take up a chair. He took up the one nearest Lucy though opposite her. Sir Robert rounded the earl's chair and moved to sit on the sofa with Lucy. She was a little shocked, especially seeing his challenging expression.

When she met Valmaston's gaze, she saw a familiar amused light in his eye and from that moment she began to relax. Whatever his reputation, Lucy trusted the earl.

During the ensuing hour a great many subjects were brought forward and during that same hour Robert's demeanor altered considerably. His stiff reserve, even ill-concealed hostility, all but dissipated. Instead, he began to speak in an open fashion that surprised Lucy. The men shared a common experience in that they had both inherited large estates that had to varying degrees been neglected by their predecessors. Of course, the earl had had a good twenty years to repair his fortunes, which he had done admirably, and in keeping with his generous temper he did not hesitate to encourage Robert in his many efforts. When the conversation soon fell to the management of their respective lands and houses, Lucy repressed a sigh and, with as much interest as she could summon, followed their conversation patiently.

"Oh, but we are boring poor *Lucia*," Valmaston said at last.

"Not in the least," Lucy assured him, but a sudden yawn, which she was completely unable to suppress, escaped her.

The gentlemen laughed.

"Will you stay to nuncheon?" Robert asked.

"I should like that."

The earl's visit extended from one hour to the next until the clock struck three. "Is it so very late?" he asked, glancing at the clock on the mantel.

"Yes, I believe it is," Robert said.

"I fear I must be going. I am engaged elsewhere for the evening."

Lucy felt greatly disappointed, for she had not had the smallest opportunity to place her request before her friend. She took a deep breath and began, "Will you not lend me five minutes? There is something I must ask you, that is if Robert will excuse us?"

Far from even the smallest show of hesitation, Robert rose and suggested they make use of the library on the ground floor, which was well suited for private conversations. Lucy lifted her brow to him, but he merely smiled as if to say he was satisfied that she was not going to be attacked by this rogue of rogues. She led her friend downstairs.

Once closeted within, she began speaking at length, albeit quickly, of the present situation at Aldershaw, most particularly emphasizing Lady Sandifort and her commanding role in the house. "Though I do not comprehend the source of her power, there can be no disputing that Robert does not disrupt her schemes, at least not so often as I believe he should."

"What does this have to do with me?"

She felt a blush climb her cheeks. "Now that I am here and speaking with you, I am rather uncomfortable addressing the truth. I suppose I should be direct."

"Yes, that would be best." He was smiling.

She released a sigh and plunged on. "The difficulty is simple. Lady Sandifort is smitten with you, or at least your reputation. Oh, dear, I am going to blush even more."

He sat down on the corner of the desk and laughed, though he crossed his arms over his chest. "Go on."

"Well, she has expressed a willingness to permit certain events if she is properly entertained, events like the come-out ball for Anne and Alice for instance, the one you have agreed to attend in a month's time." She drew in a deep breath and spoke rapidly. "If you would be willing to come to Hampshire, to Aldershaw, sooner than previously agreed upon, she will allow the twins to attend the assemblies in Bickfield."

He frowned. "Good God. She does bear an inordinate amount of power—unusually so."

"How well I know it, but Robert, as is his right, will not tell me how it has come about. He seems to be under some great obligation. Therefore, I am left to manage things as best I might."

"So naturally you thought of me." Again he laughed.

"Well, now that I am asking for your help it seems a ridiculous thing to do, and completely unfair to you."

"Let me see if I understand you. What you are saying is that you wish me to manage her ladyship until such time as—?"

"For the next month, if at all possible. Yes, yes, I know I am asking a vast deal, but if you had any notion how much the family has suffered beneath her iron hand you would understand my determination to give as much relief as I can. However, if you feel you must decline, I shan't blame you. I realize it is asking more than I ought."

He narrowed his eyes and swung his leg. His arms were still crossed over his chest. "You have in mind the promise I made to your father," he stated. "And by this you mean to force my hand."

Lucy pressed her hands to her cheeks. "You always were able to see straight through my schemes!"

"Lucy," he drawled. "What a wretch you are! Does Sir

Robert have even the smallest notion what a difficult wife you will make him?"

"What?" she cried, horrified. "We are not betrothed, if that is what you are suggesting. Good God, we barely tolerate one another."

"Oh, then I am greatly mistaken. I presumed since you were traveling together that there was some sort of understanding."

"No," she reassured him, feeling very odd of a sudden. Imagine being Robert's wife! She swallowed hard and tried not to think of the kisses they had already shared, or how wonderful they had been, and certainly not what it would be like to share his bed. No, she would not permit her mind to dwell upon these things at all! "Well, I know you must take your leave," she said, walking to the door of the library. "You may let me know as soon as pleases you whether you can accept of my invitation."

This time he laughed aloud. "Am I correct in assuming that Sir Robert knows nothing of this scheme?"

"You are correct," she stated. "I choose to cross my bridges one at a time."

"You are so much like your father. Well, *Lucia*, in part because I made a pledge to your good parent to come to your aid if required and in part because I find I am wholly intrigued by just how you will manage this present difficult situation, I shall tell you now that I do accept your invitation, but on one condition."

"What would that be?"

"You have asked me essentially to flirt with Lady Sandifort."

"Yes." She did not think her cheeks could get any warmer but so they did.

"If I find I detest her—and somehow I believe I shall— then I reserve the right to ignore her entirely."

Lucy was dismayed. Valmaston, for all his ability to beguile the feminine sex, was also rather ruthless. She did not think Lady Sandifort would like being treated with either indifference or contempt by so famous a man as the earl. On the other hand, she could hardly blame him if he found himself so disgusted he could not bring himself to do the pretty with her. At the same time, she knew quite well she had no choice but to agree to his condition. "To expect anything else would be ungenerous and certainly unrealistic. In fact, I only ask that you *manage* her, nothing more, whatever that should entail."

He smiled anew. "Then I agree." He frowned slightly. "However, I will not be able to come to Hampshire until Thursday next. Will that suffice?"

"Of course, quite beautifully, but are you certain you will do this thing without hating me forever?"

He shook his head. "I have no such certainty." But he could not contain his smiles.

Lucy laughed. "Thursday next, then. I shall send directions to Grosvenor Street before we depart."

"That will do."

She walked him to the door and he kissed her warmly on the cheek.

"You are beautiful," he said, then he was gone.

Lucy caught sight of movement and glanced up the stairs. Robert stood on the landing, frowning. What was he thinking, she wondered, and what was worse, how was she ever to explain what she had done?

Robert regarded Lucy for a long moment. He had waited a full ten minutes before venturing onto the landing. He had permitted the *tête-a-tête* because, and this had proved a great surprise, he instinctively trusted Valmaston. However, the longer they remained within, particularly with the door closed, the less certain he became. No matter how harmless the relationship seemed, Valmaston was still an acknowledged rogue.

He had arrived at the top of the stairs to watch the earl

place a lingering kiss on Lucy's cheek. He believed the image would be burnt into his mind for the next decade or two. Even now, he felt a rage within him that he could not explain, a fiery, piercing sensation that left him wanting to call Valmaston out!

Yet he knew the man to be a gentleman in the truest sense of the word and he knew the earl would never hurt Lucy, so why was he so angry by having witnessed a simple kiss on the cheek? Except that it was Lucy's cheek and Valmaston was an uncommonly engaging man. He was perhaps five and forty, but what did that matter where the feminine heart was concerned?

"Is your business with him concluded?" he asked.

Lucy nodded.

"We leave in the morning."

"Of course."

He turned away and moved, as one in the grip of a nightmare, into the drawing room.

Lucy did not know what was the matter with Robert. He seemed so strange, almost as though he had suddenly been taken ill. Certainly his complexion was rather pale, and there had been the oddest light in his eye when he spoke to her, as though he had seen a ghost.

Lifting her skirts, she moved slowly up the stairs. She tried to determine if he was angry, but the expression she had just witnessed was not his usual demeanor when he was overset. No, he seemed different somehow, but she could not quite determine in precisely what way. However, his words were straightforward and to the point. Perhaps he was anxious to return to Hampshire.

Arriving at the entrance to the drawing room, she found him reading a volume of poetry, a clear indication he was no longer interested in conversation. She excused herself, saying she was rather fatigued and would lie down before dinner. He did not look at her but nodded, his gaze fixed to the pages of his book. She turned away but turned quickly back and once more glanced at his book. She realized it was upside-down. She almost teased him about it but something warned her not to do so.

Instead, she shrugged and gave herself to her bed for the next two hours.

CHAPTER NINE

The return journey to Hampshire proved unexpectedly pleasant. Whatever had been weighing on Robert's mind the entire evening prior no longer seemed to be affecting him. He had instead become a quite enjoyable traveling companion, not only tending to her needs and desires at each posting house, but sustaining a rather personal conversation throughout the journey.

At first she had been rather skeptical about his questions, for he wished to know about her life in Somerset, about her interests, her hopes for the future. In the end, however, she had opened her budget because in her innermost heart she trusted Robert, however critical he might be of her in other ways. She remembered, too, what Mr. Frome had said of Robert, that he was concerned about being too restrained with her.

"Were you never in love, Robert?" she asked. She still did not believe that Mr. Frome was correct in saying that he thought Robert had once been disappointed in love. After all, she had never heard a whisper among the family that any particular lady had ever attached him to her side. Still, she found herself intrigued to hear his response.

"Yes," he stated simply.

She stared at him for several seconds, for she was greatly shocked. How could she not be? "You were?"

He laughed. "Why does that seem so impossible to you?"

She shook her head. "Because no one ever spoke of it, not even Hetty. I also wonder how I could not have known, since I visited at Aldershaw so often."

He smiled suddenly in that manner of his that always warmed her heart. "By my calculations, I was in the throes of a very painful calf-love when you were but thirteen."

"Well, that was a very long time ago, indeed! Calf-love, you say? It was not more serious?"

He shrugged. The coach hit a rut and she bounced in her seat. "As to that," he said mockingly, "*I* was certainly serious about loving her. Devilishly serious. I believed one day I would make her my wife, but I was quite young at the time and, as it proved, rather foolish in my hopes and expectations."

Lucy smiled and would have teased him, but there was just such a look of hurt in his eye that made her stop. "What was her name?" she asked instead.

"Amelia Damerham, and, no, I do not believe you ever knew her. She is long since married to a Major Eastleigh and resides in Norfolk, the last I heard of her."

Lucy turned this information over in her mind. She had a strong sense that there was a great deal he was not saying. "How long ago did she wed Major Eastleigh?"

"Again, you were but thirteen."

"I see." She thought of John Goodworth. "Miss Amelia was an unreliable sort?"

"She broke no vows. We were not betrothed." Yet he sighed.

Here was love, indeed, that he would speak words of such

tolerance when she could see that he was still troubled by the memories.

"Well, I dislike her immensely," she stated.

He chuckled. "You make no sense at all. You never knew her. How could you dislike her if you never even set eyes on her."

"I do not need to know her to understand that she possessed your heart but chose another. You may be forbearing with her, but I can think as ill of her as I please!" She had meant the words to be flippant and full of a dark sort of cheerfulness. Instead, she found she was rather irritated that Miss Amelia had used Robert so ill, particularly when he had been of a tender age. He would have been but two and twenty.

She remembered him as a young man, so upright and responsible, always striving to do what was right and good. He would have courted Miss Damerham quite properly and decorously.

"I should have kissed her," he murmured, more to himself, his brows parted by a heavy frown.

"I beg your pardon?"

He shook his head. "It hardly signifies."

Robert glanced at Lucy and saw that she was regarding him quizzically, trying to make him out, no doubt. *I should have kissed Amelia.* He had kissed Lucy, more than once. He had kissed her quite passionately. He had kissed her when he should not have. He had kissed her without the smallest intention of wedding her. What if he had kissed Amelia? What if he had spoken his heart with poetic words of love and obsession? Would she have married him then?

The coach halted at The George in Bickfield.

"Robert, would you mind if I went into Hart's? I should like to buy a few presents for the children."

"How could I refuse such a request?" he said, smiling.

Lucy spent fifteen minutes searching the local shop for just the right items for Eugenia, Hyacinth, William, and Violet.

By the time she returned to the coach, a fresh team had been harnessed and the final portion of the journey commenced.

With but five miles to go the coach wheels ate up the distance to Aldershaw quickly, and within little more than half an hour the manor was in sight. Turning down the long avenue, Lucy marveled, as she did quite often, at what great speeds could be achieved by a proper traveling vehicle and four good horses.

"I must say, Lucy," Robert said, his gaze fixed out the window, "that the gardens have improved tremendously. I would not have thought so much could be accomplished in so little time. It has only been a month, has it not?"

"Perhaps a little more, but then Mr. Quarley was fully prepared with scores of plants, large and small, just awaiting the orders to put each and every one in the ground. You ought to extend your praise to him. I know he would be grateful for it."

"You do that often, you know," he said, glancing at her.

"What?" she asked, surprised yet curious.

"You give me little hints about just how to manage things at Aldershaw."

She groaned. "You must forgive me, you know. It comes from having been Papa's housekeeper for so many years. I fear I am used to seeing things done a certain way. I am sorry."

"You need not apologize. I have in this moment realized that, though I am loath to admit as much, I have come to rely on you."

She saw that he was being very genuine and she did not wish to ruin the moment, but since they were getting along quite well she felt obliged to make her confession. "I am so very happy to hear you say so." How her heart began to race. "But there is something you should know."

"L-u-c-y," he said slowly. "What have you done? Does it involve Valmaston?"

She nodded and wrinkled up her nose. "I fear it does," she said hurriedly, "but not just him—Anne, Alice, and your stepmother as well. I know it was very wrong of me, but I have invited Valmaston to come to Aldershaw and reside here for," she calculated the time from Thursday next to the day after the twin's come-out ball, "three weeks."

"*Three weeks!*" he shouted.

She nodded, clasping her hands together tightly in front of her.

"How? When? With what permission did you dare—?"

She winced and closed her eyes.

"Look at me," he stated firmly.

Her eyes popped open at his command.

"You are no longer a child to be shutting your eyes like that. What the devil were you thinking?"

He was right, of course. "I had only one purpose, to persuade Lady Sandifort to permit Anne and Alice to go to the assemblies in Bickfield."

"This makes no sense whatsoever," he said, throwing his hands wide. "Of what are you speaking? Why would Valmaston persuade her to do anything?"

How was she to explain to him her reasoning? "I wanted to distract Lady Sandifort. She seems so completely intent on wounding Anne and Alice and I thought, based primarily on her own expressions of interest in Valmaston, that were he here he could keep her, that is, he could distract her from your sisters and from trying to do them injury, which I must say, Robert, seems to be one of her principle enjoyments in life. I should dearly like to know just what hold she has over them, over you, that she is allowed to be so vicious?"

"You have turned the subject quite neatly," he stated, as one injured.

"But, Robert, it is to the point," she cried.

"Do lower your voice." By now the coach had reached the house.

"Yes, of course." More quietly, she continued, "Only pray tell me why Lady Sandifort is able to rule as she does at Aldershaw?"

As the horses came to a stop, he scowled deeply. She could see that he was debating the question in his mind. He regarded her intently and finally said, but also in an exceedingly low voice, "Very well, I shall tell you, but first I wish you to be aware that there are only three others who know of this: Lady Sandifort, Henry, and Hetty. I trust, therefore, that you will keep our present conversation in the strictest confidence."

Lucy's heart had begun pounding. For the nearly six weeks she had been residing in Robert's home, she had come to believe something was wretchedly amiss at Aldershaw. Robert had just confirmed her deepest suspicions and it would seem she was now to learn what all the trouble was about. "I promise you that I will say nothing of this."

"Very well," he said gravely. "As it happens, my father left a provision in his will that Lady Sandifort would have charge of Anne and Alice in every social matter, even to the arranging of their marriages, until each was safely wed."

Lucy had never been more shocked. All this time she had thought something else was the cause of the difficulty between Lady Sandifort and Robert. "Good God," she murmured.

"Just so." He leaned back as the footman opened the door and let down the steps.

Lucy was horrified by what she had just learned. As she descended the coach, she understood finally the terrible nature of the hold Lady Sandifort had over Robert as well as the twins. She glanced at Robert, thinking that she had wronged him in her own thoughts of his character. She had been persuaded that he lacked fortitude in his dealings with Celeste Sandifort, but now she saw that in every way he tried to protect his sisters, for to cross Lady Sandifort's will was to do injury to the twins.

The youngest of the Sandiforts, apparently having seen the coach arrive from one of the upstairs windows, came racing out the front door. Violet trailed the others, her new doll clutched in the crook of her arm. "You came back!" she cried. "You came back!"

The next moment she was in Lucy's arms. Lucy held her tightly and at the same time met Robert's gaze. He smiled, if but a little sadly, and took his youngest half sister from her arms. "Is there not a kiss for your eldest brother?"

Violet kissed each of his cheeks in turn while Lucy attended to Eugenia and Hyacinth. William hung back a little, perhaps feeling both his years and his pride. He was after all six, almost seven.

"I brought gifts," she said, meeting William's gaze. His smile was worth a hundred times more than the scant fifteen minutes she had spent at Hart's searching for something for each of them.

Over the next few days, in preparation for Valmaston's arrival, Lucy vowed she had never seen Lady Sandifort so happy in the many weeks she had been at Aldershaw. Having learned that the earl was coming in but a sennight, she fairly floated from room to room and was in such good spirits that she was almost pleasant.

The house settled into a routine in which Lucy engaged contentedly, a flow of daily tasks and events that found her in company with one or another member of the family throughout each day. After breakfast she would go to the schoolroom and visit with Miss Gunville and her four charges. Hetty had command of her next, in which together they would review any housekeeping duties with the housekeeper. Afterward she would take these concerns as well as a tray of hot chocolate, apricot tarts, and the sweetest fruit to be found that day in the home garden to Lady Sandifort's dressing room, where she spent at least an hour in her company.

Early in her stay at Aldershaw she had learned that the best way of managing Lady Sandifort was to keep her very close and to offer at least half a dozen compliments on her beauty and fashion before noon. In such a way, the smoothing of her vanity seemed to create a store of cheerfulness from which she drew until she retired that evening.

"You must have slept wonderfully," Lucy said, "for I vow you have awakened prettier than yesterday."

"Oh, Lucy, how good you are to me." She reclined in bed and held a looking glass to admire her features. "My complexion is almost perfection, if I do say so myself."

"Nothing less." Lucy prepared her a cup of chocolate and brought it to her.

Lady Sandifort took it gratefully. "How glad I am that you have come to Aldershaw. You have been the greatest comfort to me."

"And I am happy you think so." She smiled and sat in a chair by the bedside, waiting patiently while she took several sips of chocolate. She said, "I noticed yesterday that you wore the yellow sprigged muslin and I kept thinking how well it became your figure. Indeed, ma'am, I have never known a lady so perfectly proportioned."

"And you never will," she stated. "Oh, yes, I suppose I should demur and titter my disbelief, but to what purpose?" She sighed again as she lifted her looking glass.

"To what purpose, indeed!" Lucy regarded her wonderingly not for the first time. There was something so childlike about Celeste Sandifort. She had noted it more than once, as though something had occurred to keep her mind in an almost infant state, for she never thought of anyone but herself. "How do you intend to have your maid fashion your hair today?"

"Well, since I have decided to wear the new lavender gown, I thought I would wear the Grecian bands."

Lucy nodded and chuckled. "I dare say you could wear your hair dangling to your waist and even uncombed and you would still be the loveliest woman in the room."

"Now you go too far in your compliments."

"Do I?"

Lady Sandifort trilled her laughter.

Lucy offered two more compliments, one on the delicate size of her hands and another on the lovely cadence of her speech. Lady Sandifort appeared absolutely serene in her pleasure. Only then did she bring forward the decisions that would need to be made about the household linens, the meals, any squabbles between servants, the children's menus, everything over which she insisted on having command but did not truly have the smallest interest. Lucy finished her list with a query as to which chamber Valmaston would be placed during his stay.

At this point Lady Sandifort sat up in bed and set aside her tray. How her blue eyes glittered. Her first choice was to have Valmaston settled in the bedchamber next to her own, but Lucy pointed out that there would be far too much gossip if she did so.

"Oh, what do I care for gossip!" she cried petulantly.

Lucy was not certain precisely what to say, but she finally made a strong point that, even if the servants were to gabble-monger, she did not think it would serve her to give Valmaston the impression she was so very eager for his society.

"You are quite right!" she cried, opening her eyes wide. "And how foolish of me. I have not taken a lover in so long, over a year and a half now, and that with what proved to be the most reckless priest who has his living but a few miles from . . . that I vow I have quite forgotten—oh, but I see I have made you blush! It is your own fault, you know, for you seem so wise in the ways of the world that I always forget you have never been married."

Lucy chose not to address any of these observations but rather rose to her feet, smiling all the while. "Shall we then see that he has the room on the third floor above yours?"

"How very sly, for then I could steal up the stairs—oh, but I shall make you blush again! Pray forget that I have said anything!"

Lucy took the tray and waggled her finger at Lady Sandifort. By the time she quit her bedchamber, she found that her cheeks were absolutely burning! And Lady Sandifort had been involved with the vicar of a local parish? She was utterly shocked and found that several minutes were required for her face to feel cool again!

After meeting with Lady Sandifort, Lucy usually spent the next hour with Mr. Quarley. He would take her to some part of the gardens in either the front of the property or behind to walk around the hedges, flower beds, shrubs, and trees in order to determine what ought to be done next. She had long since told him she relied implicitly on his discretion, but he insisted on consulting with her. "You have a good eye, Miss Stiles, and I don't see as well as I was used to." So it was that the ongoing improvement in the gardens had become a treasure to her.

Nuncheon brought most of the family together, save for the children. Rosamunde had also been absent ever since having come home foxed from Chaleford. Lucy therefore quickly acquired the habit of taking a tray to her as well, a light meal concocted by Cook to tempt her waning appetite. Of all the inmates at Aldershaw, Lucy was worried the most about Rosamunde.

On this day, a scant few days before Valmaston was due to arrive at Aldershaw, Lucy prepared her tray with a quaking heart. She had put into motion an adventure which should have been accomplished at least a twelvemonth past. She had even had the audacity to include Robert in the ruse. He had been reluctant, even hostile at first to what she wished to do, but became quickly resigned because, as he said, he had had his own unhappy suspicions for several months now.

When Lucy took Rosamunde her tray, she found her still sleeping even though it was almost noon, not an unusual circumstance since the day before had been her weekly escapade to her "infirmed" friend's home in Chaleford. Lucy found her difficult to awaken, as was also usual.

Finally, however, Rosamunde opened her eyes, yawned, and stretched. "What is the hour?"

"But ten minutes until twelve o'clock."

"Good heavens. Have I slept that long? Why, that is more than eleven hours!" She seemed surprised but quite lethargic.

"Well, you cannot keep sleeping today. As it happens I am greatly in need of a companion for a trip I must take into Bickfield."

"I do not wish to go to Bickfield."

Lucy settled the tray on the bed beside Rosamunde. "You must eat and we must take our trip. I believe Eugenia would benefit from a short drive, for she has seemed a trifle blue-devilled of late."

Rosamunde frowned. "Has she?" She knew Rosamunde would do anything for her daughter.

"Very much so. Besides, an outing would benefit you greatly as well. We could have tea at The George."

"If you say it is necessary then of course I shall go with you." With some difficulty she pushed herself to a sitting position and began nibbling on a piece of toast.

Lucy shoved the drapes back, which caused Rosamunde to groan and wince.

"Have you been at the peach ratafia again?" Lucy asked.

"No!" Rosamunde exclaimed, wincing a little more. "Well, perhaps I did have a glass or two."

Lucy chuckled. "Drink your tea. You will feel better."

So it was that in an hour, Lucy, Rosamunde, and Eugenia met Robert at the bottom of the stairs.

"Are you attending us?" Rosamunde asked, a little shocked as she glanced from Robert to Lucy and back again.

He offered his arm to her. "I hope you do not mind. But I begged Lucy to permit me to join you."

Rosamunde took his arm. "Of course I do not mind. You are always so kind to me, Robert."

Lucy followed behind with Eugenia and felt her heart swell. This much was true about Robert: he had always shown a great deal of kindness, even compassion, to Rosamunde.

When the coach reached the end of the avenue, instead of heading to Bickfield the conveyance continued in a southerly direction.

"Where are we going?" Rosamunde asked. "We should have turned left."

"We are kidnapping you," Lucy said with a smile. "We are not going to Bickfield and I fear we will be traveling well into the evening."

"I do not understand. Where precisely are we going?"

Eugenia's eyes brightened. "I know," she cried. "Baddesley! Lucy and Robert are taking us to Baddesley. Mama, we are going home!"

"I have a very intelligent niece," Robert said, smiling at Eugenia, who sat across from him.

"Baddesley?" Rosamunde queried in little more than a whisper.

"Yes," Lucy said. "We have quite gone beyond the pale and I for one have every certainty that your husband will never forgive me for concocting this scheme in the first place, but I could think of no reason not to let you at least see your home.

I am certain you do not give a fig that the house is still undergoing repairs."

Rosamunde squeaked a reply, but she had taken to crying so suddenly and violently that she could not be understood. She held a kerchief to her face and sobbed. Robert put his arm about her shoulder, holding her tightly as she promptly buried her face in his coat.

"Mama, pray do not," Eugenia said, reaching for her, but the tears did not abate for at least half an hour, after which time she must have thanked Lucy a hundred times.

"I am going home. I am going home. I will not return to Aldershaw, Robert, no matter what George says! I do not mind living in a mountain of dust so long as I can be in my own house!"

Robert merely smiled at her and patted her hand gently.

The moon was high by the time the coach drew before the gates of Baddesley. The land was drenched in a lovely pale light.

"It almost looks as though the shrubs and trees are covered in snow," Eugenia said.

The gate proved to be rusted badly and the footman, to everyone's surprise, had some difficulty opening it. At last the coach bowled through, venturing onto the rather long and circuitous drive, which in turn proved to be scandalously overgrown. Branches frequently scraped the sides of the coach.

"My poor garden," Rosamunde whispered. "What has happened here? George promised me that the gardens would be tended while I was away."

The experience in the dark, with only lamplight from the coach and faint moonlight from above to illuminate the thick growth, caused Lucy to shiver. "It is very bad. Worse even than Aldershaw was when I first arrived."

"So it is," Rosamunde said, straining against the glass in an attempt to see. "The edge of the woods and shrubs should end soon."

The coach broke out into a more open flow of land but even the moonlight showed a wretchedly forsaken garden.

Rosamunde began to weep. "It is just as I feared. The gardeners have grown lazy."

Lucy felt in her heart that something far worse had happened but she could not bring herself to say it. She glanced at Robert and even in the darkness of the coach she could see that his expression was exceedingly somber.

When at last the coach drew before the ancient Tudor mansion, built of stone, the whole party had fallen silent. Lucy felt quite sick at heart and could only imagine what Rosamunde's thoughts and feelings were at present. In the dim light Lucy could hear her sniffs and the fluttering of the white kerchief as it flew to her cheeks again and again.

Robert ordered the coachman to remain on the drive instead of seeking the stables, as would have been usual. Lucy took Rosamunde's arm and approached the door. She struck the knocker again and again quite vigorously but there was no response. She repeated the rapping. She waited. She rapped again. Finally she pressed the latch and to her surprise the door opened.

"It was not even locked," Eugenia said, clinging to her mother.

Lucy walked in, feeling as though she had stepped into a nightmare. The air smelled of damp, dust, and rot.

"My house. My poor, poor house," was all Rosamunde could say.

Eugenia had moved to the drawing room to the left of the entrance hall and peered within. "Mama, all the furniture is gone."

"What? You must be mistaken. You simply cannot see because it is too dark." She moved to stand beside her daughter and peered within. "Oh, dear God. Even the drapes are gone."

Robert entered the house last and immediately sent one of the footmen on an errand to see if he might find a stray candle or two. When at last he returned he bore a candelabra in hand. Making use of the carriage lamps, the candles were soon lit. What had already been perceived in the gloom and darkness was now illuminated.

The house had every appearance of having been abandoned, and that for a very long time, indeed.

Lucy watched Rosamunde closely, fearing that the state of the house would be the undoing of her mind. Robert led the way from room to room, holding the candelabra aloft and walking very slowly. Rosamunde followed behind, while Lucy and Eugenia trailed in their wake. Every chamber was in the same state as the one before.

Eugenia took Lucy's hand.

"Very well," Rosamunde said over and over as chamber upon chamber revealed the decay of Baddesley to her. "Very well. Very well."

To Lucy's surprise, Rosamunde's shoulders straightened and her voice grew stronger than she had ever known it to be. When at last Robert returned the party to the entrance hall, Rosamunde bore an expression of acceptance, even of relief. "I had always thought he was not telling me the truth," she said quietly. "But I had no way of proving it."

Robert was just suggesting that they return to the nearest village and stay the night at The White Horse when the door suddenly burst open.

Lucy had never been more shocked than to see George standing on the threshhold. His complexion was pale and sweat glistened on his forehead. His clothes were dusty from head to toe.

Rosamunde moved forward. "Did you ride all this distance, my love?"

He nodded.

Silence reigned in the hall for a long moment until Rosamunde ran to him. He opened his arms wide, tears now brimming in his eyes. "I am so sorry. I put every tuppence of your dowry into our home, into the surrounding farms, but I could not increase the rent rolls. We have lost everything."

"You should have told me."

George held her for a long moment then drew her to the stairs, where they sat down together, his arm tightly about her shoulders. He looked exhausted, as much from riding so far as he had as from having kept the horrible secret of his loss of Baddesley. Rosamunde sat down beside him and possessed herself of his hand. Eugenia went to him as well and took the other.

George looked up at Robert. "I owe you so much that I can never repay, brother."

"We are a family, George. You owe me nothing."

When he started to say more, Lucy quickly took his arm. He paused and glanced down at her, a frown in his eyes. She shook her head. "Will you walk out with me?" she asked quietly.

He glanced at the family nestled tightly together on the stairs. "Yes, of course." He settled the candelabra in the middle of the floor and escorted her out of doors, beckoning the footman to leave as well.

Once outside, Lucy drew him away from the coach. Her own heart was aching at the truth about George's loss.

"It is not at all uncommon in these days of failed harvests," he said somberly.

"I know," she murmured.

"You were proven right again, Lucy. I am beginning to feel completely daunted by your perceptions. I only wonder what you must think of me, since you seem to know us all so well."

She stopped him in their slow progress and turned toward him. "I think that you are a fine brother and one of the kindest men I have ever known. After all, how many gentlemen, known to take great pride in their coats, would have permitted a lady to come the watering pot on so expensive a superfine as yours?"

At that he chuckled. "Dear Lucy, how you make me laugh when you must know my heart is breaking for my brother."

"Mine as well," she said, smiling up into his face but feeling very sad.

His gaze caught and held. The moonlight was sufficiently bright for her to see the sudden glitter in his eyes. She experienced some difficulty in breathing. What was he thinking? she wondered.

Robert looked into Lucy's eyes, as much as he was able in the darkness of the night. Still, he saw the sparkle that so completely bespoke her bright temper. He was so full of affection, of gratitude in this moment that he could not find the proper words to give expression to all he was feeling. He touched her cheek with his hand. "Lucy," he whispered, leaning toward her. He felt a strong desire to kiss her, not in passion but in appreciation.

Eugenia called from the doorway. "Lucy, I am to sit between you and Uncle Robert. Papa means to ride in the coach as well."

"Of course," Lucy called back to her.

Robert did not want to let the moment slip away but he had no choice. He lowered his hand and turned back with her to move in the direction of the coach. Awareness dawned and he came to his senses. Good God, he had almost kissed her again, the lady with whom Henry was so violently in love. How grateful he was that Eugenia had interrupted them, only he could not help but wonder if Lucy would have allowed the kiss.

Lucy's heart was pounding so hard that she found it difficult to breathe. He had almost kissed her again and she had wanted him to so very much. What then would have been the result? Would he have been apologetic once more? Regretful? Or this time might he have admitted that something extraordinary existed between them? As she mounted the steps of the coach, she sighed heavily. She simply did not know.

CHAPTER
TEN

Two days later, Lucy stood on the front steps of Aldershaw conversing with Hetty.

"Did Rosamunde reveal to you where it was she went every week?" Hetty asked.

Lucy did not answer at first. Her gaze was fixed in the distance, to the coach bowling along the drive away from the manor. The large conveyance, laden with Rosamunde's, Eugenia's, and George's trunks, was just turning into the lane heading in the direction of Wiltshire, where Rosamunde's father had a fine estate. She waved one last time and thought she caught a glimpse of Eugenia's woebegone face. Though Ginny was excited about the prospect of living with her grandfather, who had always doted on her, she was very sad to be leaving Hyacinth, Violet, and William as well as her other aunts and uncles.

"No," she said at last, "Rosamunde did not confide in me."

"Well," Hetty began, her voice swelling with pride, "she did tell me. It would seem she was not visiting an invalid at all, but rather three robust friends with whom she played whist, drank a great deal of tea, and quite frequently consumed more peach ratafia than four ladies of quality ought ever to imbibe."

Lucy could only laugh. "Dear Rosamunde. Only, why would she keep secret such an innocuous weekly adventure?"

"I have come to believe that both my brother George and Rosamunde are very private individuals. I daresay Rosamunde did not want anyone knowing that she drank to excess so frequently as she did."

"No, I suppose not."

"Did George make amends, Lucy? For I know he was previously quite put out with you."

At that Lucy smiled. "Actually, he thanked me for 'interfering' in his affairs. He had abandoned Baddesley over a year past but he had found it impossible to admit the truth to either his brother or his wife."

"I still cannot credit that he kept his circumstances from all of us these two years and more. Robert told me very little and I was unwilling to pry. Did George reveal anything more to you? All I know is that the estate is ruined."

Lucy sighed. "It is not an unusual tale and I do not see that George did anything wrong. The farms on the Baddesley rent rolls were simply unable to produce sufficient income to sustain the estate, but he blamed himself particularly since he had used Rosamunde's dowry in trying to improve the farms. Perhaps there was a degree of mismanagement on his part, but then not every man has a talent for husbandry."

"He will do far better in the army. Robert was very right to purchase him a pair of colors."

"I think George will be very happy wearing a red coat."

"I could not agree more," Hetty said. "And so George and his family are gone but Valmaston arrives tomorrow."

"Yes," Lucy agreed with a smile, "and I am convinced he will greatly enhance our daily pleasures. He is one of the most amusing gentlemen I have ever known. I even predict that you will like him very much, indeed, despite his reputation."

At that Hetty lifted her chin a trifle. "I have never approved of libertines and I shan't begin now."

"We shall see," Lucy said. She had every confidence that Valmaston would eventually win Hetty's approval and possibly even her friendship. "And now I think we ought to go in search of the children. They have been very sad that Eugenia will no longer form part of their daily comings and goings."

"As well I know."

"Then I suggest we begin by having them each write a letter to Eugenia today. That will give them something to look forward to, for I know that Eugenia will have no difficulty in responding, as bookish as she is. She will treasure receiving letters from her youngest aunts and uncle. But where are they?"

"The fort, of course," Hetty said.

"Of course."

Later that afternoon, Robert begged Lucy to take a turn about the garden with him. He was oddly contrite. "I believe I owe you an apology, for I was greatly mistaken."

"In what?" she asked, uncertain what he meant.

"I believed your involvement with George and Rosamunde officious and interfering—those may have even been my words at one time."

"Yes, they were," she responded cheerfully.

"You needn't gloat."

"I think I should gloat, for you are so quick to criticize me and in this instance you have been proven wrong."

He shook his head. "You shall get no more of an apology from me than that, not if you are going to behave like a simpleton."

"Oh, do stubble it, Robert!" she cried, slinging her hands behind her back. "I must tell Quarley to trim back that rhododendron a trifle."

"The gardens are prettier every day."

"I only hope they are lovely enough to please Valmaston's eye."

"You are being quite obnoxious, my girl."

"I am, are I not?" She then laughed, but not for long. "I know I have been teasing you but I am not unaware of how painful your interview with George must have been. Were you terribly surprised to learn all the details?"

"How could I be when for the last several months he appeared so guilty when I would ask him about the repairs on Baddesley."

"Where did he go on those days he said he was overseeing the repairs?"

"He would ride out to various villages and stay at the local inn, do a little fishing, even sightseeing he told me, that sort of thing."

"You were very right to purchase him a pair of colors."

"How glad I am that you have expressed your approval," he said facetiously.

She rolled her eyes at him. "I think he will be very happy in the army."

"As do I."

"By the way, have you seen Hetty this afternoon? I have been looking for her but cannot seem to find her. There is something I would ask her."

"She has taken her walk."

"Her walk?"

"Lady Sandifort says that once each month she takes a very long walk in the direction of Bickfield, and that she has done so for years."

"Oh, yes, of course. I believe she referred to it once as her nature walk and says that, though it is very long and in its way tedious, she says that it keeps her feeling quite fit and well."

Lucy realized as she spoke that there was something odd about Hetty's *nature walk,* though she said nothing to Robert. Hetty was not in any manner a lady who enjoyed exercise. She did not mind going for rather leisurely walks with the children about the estate but she certainly never made a point of walking out merely to improve her health. And as for horses, Lucy could not get her on the back of one if her life depended on it.

However, she had little time to concern herself with Hetty's oddities since Valmaston would be arriving from London on the morrow. She could only wonder just what sort of stir he was likely to cause among the family and whether or not Lady Sandifort would be sufficiently pleased with his attentions to continue her unusual cheerfulness and good will toward the family.

"So, tell me, Robert, have you yet forgiven me for having invited Valmaston to Aldershaw?"

"No, of course not. However, I have begun to wonder just what bee is buzzing around your bonnet this time that you would have done so, for I am beginning to understand that you do very little without a strict purpose in mind."

At that she laughed heartily. "You begin to understand me."

"I believe I do," he said.

She glanced up at him and saw that he was not teasing in the least, but rather that he was quite serious in a very penetrating manner. She was completely taken aback and wondered what, if anything, he meant by saying such a thing to her. Her heart turned over in her chest and she felt a blush of hope climb her cheeks.

To be understood—now there was something, indeed!

* * *

On the following evening, Lucy entered the drawing room on Lord Valmaston's arm. If she had had any fears about just how he would conduct himself, they were allayed by his civil, proper behavior as he was introduced to everyone present. That he took Lady Sandifort's hand in his and kissed the air above her fingers was an attention that actually set her ladyship in a flutter. Lucy could not remember ever having seen Lady Sandifort lose her composure before.

Valmaston moved on and greeted Robert again. Lucy felt that the same understanding the gentlemen had reached in London had transferred to the wilds of Hampshire and she breathed a little easier. For his part, Robert showed not the smallest sign of disliking the rogue's presence.

Henry, however, was a different matter entirely. He offered but a polite bow and a stiff greeting. Lucy watched him carefully. She found herself surprised by his demeanor, for he appeared as one who would prefer to call Valmaston out rather than share the same drawing room. The earl, however, ignored him and instead turned his attention to the ladies, in particular to Anne and Alice.

Lucy, a trifle put out that Henry would snub her guest, moved to sit beside Hetty. In a low voice, she asked, "So what do you think of him?"

Hetty remained silent and that for so long a time that Lucy glanced at her and saw that she was staring rather dumbly at Valmaston.

"Hetty?"

"I beg your pardon?" she inquired. "What was it you asked?"

"What do you think of my friend?"

Hetty finally turned to look at her and yet it was as though she still did not see her. "You refer to Valmaston?" She gestured to him with a casually flung hand.

Lucy thought her comical, for she had never seen her so rattled before upon merely meeting a man. She nodded.

Hetty once more turned to regard Valmaston. Lucy for her part continued to look at Hetty, noting how her gaze took in his entire figure as he in turn seated himself between Anne and Alice, both of whom had begun to giggle. "I vow, except for my brothers, I have never seen a more handsome man. How is it he has never married?"

"Perhaps he has been waiting for precisely the right lady."

"Perhaps. His manners are so engaging. Look how Alice laughs, and she never laughs when gentlemen address her!"

"I have known him from the time I was very little and when he would speak with me, even when I was a child, I vow I always felt as though I were the only person in the world."

"Did you never fancy yourself in love with him?"

Lucy was not so much surprised by the question as by her certain response. "Never, though now that I look at him I only wonder how I could have been so stupid."

Hetty laughed. "Although, we are both presently forgetting his truly vile reputation."

"He was always perfectly civil with me."

"You had your father to keep watch over you."

Lucy shook her head. "No, you do my friend an injustice, I think. I trust him, Hetty. I always have. I would trust him with my life and I cannot say that about most of the gentlemen I know, your brothers excepted, of course."

Suddenly, Valmaston was on his feet and addressing Lady Sandifort. "My lady, your daughters have given me such a notion and I was hoping you might oblige us."

"Anything, my lord," she said, batting her lashes up at him.

He cleared his throat. "I have not attended a ball for these three months together and I fear I will miss my steps unless I have a little practice. Your stepdaughters have been so kind as to indicate that they would serve as partners for me if we were to dance this evening. Would this be agreeable to you and might I also persuade you to go down a dance or two with me as well?"

"Oh," she murmured softly. "How could I possibly refuse so sweetly proffered a request?"

After dinner, the merriment began. As Lucy well knew, Valmaston possessed an enormous ability to charm the female sex and he fulfilled his promise to her with every word, look, and gesture he extended, not just to Lady Sandifort but to all the ladies.

The armory was quickly cleared of furniture, the suit of armor was removed to the nearest antechamber, and Hetty took up her place at the pianoforte. She was greatly skilled and was able to play whatever country dance was commanded of her.

With three gentlemen present, all of whom were enthusiastic in their desire to help the twins, the dancing commenced. Lucy went down the first set with Henry, Anne danced with Robert, and Lord Valmaston partnered Lady Sandifort. The second set, Anne traded places with Alice, for it was of little use for her merely to watch. Lucy saw at once that Alice needed more practice than her sister and she believed she understood just what had prompted Valmaston's suggestion of dancing in the first place.

In the midst of the dance, Lord Valmaston feigned forgetting his steps—for it was clear he knew them as well as he knew his own name—and bumped into at least three of the other dancers. "How clumsy I am!" he proclaimed.

Only then did Alice begin to smile, to relax, and to enjoy herself.

Because Lady Sandifort had no intention of relinquishing the opportunity to flirt with Valmaston, Lucy found herself watching the dancing nearly the entire time. She noted that Robert took Alice under his wing. He gave her instruction upon instruction in a kind voice with exceeding patience. Alice bloomed beneath his tutelage. Lucy felt such admiration for him in this moment. Not all gentlemen, in fact very few gentlemen, would exhibit so much love and kindness toward a sibling. She felt her heart swell as she watched him. He was completely intent on helping Alice and once or twice, as Valmaston had done, feigned missing his steps merely to set her a little more at ease.

After nearly two hours of such exertion, as delightful as it was, Lucy ordered refreshments brought to the drawing room. A platter of fruit, sweetmeats, and ices were prepared for the dancers, all of whom expressed their appreciation for the sustenance.

During this time, Lucy found herself in a quiet corner with Robert. "You have been quite gracious this evening," she said.

He seemed surprised. "Thank you, but to what are you referring?"

"Your kindness to Alice is both remarkable and admirable. I commend you, indeed, I do." When he chuckled and appeared disbelieving, she continued, "I promise you, I am most sincere. Indeed, I am not funning."

"I can see that you are not, so I thank you, very much, but Alice is after all my sister and it is no hardship for me to offer my help."

Lucy smiled. "You were at your best, you know, when you tripped."

He met her gaze and smiled as well. In that moment, time paused for Lucy. She had forgotten how easily it was to become lost in his eyes for reasons that were as incomprehensible to her as they were magical. He continued to smile as he looked at her, which only made her smile a little more.

Hetty once more took up her place at the pianoforte and called out another country dance.

"You should dance with me this time," he said, offering his arm.

She looked at his arm and wanted nothing more, but the

dancing was not meant for her but for Anne and Alice, and certainly Lady Sandifort had no intention of giving up the set to her. "I should not," she whispered. "You know I should not."

Robert glanced about and lifted his chin in Alice's direction. "She is becoming exhausted and will benefit at this point as much from observation as from practice."

Lucy saw that Alice was indeed looking a trifle fatigued. Before she could say anything, however, Robert called to his sister. "Alice, do sit down for the next set. Lucy means to dance with me."

Even if Lucy had been inclined to object, she could not have done so in the face of Alice's expression of supreme gratitude.

"Very well," she said, taking his arm.

He chuckled. "I would not have insisted had I thought you would be so reluctant."

"You know very well why I refused. It had nothing to do with you."

"Indeed! Now you have given me a shock."

Lucy took her place opposite him and when the music began she offered her opening curtsy and he his required bow. The dance progressed in a manner that suited her quite well, for he teased her a great deal and nothing could have pleased her more.

He was quite a skillful dancer, there could be no two opinions on that score. He moved as a gentleman on a ball-room floor ought to move, with considerable grace and confidence that left his partner feeling quite secure both in her steps and in the certainty that her feet would not be bruised by his inadequacies. She realized he was in many respects just as she believed a man ought to be, and something inside her began to tremble.

After the dance, Henry demanded that he be permitted to go down the next set with Lucy. Again she might have refused, but Alice was quick to call out. "Please, Lucy, do dance with Henry. I am beginning to see where I have been erring. Indeed, it is of great use to me to watch all of you perform your steps."

Lucy smiled at Henry. "Very well."

As a partner, Henry danced nicely but not so well as Robert. His movements were perhaps more graceful but he lacked something that his brother possessed quite fully. There was a purposeful feel to Robert's dancing that as a partner gave her greater confidence.

Having sat out for two sets, Alice was properly rested and agreed to once more take up her place, this time opposite Lord Valmaston. Henry partnered Lady Sandifort and Robert offered his arm to Anne. Lucy watched with great interest as the rogue continued to charm Alice from her embarrassment and was even able to engage her in conversation toward the end of the dance. There was no surer indication that Alice had mastered her steps than when she exhibited the ability to converse while dancing. So it was that she gave a small cry of delight when Hetty played the final notes.

Two more sets convinced the party that both young ladies were well prepared for the assemblies.

Over the next several days, an air of excitement ran through the house. It seemed to Lucy that Anne and Alice were not the only ones looking forward to the local ball. The dressmaker arrived nearly every day for fittings, for the delivery of headdresses and finished gowns, for a consultation about stockings and gloves and slippers, so that the ladies especially spent much of each day traveling from one bedchamber to the next examining the latest addition to one or the other's wardrobe. Even Lady Sandifort was so happy that she forgot her usual machinations and dispensed her advice with what seemed to Lucy to be a genuine spirit of generosity and happiness.

Only one hiccough occurred to mar the joyful air of the house. Lucy had accompanied Anne and Alice to Lady Sandifort's sitting room, which overlooked the back gardens. Lady Sandifort was dancing the waltz about the chamber in a beautiful dark blue silk gown, embellished with Brussels lace that framed a quite lovely décolletage. Both the younger girls laughed and clapped their hands in three-quarter time. Anne was humming as well.

"How well you look in blue," Lucy said. "I vow I do not know which I prefer with your dark brown hair, the blue or the exquisite pink satin."

Lady Sandifort waltzed by the window, began to make her turn, and stopped abruptly. An expression of horror suffused her face as she gazed down into the garden. "Good God!" she cried.

Lucy could not imagine what had overset Lady Sandifort so severely. At first she thought perhaps one of the children had been hurt, for their playful cries had been rising from below for the past half hour. Yet this seemed unlikely, since Lady Sandifort rarely expressed even the smallest concern for her brood. No, something else had disturbed her ladyship.

She moved quickly to the second window and saw what had brought the color draining from Lady Sandifort's face. Hetty was walking toward the maze in the company of Lord Valmaston and they appeared to be deep in conversation, even though the children followed them.

Lucy wished desperately that she could slip her thoughts quite magically into Valmaston's mind and give him a hint. Beneath her breath, she murmured, "Please let her go, please let her go." She understood there was a great deal of mutual dislike between the ladies, but this trespassing upon Lady Sandifort's territory would be unforgivable in her eyes. For the present, however, the two of them were just walking and not particularly close together. If they entered the maze, however, she was convinced that the entire roof would suddenly collapse on the household!

Lucy mentally continued to speak to Valmaston and as if having heard her silent pleas, he bowed to Hetty and headed in the direction of the stables, his riding crop in hand. The children ran into the maze. Lucy was ready to breathe a sigh of relief but Hetty made the enormous mistake of glancing in Valmaston's direction. The distance was too great to possibly construe her expression or meaning, but this final glance was Lady Sandifort's undoing.

"What the devil does that horrid little wretch think she is doing?"

Lucy felt Lady Sandifort's rage flood the bedchamber. She quickly signaled for Anne and Alice to leave the room. They needed little encouragement, being well versed in their stepmother's ways, and disappeared into the hall with the force of a cavalry charge.

"She has designs on him!" Lady Sandifort fairly shouted. "That . . . that complete simpleton who cannot say two words together without sounding like a complete ninnyhammer! She means to have Valmaston, only how does she think she will win such a man as that? She has no beauty, no skills, no conversation, no grace in her countenance, and what man could ever love a woman with black hair?"

Lucy did not know where to begin. She was a little frightened by the violence of her expressions, and that over Hetty merely turning to look at the earl. "Do you think she was, indeed, looking at Valmaston? It did not seem that way to me." Oh, the whiskers she often told in her ladyship's presence.

"Do not play the ninnyhammer with me, Lucinda Stiles. You know very well she was."

"Well, there are innumerable rabbits in the garden, and snakes as well, for that matter. She could have heard something in the shrubbery and surely Valmaston would have disappeared down the path to the stables before ever she turned

to look at him. Surely! Besides, Hetty has already told me
that she is rather disgusted that Valmaston is come."

"Much she knows about anything!" she cried irrationally.

Lucy let her shoulders sag. "It is very sad, is it not?" She
was about to tell more whiskers, more horrible whiskers, for
they were wholly disloyal to one of her dearest friends. "Hetty
has been nowhere and seen nothing. Oh, I admit she has had
several Seasons, but she is hardly to be considered a woman
of great breeding, experience, and ton. Would you not agree?"

Lady Sandifort puffed her cheeks and finally moved away
from the window. "She is one of the most ridiculous females
I have ever known. Why, do you know that when her father
died, she tried to take over the management of the house in
my stead?"

"Whyever would she want to do that when you are here?"

"Precisely!" Lady Sandifort flopped down in her *chaise
longue* and popped a sweetmeat in her mouth. "I have always
disliked her. She sneers at me, you know."

"No," Lucy breathed.

"Yes, she does, quite frequently. She thinks herself so superior and yet she ought to be learning at my feet. We are of
an age, you know. But she has never been married and I have
every confidence she has never taken a lover." An odd expression, quite vile, overcame her pretty features and transformed her beauty into something quite hideous. "How well
I know she has not! I am aware of her secrets, though. Of
course, she does not know that I know, but I am well versed
in the very core of her heart and if she is not careful I know
precisely where to aim a dagger from which I know she would
never recover." She glanced at Lucy. "You see how restrained
I am? I could have hurt her quite deeply a score of times but
I withheld because she is my stepdaughter. Yet she uses me
so very ill!"

Lucy was shocked by this speech, in part because it would
seem Lady Sandifort had a weapon ready to use against

Hetty whenever it pleased her but also because she had confirmed her own suspicions. Hetty it would seem had some great secret. Knowing that Lady Sandifort had somehow become privy to it was unsettling in the extreme. Instead of revealing her disquiet, however, she glanced at Lady Sandifort's slippers. "I never noticed before how small your feet are."

Lady Sandifort sighed with pleasure. "They are small, are they not, and prettily shaped?"

"Very pretty, indeed!" With at least a dozen more compliments, Lucy was able to distract Lady Sandifort from Hetty's perfidy.

Later, Lucy related to Hetty all that had transpired and even confessed how badly she had spoken of her. Hetty dismissed this with a wave of her hand, for she understood quite well the lengths to which Lucy went in order to keep the beast tamed. She was, however, properly shocked that Lady Sandifort would have interpreted a mere glance at Lord Valmaston as interest on her part.

"Good heavens!" she cried, walking briskly from the window of her bedchamber to her writing desk and back. "I have never heard anything more ridiculous, more absurd! I could never, *never*, like such a man, nonetheless have designs on him or even *love* him." She paused and looked very odd for a moment, before continuing, "Lucy, you do know how I feel about Lord Valmaston? Have I not told you a hundred times?"

"Indeed, you have."

"Why would I have altered my opinion even in the slightest? That would be absurd! Just because he was kind to Alice when he danced with her, and to Anne as well, is no reason for any of us to think better of him. His reputation is truly horrid and I could never love such a man."

"Of course not."

"Lady Sandifort is as mad as bedlam."

"Undoubtedly, to think such a thing of you."

"I really despise him."

"Of course you do."

The day of the assemblies arrived and the excitement among the ladies rose to a fever pitch. Anne had already shed nervous tears because the pearl-studded band she had meant to wear in her hair had disappeared, only to be found after a quarter of an hour's search beneath her pillow. "I had put it there last night in hopes of having the sweetest dreams ever, but I forgot all about it."

Lucy embraced her while she shed a few more tears. "You will perform beautifully tonight."

"I do not give a fig for that," she cried, pulling out of Lucy's arms. "I only want to have more beaus than Kitty Bartley!"

Lucy laughed. "I am very certain you will if Kitty is the young lady who at church, Sunday last, pulled a face at you."

Anne gasped. "The very one, and you think I am prettier than she?" Kitty was accounted a very fine beauty, indeed.

"Have you never regarded yourself in the looking glass?"

Anne, who was wretchedly vain but a darling nonetheless, turned to her dressing table and peered at her features. With her blond hair and unusual green eyes, she would undoubtedly surpass all the young ladies at the ball in beauty as well as vivacity.

She then turned back to Lucy. "I am so excited, you can have no idea!"

Lucy laughed. "You had best finish dressing then."

"Yes, yes, of course. Robert will want to leave at seven."

"That he will."

By the time the dinner hour arrived and the ladies were dressed in their finery, Lucy called the children from the schoolroom where they had just finished their supper. She wanted them to see their mother and their half sisters before the party left for the assemblies.

Violet stood with one hand on her cheek and her doll tucked beneath her arm. "Oh, Mama," she whispered, eyeing Lady Sandifort as one completely awestruck. "You are so beautiful! You look just like a princess!"

How could Lady Sandifort resist such a perfect compliment? She approached her youngest child. "You may kiss me on the cheek if you like, but pray do not disturb my hair!"

"Oh, I would not do so, Mama." She leaned forward very carefully and barely brushed her mother's cheeks with her lips.

Lucy's heart was rent, not by Lady Sandifort, of course, but by the sweetness of her neglected children.

Hyacinth offered a similar tribute and, taking care not to touch her mother's hair, also kissed her on the cheek.

William merely smiled somewhat shyly. "I think you look very pretty."

"*Very pretty*, William?" she returned sharply. "You must learn to pay better compliments than that or you shall never win a lady's heart."

His delight dimmed. "Yes, Mama. I think you very beautiful."

"Much better."

Her duty fulfilled, Lady Sandifort swept away from her children and made her descent before the others.

Once she was gone, however, the remaining ladies gathered round them. Lucy did not hesitate to pick up Violet. "You all look like princesses," Violet said, "but I knew Mama would be angry if I said so."

The ladies giggled together. It seemed so very odd to Lucy that even a five-year-old knew better than to cross the vanity of an extraordinarily vain woman. After innumerable hugs, kisses, and compliments were passed around, Lucy returned the children to Miss Gunville.

Descending the stairs, Lucy was surprised though very pleased to find Robert and Henry awaiting them, as good brothers ought. Henry took Anne's arm and Robert took Alice's, a break with the usual order of going in to dinner, but, given that this was their first trip to the local assemblies, a not unappreciated gesture.

Lucy tried to ignore the sudden riot of butterflies swirling about her stomach as she met Robert's gaze quite briefly. He was unutterably handsome in his formal ballroom attire. Would she dance with him this evening? she wondered. He smiled, inclined his head to her, perhaps acknowledging all that she had accomplished, then moved into the dining room.

Lucy and Hetty followed and, as they crossed the threshold, Hetty tweaked her arm and said, "Robert seems properly chastened these days. I do believe he has finally come to appreciate you."

Lucy was surprised that Hetty would say so, but not a little pleased. She almost felt she might be able to truly enjoy the evening, until she chanced to look at Lady Sandifort, who was regarding her eldest stepdaughter. There could be no two opinions that the dislike Lady Sandifort felt for Hetty had turned to something deeper still, no less so than in this moment because Valmaston graciously offered to seat Hetty. Lucy had never seen hatred blaze more strongly in Lady Sandifort's otherwise lovely blue eyes.

CHAPTER
ELEVEN

Despite the tensions mounting between Lady Sandifort and Hetty, Lucy was reminded how enjoyable a local ball could be. She had certainly been to such assemblies before in Somerset, but there was something about this particular event that was unlike anything she had ever experienced. She could not quite ascertain just what that was, except that an entire family was involved in the experience, Hetty and Robert, Henry, the twins, even Lady Sandifort. And for tonight, she was part of the family as well.

She stood by Robert, watching both Anne and Alice going down their first dance.

"You must be so proud of them," she said. Alice was dancing with a shy young man by the name of James Colbury and Anne was moving gracefully with Henry. Valmaston was of course partnering Lady Sandifort.

"Indeed, more than I can say," he murmured.

The assemblies that evening were very crowded, since word had spread throughout the neighborhood that among those to attend would be the inmates of Aldershaw, as well as the renowned Lord Valmaston. In addition, Lucy discovered that

Valmaston had written to a friend of his, Lord Hurstborne, who lived not ten miles from Bickfield to the east, inviting him to attend as well. He was an engaging gentleman with a great deal of town bronze and shirt points that rose excessively high on his cheeks. Of course, after several dances they would undoubtedly wilt away from his face, but for now he appeared quite the dandy.

"Do you know Hurstborne?" Lucy inquired of Robert.

"Not very well and I must say I am surprised to see him here. He was caught recently in a very great scandal in Brighton. And no, I shan't relay the particulars!"

"Whyever not?" she asked gaily. "You know I will just tease Hetty later until I have the information I seek."

"Nonetheless, my beautiful Lucy, you shall not hear a word of it from me."

"Very well," she stated, attempting to sound disgruntled but finding her spirits so high that even to her own ears she sounded as though she were delighted with his decision.

Hurstborne was a rather intriguing creature. He was nearly as tall as Robert and quite handsome, but in a rather devilish way. His eyes were small, though, giving him the look of a Frenchman. It also seemed to her that whenever his gaze would fall to hers, as it had just now, she felt as though she was wearing nought but her shift!

She heard Robert growl next to her. "Do look away, Lucy," he whispered, "or he will think you wish to dance with him." The country dance was just coming to an end and Lord Hurstborne was eyeing her again rather scandalously.

"Perhaps I do," she teased. "Unless of course someone else were to ask me."

"I am already fatigued with dancing," he complained.

"But you have not even gone down one set!"

Since he was smiling, she took strong hold of his arm and without so much as a by-your-leave pulled him toward the floor where couples were just taking their places.

"I have not asked you," he said, appearing affronted.

"If I wait for you to ask, there will not be a place for us."

"Oh, very well." For all his pretence, she knew he was contented.

The music commenced. She made her curtsy. How happy she was. He laughed aloud, perhaps because she could not stop smiling. He danced and danced with her, first one set then the next. She felt she could have danced forever and he was such an easy partner. He quite spoiled her for all the other gentlemen present.

He was guiding her off the floor when Henry approached them. "You have taken up enough of Lucy's time."

Only then did Robert's spirits seem to dim. Lucy wondered why, but he certainly relinquished her quickly to Henry who, rather than taking her in the direction of the dancers, invited her to partake of refreshments in an adjoining chamber.

She had just sat down when she noticed Hetty standing in a corner with a man she did not know. "Henry, who is that man? There, by Hetty. He is making her laugh."

"Thomas Woolston. We have known him since we were children. He has the living at Laverstoke, just north of Bickfield." He then leaned quite close and, as she lifted her glass of lemonade to her lips, he whispered, "How beautiful you are, my darling Lucy. You have never been prettier than you are tonight."

Lucy was scarcely attending him, her attention being wholly caught by Hetty. "Never mind that, Henry. Pray tell me what do you know of Mr. Woolston?"

Henry laughed but said nothing more.

Lucy glanced at him and saw that he seemed confounded. "What?" she cried. "Do you not like Mr. Woolston?"

"I was not thinking of Mr. Woolston just now, or of my sister. I was thinking of something far more important."

Lucy glanced back at Hetty. She wondered just how well

acquainted she was with Mr. Woolston. "So, you do not know
Mr. Woolston very well?"

She heard Henry sigh, quite deeply, though she was not
certain why. "Very well, if we must speak of Mr. Woolston.
He is older than I, therefore I was never on excellent terms
with him."

"Hetty seems to like him."

"His manners I believe are reputed to be quite engaging."
He looked about the chamber and directed her attention to
the corner nearest the refreshments. "Do you see that lady
with three feathers sticking upright in her headdress? She is
speaking with, oh, now what is her name? Oh, yes, I believe
she is Colbury's mother. At any rate, the woman with the
feathers is Mrs. Woolston. She has born the good vicar nearly
a dozen children in that many years of marriage."

"A very promising brood."

"He can well afford them. She brought fifteen thousand
into the marriage."

"Good God! A fortunate match, indeed, at least for him."

From time to time as she sat with Henry, she glanced toward Hetty's corner. Just as she and Henry rose, she glanced
again and saw something extraordinary. Hetty was looking
at Mr. Woolston with an expression of distress. Mr. Woolston
immediately leaned forward, whispered something to her, then
moved away. Hetty remained as one in a deep mist, her expression rather absent.

"Henry, would you excuse me please? There is something
I would discuss with Hetty."

"But you promised to dance the quadrille with me."

"Surely that can wait," she said pleasantly. "I believe I
must go to her. Tell me you will not object."

Henry glanced at his eldest sister and frowned slightly. "I
wonder what the devil Mr. Woolston said to her, for she looks
uncommonly pale of a sudden. Yes, Lucy, do go to her."

Lucy approached her and said, "I have need of a little air

and I mean to go outside for a minute or two. Will you join me?"

Hetty's gaze cleared. "Yes, of course," she said, smiling suddenly. Lucy did not know what to make of this abrupt shift in demeanor. She had been prepared to offer her some sort of comfort, thinking perhaps Mr. Woolston had said something improper to her, but she did not seem especially overset. Indeed, the entire circumstance had a very strange air about it.

Once out of doors, she spoke on a low tone to Hetty. "I thought Mr. Woolston had said something improper to you," she began.

"Thomas? Oh, no, of course not. He never would."

Thomas. So they were on rather intimate terms.

"Yet you seemed distressed."

Hetty laughed. "Thomas and I have been very great friends these many years and more. I do not know how he bears his wife, though. She is a very coarse creature. Did you happen to see her eating? Like swine at a trough."

Lucy frowned as she walked beside her friend. "I did not notice."

"Nor should you have, I suppose. It is no one's concern, really, but there are times when I do feel truly sorry for him."

"I do not know why you should. Henry tells me that she had a large dowry and has since provided Mr. Woolston with a healthy brood of offspring."

"She has certainly done her duty by him, but he has confided in me over the years. Things have been said, so you see I am allowed to have compassion where others perhaps think it unnecessary. But come let us return. I find I am growing chilled in this night air."

Lucy walked back with her, up the high street. She realized Hetty had never been so remote as in this moment.

When she reentered the assembly room, Hetty was called away by Anne, who wanted to introduce her to friends of hers.

Valmaston approached her, expressing his desire to make her known to Lord Hurstborne.

"Indeed?"

Lord Hurstborne approached and after being introduced took her hand, promptly placing a kiss on her fingers. "Well met, Miss Stiles."

Lucy smiled and offered a curtsy.

Releasing her hand he promptly addressed his friend. "What a curiosity you have become, Val," he said. "When first you asked me to the assemblies, I thought perhaps you had gone mad, for is this not a collection of rustics? However, I vow I have not seen so many pretty ladies in all my life and therefore I believe I shall be happily entertained after all."

Lucy thought his speech put her forcibly in mind of Lady Sandifort.

Lord Valmaston merely laughed at him, told him to refrain if possible from being a pompous bore, and sauntered away.

Lucy might have been offended by Hurstborne's forthright and quite uncivil speech, but there was such in his countenance and address that did not invite offense. Perhaps this was the true composition of a rogue, that he could be wholly critical yet still invite interest, fascination, even adoration.

Lord Hurstborne did not hesitate in asking her for the next dance.

"I should be delighted," she said, taking his arm.

The viscount danced quite well and was fully able to engage her in conversation as they went down the country dance.

Lucy was not in the least disturbed by the piercing manner of his gaze as though he was utterly fascinated by her. She had already observed he looked at nearly every female in the same manner, the expression of a hawk after its prey. She understood quite well that he was the sort of gentleman who responded to even the gentlest tug on his line.

After dancing with Hurstborne, Lucy never quit the

dance floor, though she had to admit that when the assemblies drew to a close her feet ached.

By the time she climbed between the sheets, the hour was long past midnight. She had scarcely closed her eyes, however, when she heard a loud thumping sound and afterward a soft moaning. She left her bed, donned a robe, and made her way toward the dim light that showed at the top of the stairs. When she reached the landing, she listened carefully and heard another moan.

She raced down the stairs to the first floor and flew into the library, certain that someone was badly injured. The sight that met her eyes, however, made her laugh aloud, then afterward clamp her hand over her mouth. She would not for the world wake the house for this!

"Robert, whatever are you doing?" she whispered, having gained her composure. "Good God, are you foxed? Do not tell me you have been at the brandy—"

"Sherry."

"—sherry, then, since we retired?"

He squinted. "Do you know, I do believe Valmaston has the hardest head of any man I have ever known."

So, this incident must be laid in part at Valmaston's door. It would seem the gentlemen had been drinking together after the ball. "Clearly harder than yours," she responded. There was an irony to her words, since in approaching him she saw that he was bleeding from a cut on his scalp. Little red rivulets flowed over his forehead and down the side of his cheek. "Have you a kerchief?"

"Mm," he murmured, closing his eyes, but not moving in the least to retrieve it. She searched in his pocket and, finding the soft square of cambric, dabbed gently at the wound, which proved to be rather insignificant. She suspected, however, that by morning he would have a nice little bump on his head.

Once she had cleaned up his face, she said, "Come, Robert, let me take you to your bed."

"Lucy, that sounds so very nice. You have no idea just how many times I have wanted you to do just that." He touched her cheek gently.

She was properly shocked but amused at the same time. "How you flatter me," she said. She tried to lift him by sliding her arm about his but he would not be moved.

"No, 'tis I who am flattered. Will you kiss me even now before we go to my chamber?"

Before she knew what was happening he had pulled her onto his lap so that he was cradling her and his lips found hers in a horribly wonderful kiss.

"I love kissing you," he murmured, then assaulted her again.

She tried to push against his shoulder but to little avail. He held her as he always did in a powerful embrace from which she would naturally have some difficulty extricating herself. "Will you not kiss me in return?" he asked, a look of hurt in his eyes. "Do you not wish to kiss me?"

"Robert, the place, the hour, the reason, is hardly seemly."

"What do I care for that!" he cried, holding her more tightly still. He could barely keep his eyes open and every word that fell from his tongue turned sideways before hitting the air.

"One kiss, then," Lucy said, "but afterward you must promise to let me take you to your room."

"I shall, indeed," he slurred but with much enthusiasm.

The kiss that followed, tasting very much of sherry, nearly undid her senses. When he forgot himself, Robert could be incredibly passionate, a quality she was beginning to understand he held severely in check.

"Lucy," he whispered against her lips.

How tender he could be. How sensual was the manner in which he drifted his lips over hers as though savoring her. The pressure increased and her body, quite without permission, melted into his. She slipped her arm about his neck and for reasons she kept hidden from herself she kissed him quite wickedly in return, allowing his tongue to reach the depths of her mouth. She trusted or at least she hoped that he would not remember anything on the morrow. For the present, she allowed the most passionate thoughts to ripple through her mind, what it would be like to be a wife to Robert, how much she would enjoy kissing him like this day upon day, night upon night, and how often under the sanctity of marriage she would demand he take her in his arms.

"Lucy, Lucy," he murmured against her ear, placing little kisses down her cheek until he found her mouth again.

"Robert," she responded, sighing as she received his lips once more.

After several minutes had passed, after he had whispered her name a dozen times against her ear, her cheek, her lips, after he had fairly squeezed the breath from her, he suddenly moaned in a manner that had nothing to do with his desire to kiss her.

Lucy drew back to look at him. "Are you perchance unwell?" she inquired, barely restraining her smiles.

He blinked at her. "I believe I am," he said sloppily. "My head is swimming."

"You need to go to bed."

He smiled happily and nodded several. "Yes, and you are going with me."

"Only if you gain your feet," she said, not believing for a moment she could argue him from his conviction that he was taking her to bed.

With that, he rolled her clumsily off his lap so that she almost landed on her head.

"What are you doing in a heap?" he asked.

She looked up at him and saw that he had found his feet but was tottering unsteadily. "I cannot imagine," she responded facetiously.

"Well," he said, offering her his hand, "you promised to take me to bed, so now you must keep your promise."

She took his hand and he lifted her to her feet, but in doing so stumbled backward and almost fell again, except that she was able to steady him by leaning hard in the opposite direction.

She slipped an arm beneath his and held tightly to his waist. "Shall we go?" she inquired.

He kissed the top of her head. "Yes-s-s."

Lucy carefully took the candelabra in hand and began slowly guiding and supporting him back to his room.

She would never have believed that the trip to his bedchamber, which fortunately was on the same floor as the library, would have required as much time as it did. Worse, however, were her efforts to keep him sufficiently quiet in order not to awaken the entire house. Though he was in his altitudes, he did seem sufficiently aware that it would not do to bring any of the inmates from their rooms.

Once arrived at his bedchamber, she settled the candelabra on a table safely away from the bed, the draperies, or anything else that might cause a fire were he to carelessly swing his arm and send the candles flying. She reached for the bellpull to summon his man, but he stopped her, saying not only did he not wish to disturb his valet but he did not wish his valet to come anywhere near his bedchamber of the moment. With these words spoken, he grabbed her and began kissing her anew.

Oh, dear, Lucy thought. She felt a strange sort of panic and tried to slip from his grasp but he held her firmly and walked her backward to his bed. He was not himself, that was certain, but would he take advantage of her? Somehow she thought it likely he might.

Her heart beat rapidly as he pushed her back on the bed. She tried to scramble backward out of his reach but he was quickly on top of her. "Lucy, Lucy, how much I love you. I have always loved you, at least since you were grown. Not as a child, that would be ridiculous, but I love you so now. Did I tell you how glad I am that you have come to Aldershaw?"

Though he was pressed against her, he lifted himself sufficiently to look into her eyes. They were clouded but his expression was so tender, so sweet, that for the barest moment she wished what he was saying was true. "You . . . you are not yourself!" she said. "It is the wine speaking. Indeed, Robert, you must let me go."

He shook his head sloppily then kissed her anew. She wished his lips were not so perfect. She wished he had not spoken of loving her. And she certainly wished she were not pinned to his bed!

"Robert you must listen to me. You have had a great deal of brandy tonight—"

"Not brandy, sherry—"

"Yes, of course, sherry." He kissed her hard on the mouth, but she was able to push him back. "Pray heed what I am saying to you! Robert, you have drunk too much. You are quite foxed and are making no sense. You must let me go." She thought it would probably be of use to speak more loudly to him, but not for the world did she want any member of the house to see either of them in so scandalous a situation.

"No," he said, almost petulantly as a child would. "I shan't. I have you in my power and I shan't let you go. I love you Lucy. I mean to marry you. Tomorrow."

"That will be excellent. You shall marry me tomorrow and then we can share your bed, but not now. Tonight, you must let me return to my own room."

"I do not want to let you go," he laid down on her fully, his head nestled against hers. "If I do, you will never come back to me. You will go to Henry."

"No, I will not go to Henry," she stated firmly.

"Henry wants you, Lucy. He loves you but I love you more. He writes poems about you, but my heart aches so much when I look at you that sometimes I can't breathe for wanting you. Henry can still breathe. I have watched him. But I cannot. Dear Lucy, I cannot breathe."

Lucy did not know what to do. She knew he was completely foxed so that he could not be held entirely accountable for either his words or his conduct, but what on earth was he mumbling about Henry and about his own heart aching? Odd tears began streaming from her eyes. Did Robert truly love her?

She realized she understood completely what he meant about his heart aching and about being unable to breathe because more than once she had felt precisely the same way while with him. For the first time she considered quite seriously the possibility that after all of their quarrels and attempts to behave with polite indifference toward each other, that she might truly be in love with Robert and he with her. For that reason, she slipped her arms about his shoulders and held him tenderly, stroking his hair. "Robert, I do not know what to say," she murmured.

He remained silent, but kissed her neck several times.

"Do you truly love me?"

"Yes," he said in a very quiet voice. "So much, my darling."

"I . . . I think I may be in love with you as well."

"Of course you are. How could you kiss me as you do without being in love with me?" A heavy sigh followed.

She continued petting his head and stroking his hair. She hugged him and nuzzled him. A moment later, he was snoring against her shoulder.

She began to laugh, for it was absolutely ridiculous. Even her laughter did not awaken him. She swiped at her tears with the back of her hand and rolled him off her. She began scooting away from him, but he reached for her, pulling her close.

She tried again, but once more he held her tightly. Over the next hour, she tried again and again but always with the same result: he would reach for her and prevent her from leaving. She continued trying until she grew fatigued. She decided she would rest for perhaps an hour or so and try again. Perhaps then he would be so deeply in his slumbers that he would permit her to leave.

With a sigh, she gave in to the seduction of sleep until a strong light shone on her face. She blinked several times and only after a minute or so did she realize that the light on her face was coming from a sunbeam.

She thought it odd that the sun would by shining on her since her bed did not face the windows at this particular angle. And why were the curtains blue and not rose-colored?

A quick horror fi'led her. She turned abruptly in what proved to be Robert's arms. He pinned her once more. "No, do not leave me." Then his eyes opened and he looked at her. "What the deuce?" he cried.

He sat up so fast that she was able to watch as obvious pain flooded his head. "I shall be ill."

She leaped from the bed and retrieved the basin at his dressing table and ran to him. He looked as though he might be very ill indeed, but after a few moments, and several deep breaths, he set the basin aside and reclined instead against his pillows. He stared hard at her, his brow furrowed deeply. "Good God, Lucy! Whatever are you doing in my rooms? And you are in your nightdress!"

Lucy shook her head. It would seem he remembered nothing after all. "You were quite foxed and fell while in the library. Your head was bleeding. I helped you to your bedchamber but you would not permit me to leave."

"You are making no sense whatsoever. How could I have prevented you from leaving?"

Lucy did not feel it prudent to spend another moment in his bedchamber. If they were discovered, even though the situation was perfectly innocent, there would be no recourse but for Robert, a quite honorable man, to offer for her. Though she had already begun to think that she would like very much to be married to him, she was convinced no circumstance could be worse than for Robert to feel a sense of dutiful obligation.

"I must go," she whispered, and before he could argue the point further, she was gone.

Two hours later, Lucy was busily helping the children sort leaves from a recent excursion to the farthest reaches of the park, when the children suddenly squealed his name. She turned and saw that he was standing in the doorway of the schoolroom. Dark circles framed his eyes and his skin was quite pale. He very much looked like a man who had been in his altitudes on the night before.

He winced as the children threw themselves upon him, but to his credit he caught each child warmly and gave kisses all round, afterward setting each of them on their feet. Though continuing to wince, he listened quite valiantly to an enthusiastic if disjointed recounting of their adventure, for apparently just as they were flanking the home wood a stag appeared at the very edge of the meadow with at least six points to his antlers. Allowing himself to be drawn into the chamber, he took up a seat next to her. She continued sorting beneath Miss Gunville's supervision. The children once more took up their places.

After a few minutes, he bid his sisters and brother good day, promised to take William for a ride in the afternoon, then begged a word with Lucy.

She excused herself, saying she would return in a few

minutes. She could see that Robert was not fully recovered. "Is your head aching you quite severely?" she asked, barely able to restrain a smile as she looked up at him.

"Yes, wretchedly so. I . . . I came to beg your pardon. Dear Lucy, what have I done?"

"Come," she said, "and I will tell you, but not here in the hallway."

She led him to the conservatory on the ground floor where there was little likelihood of being overheard. Taking up a seat on one of the stone benches, she gestured for him to sit beside her.

"I am completely mortified," he said, not hesitating to sit down. "How could I have kept you imprisoned in my rooms?"

"Do not trouble yourself." She searched his eyes, wondering if he recalled anything of what he said to her.

"Do not trouble myself?" he exclaimed. "Lucy, you were in my bed this morning. Do not speak to me of not *troubling myself*. I shall marry you, of course, that much is determined already."

"I do not see why," she returned easily, crossing her arms over her chest.

He glared at her. "You were in my bed last night. Do not attempt to tell me nothing happened between us, for I will not believe you."

"You are so certain of your prowess that you believe you could seduce me when you were completely foxed?"

"I was not thinking of seduction," he said, his expression absolutely pitiful.

"You did not hurt me in the least, if that is your strongest fear."

He leaned forward, settling his face in his hands. "I want to believe you."

She placed a hand on his back and as she had last night she rubbed it gently. "You did nothing about which you ought to feel the least shame or mortification. The only thing you did last night was kiss me. And I was, as it happens, quite flattered by your attentions."

He turned his head to look at her. "Why, when I must have accosted you in the most ungentlemanly manner possible?"

She had debated for a very long time after leaving his room just how much of what transpired she would relate to him. She decided to hold nothing back. "Not in the least, I assure you. In actuality, you confessed that you loved me and that you believed you always had."

"I did?" he asked, appearing astonished. "I must have been very foxed, indeed." Lucy withdrew her hand. He sat up and looked at her. "I am sorry. Those words were uncalled for. Pray forgive me. I am not yet recovered."

Tears once more bit her eyes. "I will tell you everything that happened and you must judge for yourself the various meanings, for I cannot make sense of it." She then launched into an exact recounting of what had been said and done and how it had happened that she had slept in his bed, indeed, in his arms, all night, and approximately how many times he had kissed her. She felt it only appropriate that since she would have to live with the memory, he ought to as well.

When she was done, she could see that there was a very crushed expression on his face. "I do not know what to say. I have behaved abominably toward you. The only proper, the only gentlemanly thing to do is to marry. I consider myself betrothed to you."

At that Lucy rose to her feet and faced him, her temper rising. "Oh, you do, do you? Well, let me tell you, Robert Sandifort, that I would not marry you were you the last man on earth, even had your passions overcome you and I was no longer a maiden. What's more, I will never forgive you for how the only manner in which you could reveal your heart to me was in a state of complete intoxication!"

He opened his mouth to speak but she whirled away from him and left the conservatory quickly. Though she had told the children she would return to them, she could not do so because she had need of her pillow and a score of kerchiefs for the next hour or so.

CHAPTER TWELVE

"But Lucy, are you certain?" Henry appeared so hurt that she felt as though her heart would break anew. She was sitting with him in the children's fort in the center of the maze. The lower rooms of the house were undergoing a great change in preparation for the come-out ball and there had been so many servants about, besides the rest of the family, that the maze had been the only place to have a private conversation.

"Yes, quite certain. I wish I had understood your sentiments long before this. I . . . I had been so used to your attentions and that for so many years that I had assumed it was from a sort of brotherly affection."

He groaned. He was silent for a long moment, then asked, "Are you in love with Robert?"

Lucy felt stunned by the question because she had been asking herself the very same thing for two days now, two long days since she had spoken with Robert in the conservatory. There had only been one answer, one true answer, particularly when she pondered the breadth of her feelings for him; how she felt when she brangled with him, how she took such great pleasure in his kisses, how she still treasured his words on that fateful night even though he had been completely foxed, and certainly how hurt she was that he had been ignoring her since. "Yes," she responded simply. "I suppose I must be."

"For how long?"

"Forever," she said sadly. "I must have loved him forever now that I look back."

"Then you can comprehend my feelings in this moment."

Lucy turned to him, her eyes flooding with tears. "Henry, I am so sorry, but if it is of the smallest consequence, I do not believe that your brother loves me. So you see, we are both made unhappy."

"And you are absolutely certain of your feelings for him?"

She nodded and sighed.

She sat beside him for a long time.

Finally he said, "These chairs are deuced uncomfortable."

Lucy chuckled. "Well they are meant for the children, after all."

Leaving the fort, he offered his arm to her and she took it.

"Please tell me all will be well?" she queried gently.

He smiled sadly then laughed. "I must confess I never had a great deal of hope. I gave you so many hints and yet you remained completely oblivious."

"I must have, for I cannot remember your having given me a single one."

"I tried to tell you something of my feelings at the assemblies when I took you to have some refreshments but you were distracted by Hetty who was at the time speaking with Mr. Woolston. Do you remember?"

She shook her head and frowned. "I remember Hetty and Mr. Woolston, but not that you were attempting to engage my affections."

He groaned anew. "There, you see. I tried to tell you how beautiful you were, that indeed you had never looked prettier."

"You said such things to me?" she cried.

He nodded.

"How dreadful that I cannot remember your having done so. Henry, I do beg your pardon!"

"It is of little consequence and do not worry, my heart is not completely shattered."

Making the circuit back through the maze, she asked, "Were you waiting to see if I would accept of your hand in marriage before taking holy orders?"

"Of course."

"Am I right in supposing then that the sole reason you would have done so was for the sake of wedding me?"

"Precisely."

"Have you no love for the church?"

"I have no love for being a priest."

She stopped and turned toward him. "Henry, would you really have sacrificed so much for me?"

"I would have done anything."

She shook her head. "That would have been unwise, you know."

"That would have been my decision."

"But do you not see that at some point I would have disappointed you and you would have been sunk in a life, a career for which you had no true love or interest?"

He smiled faintly. "Do you think I did not consider that a hundredfold?"

"Very well. If you insist on giving me such reasonable answers then I will no longer feel so badly, since I am persuaded my refusing your offer has saved you a lifetime of regret."

"On that point I daresay we will always disagree."

The sound of a woman's voice screaming in anguish from the direction of the house disrupted their *tête-a-tête*.

"Good God," he cried. "I do believe that is Hetty!"

By the time they reached the armory, the eldest portion of the family as well as Valmaston had gathered there. The latter was walking away from the scene in the direction of the antechamber opposite. Henry quickly hurried to join Anne, Alice, and Robert, who had gathered about Hetty, who in turn was on the floor trying to collect what appeared to be over a hundred letters. Lady Sandifort stood on the hearth, imperious in her demeanor and expression.

Lucy, feeling she ought to absent herself, joined Valmaston.

"What is going forward?" Lucy asked quietly.

Valmaston drew her into the antechamber and said very quietly, "I do not know precisely what Lady Sandifort has done, or what the nature of the correspondence is, but I can tell you what precipitated this action. Lady Sandifort, I believe, has come to suspect that I have an interest in Miss Sandifort. We had come back from a walk in which we had taken the children to see Mr. Frome and to take him another basket of soup and bread and the like. I had said something that made Hetty, that is Miss Sandifort, laugh, and the next moment Lady Sandifort was standing before us. The tenor of her voice rose two pitches and she began to speak grandly about how charming it was for Hetty to be entertaining one of her guests. She was sarcastic, of course. There was no mistaking the precise state of her temper. She then begged a word with Hetty. I took my leave, as you well may imagine, retiring to the billiard room. A few minutes later, I heard Hetty crying out in a manner that pierced my heart. I have never heard such anguish before. I ran down the stairs and found this." He waved a hand at the unhappy scene in the armory.

Lucy feared the worst.

Beyond the doorway, she watched as Robert sent Anne and Alice away. The girls did not hesitate but each kissed their elder sister on the cheek and then fled the chamber.

Keeping her voice very low, Lucy said, "I fear she is a very jealous sort and you must by now know that she sees you has her particular property. One of the first days you were here, for instance, you had walked with Hetty and the children toward the maze, then you broke away to go to the stables. Lady Sandifort was watching and she might have set the incident down as innocuous, but unfortunately Hetty turned to look in your direction."

"She did?"

"Yes, I remember it quite distinctly. Of course it was perfectly innocent, for I must say," and here she laughed, but continued her whispers, "that Hetty has been quite firm in her convictions that you should not be here. However, Lady Sandifort came to believe that Hetty had an interest in you and she absolutely flew into a rage."

He scowled playfully upon her. "And you thought I might be charmed by such a vixen?"

Lucy smiled, if faintly. "I had no such notion, as well you know. I only wanted you to distract her so that Anne and Alice might be treated properly through their come-out ball, which leads me to say perhaps you ought to ignore Hetty for the present."

He turned his attention to the armory once more. Robert was now arguing quietly with Lady Sandifort. Henry was on his knees beside Hetty, helping her to gather up the letters.

Lady Sandifort caught sight of them in the antechamber. To Robert she said in a clear voice, "I meant no harm. I believed it to be a matter about which the entire family ought to be informed in order to encourage our dear Hetty in a more proper direction. Surely you must see that?"

She quit the hearth, brushing past Robert as though his thoughts were completely insignificant, and moved toward Lucy and Valmaston. She carried herself quite triumphantly. "What do you think of that?" she cried. "I had suspected it for some time, and naturally being responsible for this family I did just as I believe my beloved husband would have wished me to. I made it my business to discover the precise nature of the truth."

Lucy recalled Lady Sandifort saying that she knew a great secret of Hetty's. It would appear that she had no longer been able to restrain the impulse to expose her. Worse still, it would seem her ladyship had taken extreme measures to support what she already knew.

"You cannot mean . . ." Lucy began.

"Of course. The affair had to be revealed, the sooner the better, and I wanted more substantial proof than the gossip of . . . of old friends. You see, my dear Lord Valmaston, Hetty has been Thomas Woolston's mistress these many years and more. These are love letters she presses to her bosom."

They all turned to look at Hetty, who held some of the letters tightly as she wiped at her cheeks. Robert was beside her again and slipped a comforting arm about her shoulders.

"Love letters?" Lucy queried, shocked not only because clearly Hetty had received them from Mr. Woolston, but that Lady Sandifort in turn had apparently thrown them on the floor in front of her.

"Yes, you may read them for yourself if you are in doubt. I felt obligated to do so, of course. They are full of confessed love, a steady exchange of quite intimate anecdotes, even a recounting of secret assignations, and all this has been going on for ten or eleven years. Why there must be one hundred and fifty letters, by my count!"

"Are you saying, ma'am, that you discovered the letters?"

She straightened her shoulders. "Yes, in Hetty's bedchamber.

I felt it my duty to expose the truth. In doing so I meant it for a proper lesson for Anne and Alice." She addressed the earl, saying, "They are my particular charge, you see."

Lucy seethed with rage. She felt the strongest desire to scratch Lady Sandifort's eyes out. Her hands balled up into fists. Her breathing came in gulps.

Lord Valmaston glanced askance at Lucy, then cleared his throat. "Well, this is most unfortunate," he said hastily, addressing Lady Sandifort, all the while moving to stand between Lucy and her ladyship. "But I find I am rather parched. I should dearly love a glass of sherry. Would you care to join me?" He offered his arm.

"With pleasure," she said, taking his arm firmly. "Do you not think I did right?"

Though Lady Sandifort made as if to walk back into the armory, Valmaston held her in check. "But come, let us not pass through the armory. I find the scene rather . . . *tedious*, of the moment."

"Indeed," Lady Sandifort agreed readily. As they moved away, in the direction of the grand salon, she rattled on, "Poor Hetty! To have been so imprudent! I must say I was completely shocked. But then I am always the last to know such things, but the first I hope to place the blame where it belongs. She was always rather spoiled, though I hate confessing as much, but there it is! My husband, God rest his soul, was not the best of fathers, for he indulged them one and all, which is why—"

To Lucy's relief, her voice trailed away and she could no longer be heard. Lucy believed she owed Valmaston a great deal for taking her away so pleasantly as he had. She was still completely outraged that Hetty had been exposed so brutally. She knew it would be some time before she would be able to speak congenially with a woman whose friendship had become a critical element in keeping peace at Aldershaw. How she detested the thought, however, of continuing so hateful a ruse.

Moving into the armory, she saw that Robert was speaking quietly to Hetty. She was still on her knees and Robert had taken one of her hands in his. She could not hear what he was saying until she drew close.

"But it is my fault and I am so very sorry. I could have prevented this. I have allowed her to reign when she should not have and this is the result."

"I have disgraced everyone," she said, smoothing a tear off her cheek.

"You have disgraced no one, my dear. She is the disgrace."

Hetty looked up. "Lucy, she accused me of being Thomas's mistress and I never was. Never."

Lucy dropped to the floor as well. "We all know that," she whispered earnestly. "Indeed, we do. Anyone who is acquainted with your character knows as much. On that point, you may rest assured."

Hetty began sobbing anew. Henry came up behind her and gently relieved her of the letters.

"She went through all of my things. My bedchamber is in shambles. Is there to be nothing held sacred in this house?" she asked.

"I shall have a lock put on your door," Robert cried. "And she may go to the devil if she does not like it."

Hetty looked startled. "Robert! I have never heard you speak so severely."

"No less than she deserves. And from this moment, you have my permission not to pay her the smallest courtesy or respect, for she deserves none of it."

Hetty stared at him. "She will be very angry."

"Yes, she will, but from now on she will have to wrestle with me if she is dissatisfied."

Hetty's shoulders collapsed once more. "I am so completely mortified, but I loved him, you see."

"You always did," Robert said, stroking her hair. "We all knew you were brokenhearted when he wed Miss Rookstone. We all knew you continued to love him. Indeed, whenever he was near, you were like a torch on the darkest night. If I have any feeling at all it is that I never believed him worthy of you. You loved where your love was not valued. His greed, and greed alone, led him to marry a richer woman. Your dowry and the living at Laverstoke would have combined to provide more than most men need in a lifetime, nonetheless each year. That he married, instead, a woman with fifteen thousand pounds bespeaks his character entirely."

"I should have comprehended his baseness then, but his words were like honey."

"He never lacked for ability."

"Robert, why did you not warn me?"

"Because until this moment I only had my suspicions that you held to your love for him. But I want you to know something, which may for the present give you great pain but which I hope will illustrate Mr. Woolston's true nature."

Hetty paled. Lucy suspected she knew the truth but did not want to believe it.

"I will say nothing more unless you wish for it," Robert added wisely.

Hetty nodded her willingness for him to speak.

"Very well. Lady Sandifort took Mr. Woolston as her lover last year."

Hetty clapped her hand over her mouth but still the gasp that occurred at the same moment filled the chamber. She paled ominously. "Good God," she whispered. She shook her head, more tears seeped from her eyes, and she began to shake. "When Papa was so ill?"

"I should not have told you," Robert moaned.

She was silent for a very long time. Finally she said, "No, I am glad you did."

Lucy addressed her softly. "May I take you to your bedchamber, Hetty?"

She nodded several times in quick, painful succession.

Robert lifted her to her feet. Hetty took her letters from Henry, clutching them tightly.

Lucy held Hetty's arm the entire distance to her bedchamber. Once within, Hetty sat down on the bed and began to sob, the letters she had been holding falling to the floor.

Lucy did not leave her the rest of the afternoon or the evening. Only when she was assured that the greater part of her grief had been given its full expression did she leave her resting relatively peacefully.

When Lucy at last retired to her bedchamber, she found Robert sitting in a chair by the window waiting for her.

"Will my sister be all right?" he asked.

"Of course," Lucy responded. "Hetty has a great deal of strength." She expected him to rise from his seat and take his leave but he did not.

As though reading her mind, he said, "I saw you leave Hetty's bedchamber and I ordered a tray brought to your room. Nothing to signify, just a few cold meats, salad, and a little wine."

"Thank you." Suddenly, she was exhausted. She sat on the edge of the bed. "Did you truly know that she was still in love with Mr. Woolston?"

"As I told her earlier, I had always had my suspicions but it never occurred to me that the blackguard would have sustained her hopes in this manner, encouraging her to keep loving him. What manner of gentleman does something so wretched?"

"I do not believe I would call him a gentleman. Do you remember the walks she would take once each month? Her 'nature' walks?"

"Good God! She was meeting him, then?"

"To exchange their letters."

Robert ground his teeth.

Lucy sighed. "I cannot bear to think of him here at the come-out ball, for he has been invited, you know."

"The invitation must be rescinded," he stated sharply, "else I will not be able to account for my actions should I set eyes on him."

"I shall send a letter, if you like."

He glanced at her apace. "That is so much like you," he stated, a sudden frown between his brow. "Why is it you are so good, so willing to fill the breach, to do what it is not your duty to do?"

"How is this not my duty?" she asked. "Hetty is my friend and if it is in my power to spare her pain, how is that not an obligation of mine?"

He sighed. "You never cease to amaze me."

But not sufficiently to declare that you love me when you are sober, she thought. She wished he were not in her bedchamber tormenting her with his presence and his professed admiration of at least this quality of hers.

A maidservant arrived bearing the requested tray and settled it at Lucy's direction on the bed next to her. Once she was gone, Lucy began to nibble on the meat and celery and to sip the wine. Robert did not speak for a long time, nor did she. Fatigue was settling into her bones now. The only wonder was that Robert did not take her hint and leave.

"I suppose I should go," he said at last.

"Yes," she stated, lifting her gaze to his.

"You are still angry that I kissed you while I was foxed."

She laughed a little hysterically. "No, Robert, of course

not. I never regretted any of our kisses. I am angry that your heart is dead to me unless you are foxed."

He stepped toward her, his complexion heightened. "What does it matter to you the state of my heart, foxed or otherwise?"

She shook her head and sipped her wine. She wanted to say, "It matters to me because I am in love with you." But she did not feel he deserved to hear the truth. "I suppose it should not matter one whit and to that end I am striving to deaden my own heart. Will that suffice?"

"No, it will not."

"What do you want of me, Robert? Answer me that. I have told you what you said and what you did three nights past. Beyond that I am unwilling to discuss the matter further because you have made it clear you want none of me."

He seemed to debate within his mind just what he wanted to say next. Finally he said, "What do you want of me?"

"What difference if your heart is dead to me?"

"You keep speaking in circles."

"That is because you must earn the right to hear what my heart would say to you."

He shook his head several times. "I am convinced this would be a mistake," he stated, but she could see that he was speaking to himself.

"Go to bed," she stated wearily. "I am finished with my meal and I wish to retire."

"This cannot be the end."

"That is your choice, not mine."

"Why do you insist on being difficult?"

"I will answer you if you will answer me this: why do you refuse to speak your heart?"

He was silent for a moment, his expression serious. "There is something I truly must know."

Lucy felt greatly impatient with him, but she remained silent.

"I wish to know why you refused Henry's offer of marriage."

"So you know of that?"

"Yes, he told me at once."

"This question I will answer—I do not love him. I cannot speak more plainly than that. He is a friend, nothing more."

He nodded several times. "Very well."

With that, he turned on his heel and quit the chamber. Lucy sighed heavily. She removed the tray from her bed and, without changing her clothes, crawled beneath the counterpane and fell into a deep, if somewhat troubled, sleep.

On the following morning Lucy sought out Mr. Frome, as she often did when she was troubled. She did not necessarily always speak of what was distressing her. Sometimes his mere presence was sufficient comfort.

Today she had no words for the depth of her sadness. She was still pained by Hetty's suffering, and her conversation with Robert late last night was still weighing on her heart.

She sat on the stool and he presented her with a cup of tea. "You always seem to have it ready for me, as though you know I am coming."

He smiled and while she sipped her tea he worked at a whistle he was carving. He made his cuts slowly and carefully. "I will be leaving soon," he said quietly.

Lucy blinked at him, unable to credit what he had just said. "Indeed?" she queried in scarcely more than a whisper. Only now, with the possibility of his quitting Aldershaw, did she truly come to comprehend how much she depended upon him. "I do not know what to say except that I wish you would not! I believe I have been hoping you would stay at the very least until my own sojourn here comes to an end."

"That would be a very long time, indeed," he murmured, laughing at the same time.

"I beg your pardon?" She was certain he knew quite well she was leaving in September.

He cleared his throat. "I wish that I could stay longer but a friend in Devonshire has sent me word, by way of The George at Bickfield, that he is building a fishing boat and desires my assistance. His wife is quite ill and a son recently died. So, you see, I believe I must go."

"Of course." She had been very sad when she approached his camp, but upon hearing such news she thought her heart would break.

He reached over and pressed her arm gently. "All will be well. Sir Robert will set everything to rights. He is a good man, indeed, an admirable one. You have but to be a little more patient with him. You will see."

Lucy tilted her head at him. Was he able to read her mind that he would speak the very words she needed to hear? Whatever was she to do once he was gone? "When do you leave?" she asked

"At noon on the day of the come-out ball, I'm 'fraid."

"Oh, but you cannot!" she cried.

He pressed her arm again. "My work is finished here. Truly, I must be going. I have already bought a pony from one of Sir Robert's tenant farmers."

"Then there is nothing more to be said."

"Only this: I have enjoyed my stay at Aldershaw more than I can ever say. You have great abilities and talents, Miss Lucinda Stiles. You created an exquisite garden. I expect to hear extraordinary things of you in the future."

Lucy could not imagine to what he might be referring. "You are much mistaken," she said, her throat beginning to ache profoundly. "I play the pianoforte tolerably but not so well as Hetty and when I sing I sound like a chicken squawking. I cannot paint in the least and even Rosamunde embroiders better than I. Indeed, you are quite mistaken." Was he really leaving?

He chortled almost gleefully. "You have misunderstood me entirely. Your abilities extend far beyond musical notes or the use of watercolors. No, you have great abilities, and when you are mistress of your own home I suspect you will soon find need to express your talents in a larger community. Do not hesitate to do so. The world needs such a heart as yours. Never forget that. I know I never shall." He paused and lifted his head. "And if I am not mistaken I believe Violet is calling for you."

Lucy looked up but neither saw nor heard anyone. A moment later Violet appeared from around the corner of the maze. Even at such a distance Lucy could see that she had her doll tucked beneath her arm. She was never without it. "Lucy!" she called out. "You promised to go on our walk with us today. We are all waiting for you!"

Though Lucy wished to remain with Mr. Frome more than anything in the world now that she knew his time at Aldershaw was coming to a end, she rose from her seat, returned the cup to him, and bid him good day. "Of course, I shall see you in but a few minutes, for we are taking the western tour of the park, which as you know always ends in your camp."

Over the next few days, Hetty recovered far more swiftly than anyone would have supposed. Lucy was privy to her thoughts one moment to the next and understood quite well the journey she had taken in relinquishing the unworthy Mr. Woolston. He was the sort of man who had all the appearance of goodness but very little true character, as his conduct had proved. In quick stages she relinquished her love for him and certainly all respect, even concluding that he was perhaps the most selfish man she had ever known.

Walking with her in the garden the day before the ball, Lucy asked, "What do you mean to do with his letters?"

"I have already burned them in the grate. After all I learned of his conduct, I could only conclude that his words were worthless. There is only one thing about which I am truly curious—why did Lady Sandifort choose that moment to expose my secret?"

"I know this may come as a shock, Hetty, but I believe it is because she is convinced that Lord Valmaston has a *tendre* for you."

"What?" Hetty cried, obviously dumbfounded. "That is the most ridiculous thing I have ever heard."

"Well," Lucy mused. "I do not see why it is ridiculous since you are after all a considerable beauty, and you have a great deal of wit and charm and a very good heart. The real question is this: why would his heart not beat a little more strongly when you walk into a room?"

"Lucy, you are become as mad as bedlam!" Her complexion was greatly heightened.

Lucy only laughed. "It hardly signifies, however, what his true sentiments might be. The only thing that matters is that Lady Sandifort *believes* it to be true."

Hetty grew silent again. When they reached the maze, Lucy suggested they return to the house, since she had promised to have nuncheon with the children in the schoolroom.

As Hetty turned about, she sighed very deeply. She was silent for a long time as they made their way back up the garden. At last she stopped. Holding Lucy's gaze, she said, "There is just one thing I wish to know: how will I ever trust another man again?"

Lucy saw the tears brimming in Hetty's eyes and offered her comfort by embracing her and holding her close. How, indeed? she wondered.

From the window of the library, Robert watched the tender scene below and felt his heart beginning to ache anew.

This was what he loved best about Lucy, that her disposition was so warm, so generous that she could be such a comfort to his dear sister in what must be a most painful time. He could see Hetty's sufferings but he had been completely incapable of offering her more than a pat on the shoulder now and then and a sympathetic smile.

Only once had he been able to give her at least a portion of real comfort. He had become so enraged with Mr. Woolston and his unconscionable conduct that he had finally approached Hetty in a private moment and said, "I will call him out. That is what I will do!"

She had seemed startled but afterward had begun to laugh. "What a darling you are, Robert! How I love you!" She had then risen from her seat and clung to him for a very long time. He had not heard her crying but his coat had been nearly wet through when she finally pulled away.

Now as he watched Hetty and Lucy together, his thoughts drifted to the moment over a sennight past when he had awakened and found himself holding Lucy in his arms. He had never been more shocked. Since that time he had been trying very hard to understand his relationship with her. More than once he had mentally drawn up two separate lists, one that contained her fine qualities and the other consisting of all those ways he essentially disapproved of her. Yet what was there to disapprove of in a young woman who had so completely changed his home, his life, his family, and all for the better?

Back and forth his internal arguments drifted, but as he watched Lucy now walking toward the house arm in arm with Hetty all he could think was that he wanted nothing more than to wake up with Lucy in his arms every morning of his life.

* * *

The day before the ball, Lucy waited outside the ball-room with Lord Valmaston as well as the entire Sandifort family. Only Miss Gunville was absent. Anne and Alice had been decorating in great secrecy both the ballroom and the morning room for several days and only now were ready to reveal their efforts.

The children were fairly leaping in their excitement.

Finally the twins opened the doors.

Lucy found herself stunned by what the young ladies had been able to achieve. An enormous quantity of dark blue silk had been draped along the upper two feet of wall and caught up in festoons made of branches of fresh yew, an abundance of artificial pink flowers, and ribbons in myriad colors. In addition, Mr. Quarley had allowed several of his enormous potted palms as well as pots of flowers, ferns, and ivy to be used to fill each corner of the long chamber.

"How beautiful!" Lucy cried. "I can just imagine how extraordinary the chamber will appear when each of these chandeliers is ablaze with scores of lit candles!"

"Even the orchestra's balcony has a garland of yew and roses," Hetty said from behind her.

Lucy glanced up and smiled at the superb decorations. "Truly remarkable."

Hyacinth and Violet were twirling in circles on the ballroom floor. William's shoes could be heard clunking up the spiral staircase that led to the musician's gallery.

"There is more," Alice said, smiling broadly. She was standing by the door opposite that led into the morning room. The party trailed behind her into what proved to be a spectacle of freshly cut flowers from Mr. Quarley's cutting garden.

Violet cried, "It looks like a fairyland."

"It does," Hyacinth added.

Movement from the corner of Lucy's eye led her to watch as Lord Valmaston and Hetty emerged slowly from the ballroom. They were surprisingly deep in conversation, which lasted for several minutes until Hyacinth ran up to Hetty, took her hand, and led her to view the enormous bouquet on the table by the wall. Lucy believed she saw the future in the making but hid such a newly birthed hope deep within her heart.

Only then did she chance to glance at the doorway of the ballroom and saw, much to her horror, that Lady Sandifort had also seen enough to arouse her suspicions yet again. "Miss Gunville," she snapped, "I do believe the children should return to the schoolroom."

"Yes, of course," Miss Gunville responded crisply. She did not allow even one moan of disappointment to escape the children's lips, but ushered them quickly from the room.

Lucy felt as though a dark cloud had entered the morning room. No one spoke, not a single word.

Lady Sandifort addressed the earl. "My lord," she said sweetly, "I was hoping to engage you in a game of chess."

Lord Valmaston did not hesitate. "I should be delighted." Wisely he refrained from even looking at Hetty, but rather crossed to Lady Sandifort, offered his arm, and escorted her from the chamber.

Once they were gone, Lucy let out a great puff of air she did not even know she was holding. She felt dizzy suddenly. What would happen next? she wondered.

CHAPTER THIRTEEN

Late that night, Lucy stood on the terrace long after the others had retired. A soft summer breeze blew over the garden and because the moon was high she was able to see a great portion of the flower beds. How much had changed since she arrived at Aldershaw. The estate was looking prettier every day under Mr. Quarley's excellent guidance and tomorrow Anne and Alice would enjoy a come-out ball that had previously been forbidden them.

In the distance, to the west of the maze, a shadow moved.

Her first thought was that she was seeing a wind-blown branch from one of the beech trees, but the shadow moved steadily toward the house.

She squinted, trying to determine who it was. She wondered for a moment if she ought to raise an alarm, but she rather thought the figure could be any one of three gentlemen who might have preferred a stroll before bed.

In the end, the dark shadow proved to be Robert. He even waved to her halfway to the terrace. She waved in return and almost chose to retire before he reached her but that seemed quite uncivil, so she remained.

"The night is very beautiful," he said, joining her on the terrace.

"Indeed, very," she responded. "I had thought everyone had long since sought their beds."

"I decided to take a little brandy to Mr. Frome, for I know he enjoys it. We fell into a conversation and time escaped me. I suppose it is near midnight."

"Yes, it is. I shall miss him."

"We all will. When I said good night to the children, Violet wept into my shoulder. She said Tom would especially be sad to see him go."

"Dear Violet," she murmured.

"And what are you doing at this late hour?" he asked.

"Looking at the moon, watching the stars, admiring Mr. Quarley's handiwork. He is quite gifted, you know."

"Yes," he said, keeping his voice low for their conversation, which if too loud would certainly disturb a number of the family members through the bank of windows above them. "Quarley has been at Aldershaw forever. Have I thanked you for your help with the gardens?"

"Only a dozen times," she said, chuckling.

There was a considerable pause and Lucy sensed that Robert wished to say something to her.

She was not surprised when he cleared his throat and began, "I was hoping you might save a waltz for me. I would ask you for the first or even second dances but I am already given to my sisters."

"As you should be," she said, turning toward him. "You really wish to dance with me?"

"Lucy," he said rather abruptly. "I fear very much that were we to fall into conversation we would simply begin brangling. So I will ask again, will you save me the first waltz? Although, I wish to add," and here he touched her arm gently, "I am trying to comprehend my heart."

Lucy felt his words deeply. How her heart began to thrum.

She knew a strong impulse to say several things to him, but couldn't because they all became jumbled in her mind. "Yes, of course," she responded. Before she could say anything more, he bid her good night and was gone.

Lucy sought her bed and fell quickly into a dreamy sleep. She was certain she had just laid her head on her pillow when shouting beneath her window roused her. She could see by the moon's progress across the sky, however, that perhaps only an hour or two had passed.

She went to the window and, opening it quietly, peeked her head out. Lady Sandifort was having a fit of hysterics as she moved briskly to and fro in front of Lord Valmaston.

"Do hush, Lady Sandifort, or you will awaken the entire house," he urged her in a low tone.

"I do not care if the servants, to the last maid, hear what I have to say. I think you a vile creature, keeping me dangling and all the while never having the smallest intention of . . . of . . ."

"You are a horrid, selfish female and I only wonder that you have not driven the entire family into the madhouse!"

Lucy clamped a hand over her mouth. How many times had she wished to utter such words! How grateful she was that at last Lady Sandifort was receiving something of her due. On the other hand, she shuddered, for she understood to perfection just what sort of temper her ladyship would exhibit once the sun rose. Her vanity had been severely wounded by Valmaston's obvious rejection of her. However, he added an insult to this horrible injury by calling her a selfish female. Lucy knew quite well that Lady Sandifort saw herself as a loving, restrained, generous individual who was always being ill-used by everyone around her.

"I despise you!" Lady Sandifort cried, then stomped in the direction of the house. "I wish you every manner of evil."

Lucy withdrew into the shadows of the drapes lest she be seen and afterward gently closed the window. Climbing back into bed, she knew but one thing for certain: there would be the devil to pay in the morning.

Regardless, the moment her head touched the pillow anew, she fell into a very deep sleep until shouting, this time of an entirely different nature, awoke her.

She sat straight up in bed, wondering if she had heard correctly. She listened very hard. Yes, there it was!

"Fire!"

Lucy bolted from her bed and much to her surprise saw that sunlight streamed into her chamber. It was much later than she had supposed.

She scrambled into her robe and, regardless of her appearance, raced from her bedchamber. In the distance, Anne and Alice had just reached the landing of the stairs at the west end of the house, sleepy-eyed and sporting mobcaps.

Lucy descended the east staircase and a moment later followed Anne and Alice down the central staircase from the first floor to the ground floor. At the bottom of the stairs, servants raced to and fro, all carrying either empty buckets in one direction or buckets sloshing with water in the other.

Henry was stationed in the entrance hall, his complexion pale. Anne and Alice were both clinging to him and weeping. He caught her gaze. "It is the ballroom and, I fear, the morning room."

"Ablaze?" Lucy inquired, much shocked.

He nodded. "Yes, but I believe the fire will not spread."

Lucy thought of Lady Sandifort and shuddered. Would she have done this?

Robert was in his shirtsleeves when he descended the stairs. In tow were the youngest Sandiforts. He held Violet in his right arm while shepherding Hyacinth and William before him. Hetty followed, also wearing a robe over her nightdress.

"What is going forward?" she asked.

Henry repeated the wretched news. Hyacinth looked up

at her eldest brother, "Will there not be a ball for Anne and Alice?"

Robert held her close to his side. "I do not know, dearest, but right now our greatest concern is that everyone is safe."

Hyacinth looked around. "Where is Mama?"

Lord Valmaston arrived at the top of the stairs and searched the group. "I see everyone is present save for Lady Sandifort. Does anyone know where she is?" He was dressed in riding gear and walked briskly down the stairs.

"We have not seen her," Lucy said. "What of you, Henry? Was she about before I descended the stairs?"

He shook his head.

As several servants hurried by, Robert said, "Let us all move into the garden. We will be safe there and out of the way of the staff."

The party filed out, moving first onto the terrace and then down the three steps to the lawn. Robert, Henry, and Valmaston agreed to see if they might be of use in the ballroom as well as discover the location of Lady Sandifort.

Once they were gone, Anne began to weep. "I suppose there cannot be a ball now. Hyacinth was right."

"Where is Mama?" Violet asked this time.

Lucy exchanged a meaningful glance with Hetty. She suspected they shared the same thought. Movement caught Hetty's eye and she whispered to Lucy, "Do but look."

Lucy glanced up at the window. Lady Sandifort's rooms were as far from the ballroom as any in the house. She was presently waving to them and smiling all the while.

"There she is, Violet!" William cried.

Lady Sandifort opened the window. "Is there really a fire? I thought Henry was funning, for I heard him earlier but did not believe him."

"Yes, Mama," Hyacinth cried. "In the ballroom."

"How dreadful," she said, clucking her tongue and shaking her head. There was nothing of real concern in her expression. "Well, I suppose I ought to join you. I will be down in a moment."

In the end, the fire was put out quickly so that neither blaze had affected any other room in the house. However, the damage to both rooms was truly horrendous. Everyone took turns viewing the results of the fire. Several of the decorations were charred badly. None of the adults spoke of the possible origin of the fire. There did not seem to be the smallest doubt as to how such a tragedy had occurred. Unfortunately, though the damage from the fire itself was fairly minimal, the greater destruction was caused by the ensuing smoke and water. The result was a sodden, black mess that smelled utterly wretched.

Though Alice was not deeply affected by the certainty that there would be no come-out ball after all, her sister was in near hysterics after seeing the once beautiful chambers. Alice and Hetty took Anne from the room, but in her distress she cried out several times, "She did this! She never wanted me to have a ball! She did this to me!"

Lord Valmaston drew close to Lucy. "I fear this is my fault. I believe I have failed you all."

Lucy could only shake her head at him. She led him across the back entrance hall and into the armory. "I have a confession," she whispered. "I heard you quarreling with Lady Sandifort last night. You happened to be doing so beneath my window."

"Indeed? Then I do apologize."

"It hardly matters. With that said, I wish to assure you that I had no intention of your surpassing the dictates of your conscience where she was concerned—"

He lifted a brow.

"And yes, I know quite well that you have a conscience, a very proper one. However, I believe I may have underestimated just how low her ladyship would sink in attempting to gain your favor."

He shrugged. "I beg you will not believe there was any great chivalry on my part. Had I been younger, a great deal younger, I would have been unable to resist her . . . lures."

"Even as heavy-handed as they were."

"Quite." He laughed and withdrew his snuffbox from the pocket of his coat. He took a pinch and inhaled deeply. "Although, I must say, I am not at all regretful at having agreed to come to Aldershaw."

"No," she observed dryly, "I dare say you are not."

He met her gaze fully. "Do I have even the smallest hope?"

This time Lucy shrugged. "I have not the faintest notion, but if you do achieve your object I can promise you that to whatever lengths you go to win her heart, she will be well worth even the most determined pursuit."

"She is a darling."

"She is an innocent."

"Yes, and I so undeserving."

"Then you must become deserving."

He narrowed his eyes slightly. "And is there something you have in mind?"

Lucy smiled. "Look out the window. Tell me what you see."

"A beautiful garden."

"You know, I truly despise the thought of Anne and Alice having to forego their ball."

He glanced at her sharply and then he smiled, quite broadly. "I have an idea."

"I believe you do and I think we should share it with Robert at once and then of course, Hetty!"

Valmaston laughed. "You know, you would do well in Parliament, I think."

A few minutes later, after having spoken with Robert and received his approval for their scheme, both Lucy and Valmaston scratched lightly on Anne's door. Hetty met them but would not permit them to enter.

She whispered, "Anne cannot receive anyone. She is greatly overset, as you may well imagine."

Lucy nudged the earl.

He said, "We have good news, Hetty. It involves the come-out ball."

Hetty frowned. "Indeed? Whatever do you mean?"

"Well, what do you say to having the ball in the garden?"

"The garden," she stated. "Yes, of course! The garden! What an excellent notion. Was this your idea, my lord?" How bright, how hopeful the expression in her eye.

He hesitated. "Only in part," he said at last. He then inclined his head to Lucy. "I believe I may have been given a hint in that direction, but I do believe the notion has merit. It can be done."

"Even with dancing?"

He nodded. "Even with dancing."

"Well . . . well, it is very kind of you. Very kind, indeed!" Hetty appeared rather breathless.

For his part, Valmaston fell silent. He stared at her, apparently unable to speak. Only then did Lucy realize just how smitten he truly was.

Hetty extended a hand to him. "Anne will be so happy!"

He took her hand and kissed her fingers. Lucy heard Hetty's breath catch.

Composing himself, he said, "Pray tell her at once so that she may be made comfortable."

"Of course."

When Lucy walked with Valmaston down the hall, she nudged him again and laughed.

He laughed as well. "I am enslaved," he cried. "She has enslaved me."

"If that is so, then you could not have found a better master!"

* * *

When Robert went to Lady Sandifort's sitting room to inform her there was to be a ball after all, he later reported to Lucy that she threw a ceramic vase at his head. Fortunately, he ducked and the vase shattered forthwith on the hearth.

At noon Lucy, Valmaston, and the family, save for Lady Sandifort, had gathered about Mr. Frome. Even Anne, with her puffy eyes, felt compelled to join in saying farewell. His new brown pony was harnessed to his caravan, he held the reins in check, and with a warm smile and twinkling gray eyes he set the horse in motion.

Lucy dabbed at her eyes more than once as the caravan lumbered across the uneven grass in the direction of the stables, which were not far. The party followed after him, the ladies waving kerchiefs, the gentlemen their hats. Only William, with his strong young legs, kept pace until the caravan left the stableyard entirely.

"I feel as though I have lost a very dear friend," Hetty said, undoubtedly expressing the views of all.

Lucy could not credit he was gone. To some degree, she felt as though she had lost her father all over again. She supposed in that sense Mr. Frome had indeed been a parent to her in his many kind words and helpful suggestions. She would miss him, but as he said, he had more work to do, this time building a boat. Regardless, she felt it would be some time before her sadness would begin to abate.

That evening Anne and Alice walked down the stairs together, arm in arm. Lucy thought that never had a young lady recovered so completely as Anne. Though her eyes were still a trifle red-rimmed, she was in a glow of happiness, enhanced by the exquisite nature of her hair bearing its beaded band.

She wore a gown of white silk covered in spangled gauze and pearls dangling from her ears and draped about her neck.

Alice was equally as pretty in her lavishly embroidered white muslin, but since her interest in the affair was not even half of her sister's, she did not have the same sparkle in her eye. She did, however, evince a great deal of confidence, largely because she had performed quite well at the assemblies a fortnight prior.

Hetty led them to look at the garden where the orchestra had already assembled on a portion of the west lawn. As they stepped onto the terrace, the delicate strains of Mozart commenced, drifting with the soft evening currents. Lucy went with them, wanting to see just how the young ladies would respond to how beautifully Mr. Quarley and all the household servants had transformed the already pretty gardens into a wholly magical place.

Anne held her hands to her cheeks. "Why, it is like paradise!"

Hetty laughed. "I think the Vauxhall Pleasure Gardens never looked so pretty."

"I wonder how many Chinese lanterns there are and where did they come from?" Alice queried.

Hetty turned to Alice and smiled softly. "The lanterns were Valmaston's notion. He had been to a fete at Lord Hurstborne's in late June. He remembered that the garden had been lit in just this way and sent a servant to inquire if Hurstborne would permit us to make use of them. You see his generous answer before you."

"We must write a note of appreciation," Anne said, "for I vow I have never seen anything so lovely."

"You may tell Lord Hurstborne as much when he arrives," Hetty said. "I made certain Valmaston extended the invitation to your ball once I knew he meant to ask such a great favor of him. I received a missive the next day saying he meant to attend."

The terrace had been arranged with small tables and chairs, not just for supper later but for viewing the dancing as well. On the lawn, a makeshift floor had been built of finely milled lumber and afterward sanded and rubbed with beeswax to a smooth sheen. A great number of chairs, tied festively with blue ribbons, lined the long floor, which Lucy thought appeared to be at least twenty yards in length.

In the distance, toward the maze, servants were setting up a row of flambeaux that when lit would lend a truly festive backdrop to the ball.

Alice said, "I think this might even be prettier than the ballroom."

A few minutes later, dinner was served. Except for Lady Sandifort's obvious absence, there was joyfulness in the air, of congratulation to the twins and of the pleasure of being together, that extended through every thread of conversation.

More than once, Lucy found Robert staring at her. She could only wonder at his thoughts, for he still had not spoken to her from his heart. She wondered if he ever would.

As the second remove appeared, and Lucy was sliding a fine piece of roast beef onto her plate, she noted that Alice and Henry opposite her were staring at the doorway and appeared rather shocked. Lucy realized Lady Sandifort must have finally arrived. She turned to look as well and promptly dropped the large serving spoon, which clattered first onto her plate, then banged against the side of her chair and finally landed on the floor. Even the footman did not at first move to retrieve it. Lucy could hardly blame him, for she did not know when she had seen such a disgraceful gown.

Scarlet, she thought, *and more wicked than anything she had ever before witnessed.* The décolleté was so severe that Lucy touched her own bosom quite absently as though to make certain she was covered. There was nothing left to one's imagination with regard to Lady Sandifort's figure. The white undergown clung to her, a circumstance that led Lucy to believe she had actually dampened her gown!

"I see I have given you all a shock!" she cried out gaily. She extended her arms. "Do you not like . . . my gown?"

No one uttered a single word.

No one seemed to know what to say or even do.

Finally, Valmaston rose and approached her, offering his arm. "May I escort you to your seat?"

"Of course," she said, though pouting a little. "I do hope you have not taken our little disagreement of last night too seriously?"

Valmaston smiled. "I cannot imagine to what you might be referring."

"How very gentlemanly of you to say so." As she sat down, she looked up at him. "I trust you mean to dance with me."

"I have no other object in mind."

She smiled happily. "Then I am content." She turned to look at Robert and lifted a brow.

Lucy saw a hard light enter his eye and a very strong suspicion struck her in that moment, that Lady Sandifort was in pursuit of him and probably had been for a very long time! Of course! How much of her conduct, even of her remaining at Aldershaw, was explained in this moment! Even her desire to have Valmaston in the same house took on a new meaning. Worse was the realization that, since Lady Sandifort had power over Anne and Alice, the girls had undoubtedly been her principle choice of weapon in all her dealings with Robert. She thought back specifically to her original refusal to allow the come-out ball, how Lady Sandifort had cast Robert such a look! Lucy could recall it even now as though it was but yesterday, and yet that was so many weeks ago, nearly ten by now. She could only imagine just how many times she had threatened to do some injury to the girls in an attempt to gain control of Robert.

She glanced at the twins and saw that Anne was staring at her plate, her joy having dimmed greatly, but that Alice was regarding her stepmother rather speculatively. She was the first to resume eating.

"Have you seen the gardens, my lady?" Lucy asked. Because there was nothing to be done about Lady Sandifort in this moment, she chose instead to attempt to divert her attention. "Lord Hurstborne lent us a great number of Chinese lanterns. The entire lawn is in a glow."

"How lovely," she returned, but she sounded bitter. "And how clever that there is to be a ball after all. Was that your doing, Hetty?"

All eyes turned upon Hetty, who in turn lifted her chin. "Will I take credit for it? No, but I am certainly grateful that this miracle has been achieved for my sisters. In the end, I would say we all contributed."

"Indeed, we did," Henry cried. "I helped make the floor. I have never hammered so much in my life."

"You did not!" Anne cried, laughing. "Oh, my dear Henry! How difficult it is to picture you with a hammer. A pen, yes, but a hammer, no!"

"I was never so sore," he stated, rubbing his shoulder.

Alice, who sat next to him, said, "And I am very appreciative."

"Anything for you, dearest," Henry said, chucking her chin. "So, you are having your come-out ball at last. You are now officially grown and I daresay you will both be married quite soon."

"Indeed, yes," Lady Sandifort said. "I hope to see both the girls wed before they become spinsters like one particularly ridiculous female at this table whose name I need not mention." She cast Hetty a darkling look over the rim of her glass of champagne.

Anne gasped. "How can you speak so?" The words were out before she could check them.

Lady Sandifort glared at her then ordered her wine glass to be refilled with champagne.

Lucy was afraid that her presence would dim the exuberance of the party, but save for this single arrow aimed at Hetty, Lady Sandifort apparently had chosen to be on her very best behavior. She especially offered more than one compliment to Robert and insisted upon keeping him company in the receiving line.

The guests started arriving at just past seven and since over two hundred had been invited, Anne and Alice remained with Robert and Lady Sandifort greeting all their guests for well over an hour. Once their duties were fulfilled, however, Henry graciously made it his purpose to keep Lady Sandifort entertained and away from the twins.

He found partners for her for dancing and more champagne for drinking, though Lucy knew he had no pleasure in it. "But at least," he said, having sent Lady Sandifort onto the makeshift ballroom floor with an older gentleman who was obviously delighted to be dancing with her, "it is something I can do for my sisters so that they may enjoy the night."

"You are a good brother," Lucy said. She glanced at the doorway. "I see Lord Hurstborne has arrived." Alice appeared to be engaged in conversation with him at present. She was speaking with him quite intently, as was her way, probably thanking him for the generous use of his lanterns. She watched the younger of the twins thinking that Robert had much to be proud of in the girls.

The most recent dance ended and Lucy felt a pressure on her elbow. She turned and saw that Robert had found her. "The next is a waltz. Remember your promise?"

"Of course," she said, smiling. She again thanked Henry for his sacrifice.

"What sacrifice?" Robert asked as he led her onto the floor.

"Have you not noticed?" she queried. "He has devoted

himself to your stepmother nearly the entire evening thus far."

He glanced at Henry and saw that he had indeed hurried to Lady Sandifort's side and was even now wrapping her arm about his. "How very good of him. I ought to relieve him at some point."

"I would not recommend it, for I have not failed to notice that you seem to be an object of hers as well, or am I mistaken?"

He was silent for a moment then said quietly, "Do I understand you to have apprehended my greatest difficulty at Aldershaw?"

"I do not know why I did not see it before, nor can I comprehend how you have borne her presence here."

He sighed. "In that I had no choice."

"No, I suppose you did not."

The dancers assumed their positions. Robert took her hand in his and slipped his arm about her waist. Lucy felt very odd suddenly, as she so very often did when she drew close to Robert, even though this was merely a dance. She chuckled inwardly, for she recalled hearing that Lord Byron had once said the waltz was merely an excuse for hugging. Perhaps he was right, but a very fine excuse after all. She looked up into his eyes, the music began, and from that moment she knew herself to be completely and utterly lost.

Her concerns at Aldershaw were many, but they were forgotten. The quarrels she had had with Robert were too numerous to be counted, yet she could not recall even one to mind in this moment. Lady Sandifort's worsening state should have been her primary object, instead she felt as though no such lady even existed. Up and back, round and round he moved her and turned her. All the while her gaze was fixed to his, and during those few minutes he was the only real part of her life. Everything else was a distant, faint memory.

Robert held Lucy's gaze as though he was holding her

soul. Even in the flickering light of the flambeaux he could see the sparkle of her eyes, that quality which best reflected how she confronted her world, wherever she happened to be. He was in awe of her, for she never seemed daunted and always contrived a solution, however creative, for any difficulty she encountered. The fact that he was dancing with her now was a perfect example of what she was able to accomplish with seemingly little effort. Here was not only a come-out ball for his sisters, something that had been previously forbidden them, but even with a fire that morning a veritable dream had been created in his own gardens.

"Thank you," he murmured, twirling her round and round, up and back.

"For what?" she inquired, seeming surprised.

"For this ball, for tonight, for a garden full of people and dancing, and for the happiness of my sisters."

"But I did so little," she countered.

He could only smile. "Perhaps it appears that way to you, but you are undoubtedly unaware that it is your *joie de vivre* that has moved through this house so that, even in the face of a fire meant to ruin the ball, we are yet dancing." He laughed.

Lucy felt her heart grab and hold. How she loved to see Robert laugh. He had been so dark, so serious in his obligations when she had first arrived in June, but now delight was in his eyes.

Perhaps it was the music, or the moon overhead, or the evening breeze that swept her skirts against Robert's legs, or perhaps simply that she had known him since childhood, but Lucy acknowledged freely, at least within the confines of her own mind, just how much she loved Robert Sandifort.

He drew her more closely to him, whirling her around and around. "What are you thinking?"

"That I am a very great fool," she said, wondering if there was even the smallest hope that Robert could return her regard openly.

He laughed, drew her up and back, round and round. "Then I believe we are a pair."

Over the next hour, Robert watched Lucy. He had much to say to her, but he truly did not know how to go about the business. When she had completed a dance with Valmaston, he approached her, offering his arm. "Will you walk with me?" he inquired gently.

Though the light was but a scattering of flickers from the flambeaux, he saw the unmistakable answer in her eye. She took his arm quite willingly. "A stroll would suit me to perfection," she said.

He led her in the direction of the maze, beyond the flambeaux, deeper and deeper into the shadows. The laughter from the revelers grew quieter with each step they took. When they were at last on the far side of the maze, and some distance from the ball, he heard Lucy sigh.

He whispered her name, turning toward her and placing his hands on her shoulders. He was strangely nervous and began haltingly, "I know that I have not always been . . . that is, I am not a gentleman of mild opinions and temper. I often speak my mind more forcefully than I ought, but I wish to assure you . . . Lucy, I wish to marry you!" The devil take it! When had he become so cowhanded that he must blurt out an offer of marriage as though he were calling the pigs to supper?

"What?" she queried, obviously stunned.

"Yes. I wish to marry you. I have for some time, well perhaps not a very long time, but recently when I realized how much I loved you."

"You love me?"

He gripped her arms more tightly still, as though holding onto the sides of a small boat in heavy seas. "Yes. I love you . . . passionately." To his own ears he sounded ridiculous.

"Passionately?"

"Yes. I have said so." He groaned. "I am making a terrible mull of this."

Lucy frowned. Even in the shadows he could see that she was frowning, as though suddenly full of doubts.

Well, there was one thing he knew how to do. Though every word and expression to be found in the English language failed him, he knew how to kiss her. With that, his body relaxed and he slipped his arms about her, holding her tightly. He found her mouth, kissing her hard until she parted her lips. He kissed her more deeply still, so that familiar warbling coos began gathering in her perfect throat. How he had grown to crave those sounds. How happy he was to be holding her in his arms once more.

"Lucy," he whispered. "I do love you."

"And I love you, Robert, but—"

He stiffened slightly and released her, but only sufficiently to once again hold her shoulders in his hands. The feel of the seas were heavy beneath him once more. He swallowed hard. "What is it?"

"I . . . I do not mean to offend you, Robert, but though your kisses are like heaven, I am not persuaded, that is, what if tomorrow we begin brangling anew? Though I do hold you in great affection and esteem, though I love you, I do not trust that we could ever be truly happy together."

His hands slid down her arms as if of their own volition. "I would not press you to marry me for the world." He felt he should say more, that he should offer a speech from his heart, words that would persuade her that the love they shared would overcome their tendency to quarrel, but he could not.

He watched as she breathed a deep sigh of relief. "Then we understand one another?"

No, we do not understand one another at all, he wanted to say. Instead, he let her go. She turned away from him and only after several minutes had passed did he find he could make his feet move. He then returned to the ball.

Henry found him shortly after and was scowling. "What the devil did you do?" he cried. "For I can see that you must have done something. When I asked her what was amiss she simply spoke your name."

"I have not your abilities. I am sadly unskilled. Henry, you would have been ashamed of me. I asked her to marry me as though I had not a single thought for her feelings, then I kissed her. The kiss was well enough, I suppose, but in the end she refused my hand in marriage because she said she did not believe we could be truly happy together."

Henry appeared utterly aghast. He caught his arm hard. "Robert, am I hearing you correctly? Are you now telling me that you just proposed to and kissed Lady Sandifort?"

"What?" Robert exclaimed, aghast. "Good God, no! I was speaking of Lucy. Why would you think even for a moment I was referring to Lady Sandifort?"

"Because *I* was!" he cried.

"I am completely lost. I do not take your meaning."

"Then you did not speak with Lady Sandifort just now, in the last ten minutes?"

"No. Lucy and I walked just past the maze and that is when I proposed to her."

"I see," Henry said, nodding slowly. "Then I now must warn you that Lady Sandifort had just come from the direction of the maze when I spoke with her. She must have seen you kissing Lucy. I tell you, brother, she looked as mad as fire."

Robert shook his head. "Good God!" he whispered, horrified.

CHAPTER
FOURTEEN

"Well," Lady Sandifort said, hooking Lucy's arm and drawing her into the house. "Are you not the most clever girl! You quite put me to shame."

Lucy immediately felt uneasy. Lady Sandifort was smiling but there was just such a look in her eye and a cold tone to her voice that she knew something was amiss, only what? She could see that she was offended, but in what way? Unless . . .

Lucy therefore asked quietly, "What do you mean I am a *clever girl.*"

Lady Sandifort drew her up the stairs and into the library where, once within, she closed the door. "Have you never wondered why I was particularly interested in Valmaston?"

Lucy felt a sudden chill that had nothing to do with the temperature of the chamber. "You wished to make Robert jealous," she said.

Lady Sandifort stared at her for an intense moment. "Then you can understand now why I am overset, for I counted you a friend."

Lucy saw the venom in her blue eyes and realized that her worst fear was true—she must have seen Robert kissing her. She did not even know what to say to her ladyship except, "I did not know of your interest in him, at least not until this evening at dinner."

"Then why, once you knew, did you kiss Robert, and do not deny it, for I saw you?"

"You saw us just now?" Lucy asked, gesturing in the direction of the gardens. Her heart was pounding. She did not know what else to say to her.

"Forever the innocent. Well, I fear I have grown weary with being so patient with everyone. No one knows the trials I suffer. In you, I thought I had at last found someone who understood my sacrifices as well as my desires. Yet, you would use me as badly as Valmaston."

A scratching sounded on the door.

"Come," Lady Sandifort called out.

Mr. Colbury entered the chamber. He was a tall, thin young gentleman who had been in attendance at the assemblies. He was the third son of the vicar of a neighboring parish and appeared quite nervous as he made his bows.

"Lucy, I beg you will fetch Alice and Robert, for I have something of import to say to them both," said Lady Sandifort.

Lucy glanced at Mr. Colbury and understood instantly what it was that Lady Sandifort meant next to do. Lucy left the chamber at once and the moment she quit the room, panic seized her. How on earth was she to prevent so unexpected a betrothal?

She found Alice first and as calmly as she could explained that Lady Sandifort was quite overset for her own peculiar reasons, that she had Mr. Colbury with her, and that she most particularly wished to speak with Alice and Robert, together.

Alice paled, a certain sign that she too apprehended the implications. "I see," she murmured. "Very well."

"You know about this then?" She was not certain if Alice knew of the conditions of her father's will.

Alice nodded. "A few minutes ago, Lady Sandifort said that she thought I should be married off before I was allowed to ruin my life. She seemed very angry. I know Robert thinks that Anne and I are in ignorance of the fact that Lady Sandifort has the right to arrange marriages for us both. But because neither Anne nor I could comprehend why he was not more forceful with Lady Sandifort, Hetty felt compelled to tell us the truth not a sennight past." She appeared very sad suddenly. "I do not know how my brother has borne this burden over the past twelvemonth."

"For your sake and Anne's I believe he would have borne anything. Only what is to be done?"

"Lucy," she said, taking her arm strongly. "Do not be overly concerned. I . . . I believe all will be well."

"But I suspect she means to arrange, perhaps even announce, the betrothal tonight."

"So I understand, but even were she to do so . . . well, let me just say that whatever schemes she hopes to accomplish tonight can be undone later."

Lucy marveled at her. "I wish I could be so certain, but for the first time since my arrival at Aldershaw, I am truly frightened."

Alice merely smiled in her stoic manner. "Again, I beg you will not distress yourself. Instead, if you will find Robert, I will meet you both in the library as Lady Sandifort has requested."

"Yes, of course."

With that Alice turned on her heel and was gone.

Lucy moved to the center of the terrace and searched through the lively dancing crowd for Robert. He was going down a set with Anne so there was nothing for it, she must wait.

She moved to the lawn and positioned herself so that the moment he finished dancing she could take him aside. How the music played on and on! She vowed she had never before realized just how long a country dance could be!

Finally the music drew to a close and Lucy fairly pounced on Robert. "Forgive me, Anne, but there is something of great import I must say to your brother."

"Of course," she said. Since three young gentlemen approached her, each begging for the next dance, Lucy did not give her another thought.

"What is the matter, Lucy?" Robert asked, obviously concerned. "What has happened?"

Once away from the crowds, Lucy whispered, "I believe Lady Sandifort is about to betroth Alice to Mr. Colbury. She asked me to bring you and Alice to the library. I have already sent Alice to her."

Robert shook his head. "Who is Mr. Colbury?"

"He was at the assemblies, the vicar's son?"

"Colbury," he mused. "Do you mean that sallow young man with scarcely two words to say for himself?"

She nodded. "The very one. I . . . I believe she means it as a sort of punishment to you. She saw you kiss me."

"So I have been given to understand," he said.

Lucy turned to walk in the direction of the house. Robert walked beside her, even taking her arm. She had never felt so helpless. Panic still rippled through her, for she could not think of a single thing she could do to alter the situation. Not one! "I do not know what to do," she cried.

She heard Robert chuckle and looking up at him she saw that he was watching her closely and shaking his head.

"What is it?" she asked.

"I believe this may be the first time since your arrival at Aldershaw in which I have seen you at a loss."

She waved a dismissive hand. "Why are you speaking of me in this moment when Alice's entire future is at stake?"

"You are right, of course," he murmured. Yet again he chuckled.

"Why do you laugh? Why are you not overset? For I vow I am ready to scream in vexation!"

"Lucy, pray calm yourself. If I do not seem so wretchedly overset it is because you have taught me that even the most hopeless situation can have a solution. I think we must be patient."

She was dumbfounded.

"Let us hear precisely what it is Lady Sandifort has to say to us."

Once within the library it was as Lucy had feared. Lady Sandifort stated her case, that Sir Henry had given her the right to choose husbands for both Anne and Alice if she felt it necessary. She had therefore decided it would be best if Alice accepted Mr. Colbury's hand in marriage. "Tomorrow we shall settle the matter with Mr. Colbury's father—who was unable to attend the ball because of the gout—and begin the process of having our solicitor compose the proper papers. Is that clear?"

Robert stood beside Alice and spoke softly. "Whatever you wish me to do, I will do."

Alice smiled faintly. "I beg you will say nothing, Robert," she responded in her quiet, studious manner. "My stepmother was given the right to choose a husband for me. There can be little use to argue the point now."

Lucy saw that Robert was rather awestruck by his younger sister's demeanor and speech. "As you wish," he responded, but he was frowning.

"I see you mean to be sensible," Lady Sandifort said, addressing Alice.

"Indeed, I strive to be. But I do request that any announcement of the betrothal be delayed until the engagement papers have been signed. Will that suit you, ma'am?"

Lady Sandifort lifted a brow. "Since you are being so reasonable, I do not see why I should oppose the idea. Mr. Colbury, I suggest you take your bride-to-be to the garden and dance with her."

Alice waited for him to approach her. He was nervous and the tips of his ears were bright red. As he led her from the chamber, he was heard to whisper, "Miss Alice, I am sorry . . . I had not the smallest notion . . . I did not know for what reason she asked me to come to the library . . ."

Lucy watched as Alice patted his arm. "Pray be easy, Mr. Colbury. All will be well."

With his free hand he ran his finger around the inside of his neckcloth. "I hope you are right!"

Lucy did not wait but followed them out. A new panic seized her. She would have asked Alice to stay a moment and speak with her, but Alice was busily engaged in whispering to Mr. Colbury as they made their descent down the stairs. She wondered if Alice had some scheme of her own in mind.

For that reason Lucy followed them onto the terrace and watched with some interest as Alice sent Mr. Colbury off to amuse himself however he wished. Alice in turn began wending her way through the crowds, not stopping until she had found Lord Hurstborne. She drew him aside and spent at least ten minutes speaking rather intensely with him.

The horrible thought went through Lucy's head that Alice was arranging to elope with Lord Hurstborne, but that was ridiculous. Alice would never do so. For one thing she was far too sensible, and for another her object was Cornwall, not any sort of romantic attachment.

What then was she about?

In the end, Lord Hurstborne smiled broadly upon Alice, bowed to her, and quit her side. Lucy found herself utterly intrigued and, rather than dance, set about to watch what next would happen.

Interestingly, Alice went about her business, continuing to enjoy her come-out ball as though nothing untoward had happened. Even Mr. Colbury, who fairly ignored his "bride-to-be," seemed to take pleasure in the ball. As for Lord Hurstborne, he greeted Lady Sandifort shortly after leaving Alice's side and from that moment danced attendance on her.

Lady Sandifort accepted his attentions with pleasure, even permitting him to dine next to her at supper.

When the hour neared midnight, Lucy was again speaking with Robert about Alice's betrothal. "But what can be done?" she asked.

He shook his head. "I have not the faintest notion. However, Alice does not seem to be concerned in the least. Indeed, I have never seen her so . . ." He seemed to be searching for the right word to describe her.

"In command of herself and her surroundings?" she queried.

"Precisely so!" he cried.

Lucy caught sight of Alice waving to them.

Robert waved as well. "I wonder what she means to do now," he mused as Alice made her way to them.

"I need your help, Robert," she said. "Will you oblige me with something?"

"Yes, of course, dearest," he responded. "You have but to tell me what it is you wish me to do."

"As to that, I have put a scheme in motion and you have but to follow my lead."

Robert appeared as though he wished to inquire further, but she laid a quick hand on his arm. "Please, Robert. Will you trust me?"

At that Robert relaxed. "Of course."

"And Lucy, I most especially wish you to come join us,"

here she smiled, "merely to observe that I have learned a great deal from you."

"As you wish," Lucy said, but she could not imagine what Alice meant to do or why she had spoken of having learned "a great deal" from her.

Alice then smiled and in her eyes was such a look of joyful mischief that Lucy could only turn to exchange a wondering glance with Robert.

"Follow me," she said, lifting her lovely muslin skirts carefully and turning to walk back to the terrace and into the house.

A minute later, Lucy found herself once more in the library. Mr. Colbury was present again, but this time he sat in a chair and appeared absolutely miserable. Hetty, Henry, and Anne stood to one side near the windows. None of them seemed to know what was going forward. Surprisingly, Lord Hurstborne stood next to Lady Sandifort. He whispered to her, though what he was saying could not be heard.

Alice directed Robert and Lucy to a sofa near the door. Robert obeyed and Lucy followed suit. Once seated, they again exchanged a surprised glance.

"What is the meaning of this, Alice?" Lady Sandifort cried haughtily. "You said earlier you did not mean to contest the betrothal. If that is so, I cannot imagine why you summoned all of us here."

"I did not come to argue, contest, or quarrel, merely to inform you that I have no intention of wedding anyone at present."

Lady Sandifort smiled in her habitually high-handed fashion. "You have no say whatsoever in the matter. Your father gave me the power to select a husband for you and so I have. Mr. Colbury will suit you far better than the Cornwall sea cliffs."

Mr. Colbury found his voice. "If Miss Alice is not wishful of marrying—"

"Silence," she cried, turning sharply toward him. "This does not concern you!"

Mr. Colbury appeared properly shocked but, given Lady Sandifort's heightened complexion, he refrained from speaking further.

Alice moved to stand but three feet from her stepmother. Lucy noted that a faint sliver of doubt entered Lady Sandifort's eye. Alice said, "I have no intention of obeying you, *Stepmama*, for you do not have my interests at heart. You never have."

"How dare you speak to me in that insolent manner, ungrateful girl!"

"You are correct. I am not grateful. What have you ever done for me that was not a matter of self-interest?"

A lovely shade of red climbed Lady Sandifort's cheeks. "Why I . . . I have never heard such words from you! You who were always a mouse, never speaking save to echo Anne."

"You have the right of it, but I am a mouse no longer. I will not marry Mr. Colbury and all your fussing will not see the deed done."

Lady Sandifort turned suddenly to Lord Hurstborne. "You see how badly I am treated at Aldershaw, I who have sacrificed everything to continue being a mother to these wretched, horrid girls!" She threw her arms wide, the very specter of martyrdom. However, Lucy thought the effect would have been better achieved had she not been wearing her scarlet gown.

Lord Hurstborne clucked his tongue and shook his head as one in complete agreement with her. She gained courage from his support and turned back to Alice. "Well, you may refuse all you like, but after the banns have been properly read you will marry Mr. Colbury."

"No, she will not," Robert said, rising suddenly from the sofa to stand beside his sister.

Again a new flush of color rose to consume Lady Sandifort's

complexion. "And you . . . you would speak to me this way when I have always loved you?"

Lucy was shocked that Lady Sandifort would make such a confession before the family. Both Anne and Hetty gasped. Henry snickered his disbelief.

"You never loved me," he returned coldly. "You do not comprehend the meaning of the word. Why, you treat your own children as though they were dogs to be kicked about."

"I never kicked my children," she returned, her head held high.

Robert was silent for a moment before saying, "You might as well have."

At that Lady Sandifort's eyes grew quite large. Lucy thought they might pop from her head did she not have a care. Instead, she did the only thing she could and promptly burst into tears.

Lord Hurstborne was at her side immediately. "You must pay no heed to what any of them say, dearest Celeste. They do not understand you, nor appreciate you even in the slightest. But I do. I have not lived in the world so many years without having seen this sort of thing before."

She wept into his shoulder and clung to him. He patted her back and stroked her neck. "There, there, my darling." He then glanced at Alice, smiled, and winked. To Lady Sandifort he added, "You ought to leave this place, the sooner the better. My sister wishes to extend an invitation for you to sojourn at Highcliffe for as long as you desire."

"I should like that," Lady Sandifort said, pulling back slightly and looking up into his face. "You are the kindest man I have ever known."

He dabbed at her eyes with a rather lacy kerchief. "And you are the only lady I know who can weep without losing one particle of her beauty."

Lady Sandifort smiled, laughed, and sniffed. "How very gallant of you, my lord."

"What do you say? Will you not pay my sister the honor of a visit?"

She nodded. Again Lucy thought she appeared like a little girl.

Alice tugged on Robert's sleeve and whispered something in his ear. Robert nodded to her, then said, "Lady Sandifort, should you leave, you must remember the terms of my father's will."

"Oh, I do not give a fig who your brat of a sister weds. She may go to the devil, for all I care."

"But what of your children?" he asked.

"When I am free to do so, since it would appear I shall be quite busy in the coming months, I shall visit them, of course."

Lucy stared at Lady Sandifort in some astonishment. She knew her mouth had fallen agape but she could not seem to close it. She had always understood that Lady Sandifort was not particularly attached to her children, but she was still shocked that she could dismiss Hyacinth, William, and Violet without so much as a blink of an eye.

"As you wish," Robert said somberly.

"Come, Hurstborne. I believe I do not desire to remain another moment where I am least wanted."

"Very wise, indeed." Once by the door, he added, "I encourage you to ignore them all, for it is clear to me they are a rather vulgar lot."

Lady Sandifort smirked as she addressed Robert. "You may send my trunks to Highcliffe on the morrow."

"If Lord Hurstborne will be so good as to leave directions with Finkley, your wishes will be attended to."

Lady Sandifort cast a triumphant glance all round the library before she passed into the hall.

Lucy noted that, as one, she, Hetty, Robert, Henry, and Anne all turned to stare at Alice, for she had accomplished in the space of a scant few minutes what no one had been able to do since Sir Henry paid his debt to nature. She had got rid of Lady Sandifort!

Alice addressed Mr. Colbury first, however. "You are free now," she said. "And as you can see, Lady Sandifort will not trouble you again."

He rose from his seat and, after bowing to them all, fairly ran from the room.

Anne raced to the door and closed it softly, then turned back to rejoin the group now clustered about Alice. "How did you know what to do?" she asked. "But then of course you do have a superior intelligence, but how did you know to involve Lord Hurstborne?" She sounded as dumbfounded as Lucy felt.

Alice smiled somewhat shyly, then turned to Lucy and quickly possessed herself of her hands. "I simply asked myself, 'What would Lucy do?' and then I had my answer. That was what Mr. Frome suggested to me when I told him how horrid Lady Sandifort was being."

"He said that to you?"

Alice squeezed her hands. "Yes, indeed he did and, Lucy, I do wish to thank you ever so much. You took us over a hill we had not been able to surmount by ourselves."

"Indeed, you did," Henry said.

Hetty added, "I believe we were too lost in our grief to know how to counter Lady Sandifort's unhappy presence here."

"But what of Hyacinth, William, and Violet?" Anne asked. "What is to become of them?"

At that Robert stared at her as one wholly confounded and then he began to laugh. He laughed until tears streamed down his cheeks. "I understand now!" he exclaimed, sinking down into a chair. "Papa was so much wiser than I ever comprehended until just this moment."

Hetty patted his shoulders. "Robert, you are not well."

"I am quite well, indeed. You see, he gave me guardianship of the children—something our stepmother would never have forgiven except that he softened the blow by giving her the power to marry off Anne and Alice, unless of course she chose to leave my house. Had she been left with no rights, there would have been no end to her displeasure. Her pride would never have allowed it. How clever my father proved in the end."

Lucy nodded. "Yes, perfectly concocted, indeed! It would seem he comprehended her character after all, that she would not choose to live forever at Aldershaw, but once gone, not only would she forfeit her rights over Anne and Alice but she would be forbidden by law to take her children with her. She might have done so, otherwise."

"I believe she would have, merely to spite me," he said.

"Robert," Anne said, drawing close to him and slipping her hand in his, "she will not come back, will she?"

"Of course not. She will discover other pleasures more in keeping with her, er, *interests*. However, just on the smallest chance she should decide to revisit Aldershaw, I believe I shall have a very deep moat dug, and the drawbridge always up, just to keep her out!"

"You know, the sun rises with you," Robert said.

Lucy stared at him, a now quite familiar shiver going through her. Robert had been saying such things to her of late, nearly every day since the come-out ball. "I beg your pardon?" she inquired, fiddling with the roses she was arranging in one of the succession houses. She was quite alone with him and more nervous than she had ever been. She did not look at him.

"I believe you know very well what I mean," he said, drawing close to her from behind and taking her shoulders gently in hand.

"Robert, you should not!" she cried, ducking down swiftly and coming up beneath his arm. "It is most unseemly!" She passed behind him and went out of doors to collect some ferns that grew in a long row outside the hothouse.

"You cannot run from me forever," he said, trailing after her.

She glanced at him and saw that he was smiling in that wretched manner of his, as though he knew what she was thinking. Only what were her thoughts, since she felt so confused of late? He was tall and handsome and had beautiful brown eyes into which she seemed to sink every time she looked at him. He was a man she could admire because he tended his lands, his family, even his half brother and sisters. He seemed to fit to perfection her sense of the ridiculous. He was all she had been thinking about for the past sennight.

"I know what you are thinking," he said, as she bent over the ferns and clipped one frond after another with a pair of rather dull scissors.

"No, you do not," she returned flatly.

"You were thinking that I am quite good-looking, that you approve of the manner in which I conduct my house, and that we share a great many things in common. Admit it is so!"

She stood upright and faced him. Had he read her mind? Again, fear rippled through her. "You are being quite absurd." Once more she pushed past him. "And now I beg you will permit me to complete my flower arrangement." She returned inside and went directly to her bench. She thought he would follow her but instead he remained standing at the door. Her heart was hammering against her ribs. Her breathing grew shallow and labored. Tears struck her eyes.

"I fear I cannot wait forever, Lucy," he said, his tone suddenly sorrowful. "There are circumstances, as well you know, that demand I continue to fulfill my obligations to Aldershaw and to my family."

What was his meaning? She found her hands frozen above

the roses. Finally she whirled around to ask him what he was trying to say, but he was gone.

Lucy sank into a heap on the brick floor and began to weep. She did not know why she was crying nor why his words had felt like a sword he had thrust all the way through her. What did he mean he would not wait?

Ever since the come-out ball and his abrupt declaration of his feelings, he had been tormenting her with an elaboration of his sentiments. Whenever they were alone, he did not hesitate to express his love for her, indeed, his passionate feelings for her and often in so romantic a mode that she frequently fled the chamber on one excuse or another.

He had also taken to stealing kisses from her, a circumstance that further disrupted the peaceful, secure state of her heart. She had been afraid he would do so this morning and even as she wept she wished he had kissed her, for then she would not feel so desolate. Only, what was the matter with her? Why did she toss about on her bed all night, unable to sleep for reviewing the day's events in which he told her he loved her, or begged forgiveness a hundredfold for any slight or criticism he had ever given her, for he understood now that his object in doing so had been to keep his heart safe. He understood now that he had no need of keeping his heart safe from so sweet, generous, and genuine a lady as Lucinda Stiles.

Oh, why did he torment her with such speeches and why were his kisses like whispers of fire on her mouth and in her soul? She desired him but she feared him, because they had brangled so much and because he criticized her, because he had once said she was vulgar and interfering. Yet he had asked her to forgive him and had even offered reasons for his conduct, which he assured her were no longer difficulties for him. He loved her, he wished her to be his wife, and now . . . now he was telling her he would not wait forever!

That evening he was strangely remote from her. He smiled

politely, if sadly, but withheld his expressions of affection and love. When he bid her good night, he took her hand tightly in his and though he said nothing there was such a look of longing and regret in his eyes that now she was frightened indeed.

On the following morning Hetty awoke her from a very deep, if troubled, sleep. "Lucy!" she cried, shaking her abruptly.

Lucy sat up blinking several times and pulling a tousled mobcap from her blond curls. "Whatever is the matter?"

"Robert is leaving for London, even now!"

"London? What for?"

Hetty's lips trembled and tears rolled from her eyes. "He says he means to find a mother for the children."

Lucy weaved and felt suddenly ill, as though she might cast up her accounts. "A mother for William, Hyacinth, and Violet?"

Hetty nodded.

Lucy recalled what he had said to her on the previous morning about obligations to Aldershaw and to his family. A new fear pounded in her head. "He means to marry?"

"Yes," she said, pressing her kerchief to her eyes. "Oh, Lucy, was it a foolish thought of mine that I wished for you and Robert to wed, that I believed you were made for him and he for you and that then I would always have you as my sister?"

Lucy slipped her legs over the side of the bed. She could now hear the horses stomping on the drive. She ran to the window and looked down. There was Robert, standing by the door of the coach and pulling on his gloves. He had harnessed three teams to the coach—clearly he meant to get to London as quickly as possible. Something about that both incensed her and yet made her fears all the worse. Robert was leaving? Now?

She moved back from the windows, her hands shaking. She did not know what to do. If only Mr. Frome were still here, he would know what she should do, only, what should she do?

Hetty stood by the bedpost weeping into her kerchief.

Lucy slipped on her robe, her mind whirling. All her experiences at Aldershaw from the time she was a little girl and sitting on Sir Henry's lap, to the many years she spent in childhood tormenting Robert, who was nine years her senior, to developing the worst *tendre* for him when she was seventeen, to the many years betwixt, brangling and holding all her feelings for him at bay, especially after her failed romantic entanglement with John Goodworth. John was the cause of this, all her hesitation. Mr. Frome had hinted at this truth, but she had not realized it until now. She was not afraid of Robert. Instead, she had been afraid of being hurt again as she had been hurt by John. But Robert was not John, he was not a halfling under the hateful command of an unreasonable parent. Robert was his own man and always had been, for Sir Henry would never have raised him in any other manner.

She understood at last and a great weight slid from her shoulders.

"Robert!" she called. She could hear the roll of the coach wheels.

She ran faster than she had ever run in her life. She flew down the stairs on feet swifter than even Mercury's. She flew down the second set of stairs, her bare feet padding softly across the tiled entrance hall. From the corner of her eye she saw that the family, the entire family including the children, as well as Lord Valmaston, were waiting nearby but she ignored them. She opened the door. The coach was already moving, if slowly down the drive.

"Robert!" she called out loudly. "Wait! Please wait!"

The coach did not stop. She began to run after him, only

the gravel bit at her feet. She ran to the bordering grass and picked up speed, her robe flapping behind her.

"Robert!" she cried again and again.

Finally she heard his voice, a single sharp command to the coachman, and the equipage drew to a halt. She was breathing hard as she slowed to a walk some twenty feet from the vehicle. He descended, a broad smile on his face and so much love in his eyes that she decided she needed to run a little more. She raced to him and threw herself into his arms. He held her tightly. "Do not leave me!" she cried. "Please, Robert, I do not know how I would go on without you. I love you so."

He promptly devoured her in a kiss from which she did not emerge until shouting and cheering reached her ears. Only then did she draw back and note that the family party assembled on the front drive was waving, whistling, and cheering a little more.

Lucy drew back and looked up at Robert. She then peered into the coach and, removing herself from his arms completely, scrutinized the outside of the coach as well. "Where are your trunks, your portmanteaux?"

Robert merely smiled upon her.

She gasped and planted her hands on her hips. "You had no intention of going? This was merely a ruse!"

He shook his head. "You are very right. I had no such purpose."

She gasped. "I have been tricked," she cried, "quite vilely so I must say." She turned on her heel and began walking toward the house.

After giving orders to the coachman to return to the stables, he followed after her. "Now, Lucy, do not take a pet. You know you love me. You know it is inevitable that we marry."

"I know no such thing," she said, lifting her chin. But there was so much joy in her heart that she felt as though she would break out singing and shouting at any moment.

"I only showed you your heart. How can that be a bad thing?" He caught her suddenly about the waist and turned her into him. "Besides, if you do not agree at once, I shall tell everyone that you once slept in my bed, all night, and I would like to see you deny it."

She gasped loudly again but she could not keep her countenance. She leaned into him. "I should be angry with you for such a trick but Robert I cannot. How happy I am! How much I have always loved you."

He sighed happily, and though he rather shocked the youngest of the Sandifort children, he kissed her again quite thoroughly.

A fortnight later, Lucy sat with Robert on the terrace. He held her hand gently. "We must think of some way of keeping him here," she said.

"He has stayed long enough."

She watched Valmaston pick up Violet and plant her carefully on his shoulder. Violet wrapped her arm about his head. Hetty looked up at them both and laughed. They were walking in the direction of the maze, Hyacinth and William before them.

"Another sennight and the trick will be done," she said. "Besides, I wish him to stay for our wedding."

"Then he shall stay, though I know very well it is not because of our wedding."

Lucy giggled. "Of course it is not, but will not Hetty be delighted?"

"Yes, I believe she will. She grows more in love with him every day."

Once the small party disappeared into the maze, he reached over and stole a kiss from her. He often stole kisses as soon as the family absented themselves, which seemed to be quite frequently of late. "I should have gotten a special license," he whispered.

"So you have said every day since we became betrothed." She touched his face lovingly. "And to confess the truth, though I shiver at telling you as much, I wished we had as well."

"Darling!" he cried, kissing her again.

More Regency Romance From Zebra

__A Daring Courtship   0-8217-7483-2 $4.99US/$6.99CAN
  by Valerie King

__A Proper Mistress   0-8217-7410-7 $4.99US/$6.99CAN
  by Shannon Donnelly

__A Viscount for Christmas   0-8217-7552-9 $4.99US/$6.99CAN
  by Catherine Blair

__Lady Caraway's Cloak   0-8217-7554-5 $4.99US/$6.99CAN
  by Hayley Ann Solomon

__Lord Sandhurst's Surprise   0-8217-7524-3 $4.99US/$6.99CAN
  by Maria Greene

__Mr. Jeffries and the Jilt   0-8217-7477-8 $4.99US/$6.99CAN
  by Joy Reed

__My Darling Coquette   0-8217-7484-0 $4.99US/$6.99CAN
  by Valerie King

__The Artful Miss Irvine   0-8217-7460-3 $4.99US/$6.99CAN
  by Jennifer Malin

__The Reluctant Rake   0-8217-7567-7 $4.99US/$6.99CAN
  by Jeanne Savery

Available Wherever Books Are Sold!

Visit our website at **www.kensingtonbooks.com**.

More Historical Romance From
Jo Ann Ferguson

__A Christmas Bride	0-8217-6760-7	$4.99US/$6.99CAN
__His Lady Midnight	0-8217-6863-8	$4.99US/$6.99CAN
__A Guardian's Angel	0-8217-7174-4	$4.99US/$6.99CAN
__His Unexpected Bride	0-8217-7175-2	$4.99US/$6.99CAN
__A Rather Necessary End	0-8217-7176-0	$4.99US/$6.99CAN
__Grave Intentions	0-8217-7520-0	$4.99US/$6.99CAN
__Faire Game	0-8217-7521-9	$4.99US/$6.99CAN
__A Sister's Quest	0-8217-6788-7	$5.50US/$7.50CAN
__Moonlight on Water	0-8217-7310-0	$5.99US/$7.99CAN

Available Wherever Books Are Sold!

Visit our website at **www.kensingtonbooks.com**.

Discover the Romances of
Hannah Howell

My Valiant Knight	0-8217-5186-7	**$5.50**US/**$7.00**CAN
Only for You	0-8217-5943-4	**$5.99**US/**$7.50**CAN
A Taste of Fire	0-8217-7133-7	**$5.99**US/**$7.50**CAN
A Stockingful of Joy	0-8217-6754-2	**$5.99**US/**$7.50**CAN
Highland Destiny	0-8217-5921-3	**$5.99**US/**$7.50**CAN
Highland Honor	0-8217-6095-5	**$5.99**US/**$7.50**CAN
Highland Promise	0-8217-6254-0	**$5.99**US/**$7.50**CAN
Highland Vow	0-8217-6614-7	**$5.99**US/**$7.50**CAN
Highland Knight	0-8217-6817-4	**$5.99**US/**$7.50**CAN
Highland Hearts	0-8217-6925-1	**$5.99**US/**$7.50**CAN
Highland Bride	0-8217-7397-6	**$6.50**US/**$8.99**CAN
Highland Angel	0-8217-7426-3	**$6.50**US/**$8.99**CAN
Highland Groom	0-8217-7427-1	**$6.50**US/**$8.99**CAN
Highland Warrior	0-8217-7428-X	**$6.50**US/**$8.99**CAN
Reckless	0-8217-6917-0	**$6.50**US/**$8.99**CAN

Available Wherever Books Are Sold!

Visit our website at **www.kensingtonbooks.com**